Something TO PROVE

Also by Shannyn Schroeder

More Than This

A Good Time

Something TO PROVE

The O'Learys

SHANNYN
SCHROEDER

Kensington
KENSINGTON PUBLISHING CORP.
www.kensingtonbooks.com

KENSINGTON BOOKS are published by

Kensington Publishing Corp.
119 West 40th Street
New York, NY 10018

All Kensington titles, imprints, and distributed lines are available at special quantity discounts for bulk purchases for sales promotion, premiums, fund-raising, educational, or institutional use.

Special book excerpts or customized printings can also be created to fit specific needs. For details, write or phone the office of the Kensington Special Sales Manager: Kensington Publishing Corp., 119 West 40th Street, New York, NY 10018. Attn. Special Sales Department. Phone: 1-800-221-2647.

Kensington and the K logo Reg. U.S. Pat. & TM Off.

eISBN-13: 978-1-60183-183-5
eISBN-10: 1-60183-183-8
First Electronic Edition: January 2014

ISBN-13: 978-1-60183-184-2
ISBN-10: 1-60183-184-6
First Print Edition: January 2014

Printed in the United States of America

CHAPTER 1

Elizabeth drove up and down Addison, west, then east again, watching the addresses. No matter which way she went, the gray slab of a building had to be the right place. She parked and climbed out of the rental car. Motorcycles leaned against the building—not at the curb, but on the sidewalk actually touching the building.

Why the hell would Dad own a biker bar?

She glanced up at the rusty sign, THE IRISH PUB. It didn't look much like anything Irish. She pushed through the door and a cloud of smoke smacked into her lungs. Chicago was supposed to be smoke-free. Didn't the manager know this? That alone was fine-worthy. Trying to keep her breaths shallow to avoid inhaling too much smoke, she walked toward the bar, hoping to find someone in charge. The room, what she could see of it, was dark and tables were scattered haphazardly.

"Excuse me, I'm looking for the manager," she called out.

"Are you the health inspector?" a grizzled man asked while drying a glass with a dirty cloth. His pasty skin reminded her of a vampire's, but she doubted he'd sparkle if she took him into the sunlight.

"No, I'm the owner."

He laughed and the men sitting on stools at the opposite end of the bar joined him. She stiffened. It wasn't like this was the first time she'd been laughed at, and it undoubtedly wouldn't be the last. She produced a card from her suit coat pocket and slapped it on the bar.

"Elizabeth Brannigan. My father has owned this bar for more than ten years. Feel free to call the office to check."

She prayed her bluff would work. If he made the call, she'd be caught.

The man sobered and took the card. He brushed his stringy salt-and-pepper hair from his eyes. "So you're here to finally sell?"

"No. I'm here to save it." Until the words left her mouth, she didn't even know that was her plan. She had arrived in Chicago thinking she wanted to know more about this property, but now she knew it would be her mission. Her chance to prove her worth to her father.

Her statement set off another round of laughter.

"Then, when it's turning a profit, I'll sell."

The man leaned forward and extended his hand. "Mitch, your manager. I was hired on about ten years ago and have seen many men come through from your daddy's company talking about change. It ain't happened yet."

She shook his hand, trying to ignore whatever diseases she was accepting in the action. "Maybe that was the problem."

"What?"

"They were all men." She paused. "I'll need to see the books and any other pertinent information. I'll be back tomorrow morning at nine a.m."

"We don't close until two. I won't be here at nine." His eyes were already bloodshot, so she couldn't imagine him more sleep-deprived.

"Then give me a copy of the key and leave the information in the office. I assume there is an office?"

"You got ID on you? It'd be just my luck to give keys to someone who isn't the owner."

Elizabeth reached into her wallet and slipped out her driver's license. Mitch took it from her hand and tilted it in the light, glancing from the card to her face. Satisfied, he tossed it on the sticky bar for her to retrieve.

"Hold on." He walked to the end of the bar and flipped up a piece of the counter. He disappeared into the back and returned a few moments later with a ring of keys. He tossed them on the bar.

"Thank you." She slipped the keys into her pocket and walked back outside. Within a few minutes she had already learned more about the bar than the audit of her father's properties had taught her.

From behind the wheel of the rented Mercedes, she stared at the building. It must've meant something to her dad. He'd never done any work on it, but never sold it either. If she could turn this place around, prove to him that she could handle this task, he would have to hand the reins of the business over to her instead of Keith.

She'd never taken the lead like this before. They tended to treat her more like the clean-up crew. Dad didn't even know she was here. He'd been keeping this place a secret. This was her moment to shine. If she fixed this, he'd have to see that she could handle doing it all.

And if he didn't?

She shook her head. She'd cross that bridge later. Right now, she needed to do some research, starting with finding a place to live.

While allowing her GPS to guide her to a hotel, she called the office. "Hi, Meg."

"How was the flight?"

"Fine. Listen, I need you to get some information for me about a property." She heard some rustling and knew Meg was getting her notepad out.

"Shoot."

"My dad owns a bar called The Irish Pub here in Chicago. It's part of his personal holdings, not Brannigan Enterprises."

"I don't have access to his personal information," Meg said, uncharacteristically nervous.

"I want you to talk to Claire. She's been with my dad forever. Talk to her, assistant to assistant. Tell her that I need whatever information she has."

"Can I ask what's going on?"

"I'm not sure. I'm going to call my dad, but I have a feeling he won't give me all the details, so I'm making a preemptive strike. I also need everything you can get me on the codes for bar ownership in Chicago."

"Anything else?"

"Not yet. I'm sure that once I hit the ground on this, I'll need some more support."

"I could do my job from Chicago. I've never been there."

Elizabeth smiled. "I'll let you know if I need you. In the meantime, if Keith asks, play dumb. I don't want him following me here trying to help."

"Okay."

They clicked off, and Elizabeth pulled into the lot of a chain hotel. No five stars here, but it would have to do. Her mother would choke if she knew. At the reception desk, she negotiated a month's stay for a decent price and went to her room to set up her office away from home.

She tossed her suitcase on the brown paisley bedspread and pulled her laptop from her shoulder bag. While the computer booted up, she hung her suits in the minuscule closet and placed the remaining clothes in the dresser. From the front pocket of her suitcase, she pulled the frogs. For this trip, she had four.

She set the frogs beside her computer: two plastic, one stuffed, and one metal. It was her niece's way of making her feel at home. Before every business trip, Melissa snuck some frogs into the suitcase. It had started when Mel was little more than a toddler and offered Elizabeth her stuffed frog to keep her company. She'd just moved into Keith's carriage house, and her relationship with Mel was nonexistent. What did she know about kids?

But they'd bonded over frogs.

Over the years, it had bloomed into a collection. Family now gave Elizabeth frogs for gifts. It was almost a competition to see who could find the ugliest one.

Smiling at her family of frogs, she set to work. Her first order of business would be to check out the competition. Returning to the computer, she Googled Irish bars in Chicago and then narrowed her search for the neighborhood.

The results stared at her, a mass of red pushpins on the screen. "How can there be so many damn Irish bars in one area?"

She expanded the map and looked closely. In a ten-mile radius, she counted twenty-three Irish pubs. She'd bet she wouldn't find that many in the entire state of Florida. Zooming in on the map, she copied the addresses of the five closest to The Irish Pub and sent the information to the GPS on her phone.

The Irish Pub.

What a dumb name. The total lack of creativity or originality grated on her nerves. She checked the time. Six o'clock. After-work hours for most. Tucking a notepad into her purse, she headed out to the first bar, figuring she'd get dinner along the way. The research and reconnaissance was the worst part of the job. Keith usually handled it. He was good at reading people.

She was better with the finances, which was why Brannigan Enterprises should be hers. The CEO didn't need to be a people person. The job required an understanding and ability to wrangle the bottom line. Definitely her forte.

Pulling into the lot alongside a bar called Duffy's, her stomach growled and her eyes felt dry. It promised to be a long night, and she planned to be back at the bar at nine. She climbed out of her car and pushed on. The sooner she got started, the sooner she'd be done.

For a Monday night, she hadn't expected to find crowds at any of the bars she'd chosen to investigate. She pushed through the glass doors of the bar and was met with chaotic noise. The crowd wasn't huge and the patrons were mostly young, early twenties. Two TVs blared in competition with the jukebox that played some kind of rock. As she moved toward the bar, her feet squeaked in the stickiness of the floor, and she cringed.

The lighting wasn't bright enough for her to see what made the floor gross or for her to make sure there wasn't anything stuck to the stool as she took a seat. The bar itself was made from a nice dark wood, walnut, if she had to guess, but puddles of some indeterminate liquid lingered across the surface.

Not very inviting.

She slung her purse over the back of the stool and waited. Within moments the bartender asked what she wanted.

"Do you have a menu?"

He slapped a laminated sheet of paper down in front of her. The menu consisted of the usual bar food: hot wings, burgers, nachos. "I'll have a burger, everything. Do you have a drink menu?"

"Huh?" His eyebrows rose with the question.

"A drink menu? So I can decide what to drink?"

"Uh, no."

Huh. How was a customer supposed to know what to order if choices weren't presented? "Can I have a wine spritzer?"

"Coming right up."

While she waited, she took in the atmosphere. Tuning out the noise, she focused on what she saw. Young people, dressed casually, congregated in clusters at tables. Waitresses circulated, but the only thing that distinguished them from the customers were the aprons tied around their waists. No uniforms, no name tags. Cardboard decorations hung drunkenly from the soffit above the bar. Beer promotions and green-clad leprechauns dangled lopsided, and their discoloration told her they'd been hanging there far too long.

Her drink was delivered. She only took a small sip to find it relatively tasteless. When her burger arrived, it wasn't much better. She tossed money on the bar beside her half-eaten food. Regardless of location, when she was done, Duffy's wouldn't be much competition.

Four hours and three bars later, Elizabeth was ready to call it quits. She was tired of drinking cheap alcohol and being hit on. Her last stop for the night was O'Leary's. She'd almost decided against it, but after checking out their Web site on her phone, it looked too promising to pass up. Cars filled most of the lot, but spots were still available. She tugged the heavy oak door open and walked through, pleasantly surprised. No cigarette smoke and the noise level was tolerable. She eased her way toward the bar, scanning the crowd as she moved.

The main bar area had a variety of seating from booths to tables and in the back area she saw high-top tables and dartboards. All of the waitresses wore O'Leary's Pub T-shirts with jeans and they each had a name tag. She took a seat at the end of the bar. On a small stand was a menu for both food and drinks.

This bar was doing something right.

The bartender came over as she was reading the menu. "Hi. What can I get you tonight?"

She looked up and swallowed hard. The man in front of her was mouthwateringly gorgeous. His mussed black hair framed a face dominated by a happy-go-lucky smile. She lost her ability to form coherent sentences. "Uh . . ."

He tilted his head and studied her face. "You look beat. Tough day?"

She nodded. What was wrong with her? She didn't do this around men. She'd had no fewer than eight different men try to pick her up tonight. This one was just doing his job, and she had to fight for focus.

"How about an Irish coffee?" Dark brows arched over navy eyes.

She cleared her throat. "Sounds good."

He walked away. She studied the menu. It wasn't fancy. Like the rest of the bars, it offered burgers and hot wings, but they had more traditional pub fare, like fish and chips and shepherd's pie. Her mouth watered at the thought of real food. The drink menu was plain as well, but at least displayed a list of drinks with the basic ingredients. Pictures and descriptions would've been better, but this bar had already exceeded the competition from the other Chicago neighborhood pubs she'd visited.

The bartender returned with her Irish coffee. She sipped and found it perfect. The whipped cream puffed and floated on top and she used her straw to scoop some up. She ran her tongue over the cream-laden straw and heard a groan.

She looked up to find the bartender looking at her. Replacing the straw, she waited for an explanation.

His mouth quirked up at the corner. "Sorry. I couldn't help it. That was downright sinful."

Her cheeks flamed. She was blushing? No. The alcohol from earlier in the evening was catching up with her and colliding with her exhaustion. He broke eye contact and mumbled, "Give me a holler if you need anything else."

He walked away and picked up a conversation with other customers. She tried not to be obvious in studying him and the way he interacted with people. This was something the other bars had been missing as well. A personal touch.

She finished her drink, tossed cash on the bar, and took a few moments to wander toward the back of the bar. There was a small stage, a jukebox, and dartboards. Down a dimly lit hallway were the bathrooms. Too tired to think, she opted to leave. Part of her wanted to talk to some of the patrons, get their perspective as to why they came here, but it would have to wait.

By morning, hopefully Meg would have information about The Irish Pub and, with any luck, the books wouldn't be as bad as she imagined. As she wound her way back toward the front, raucous laughter exploded at the bar. The sexy bartender was enjoying something.

He caught her eye as she passed. His laughter made his eyes twinkle with mischief, his smile lighting his face, like he had the best life in the world. She wondered what it would be like to feel that even for a night. It wasn't that she was unhappy; she liked her life very much, in fact, but it had been too long since she'd experienced a laugh that shook her whole body.

* * *

Morning came much too soon for Elizabeth, especially when she realized that she hadn't thought to pick up her own coffee for the maker. Now she'd be stuck with whatever the hotel offered. The coffeemaker didn't brew fast enough for her sloggy brain, so she put her cup directly under the drip. After a measly half-cup, she took her shower and prepared for the day.

Meg hadn't called, so she dug around a little on her own, gathering information on both IP, as she'd begun to call The Irish Pub, and O'Leary's. Something about that bar had stuck with her into her dreams last night. She couldn't call it a classy bar; it wasn't. It was more like a neighborhood hangout for adults. Truth be told, she wouldn't have ever stepped foot in the place if she hadn't been doing research. It wasn't the kind of establishment she normally frequented, at least not since college. Maybe that's why she liked the place.

She toyed with the frogs on the small table that acted as her desk. Before heading to IP, she sent a quick e-mail to Meg. She hadn't even gathered her keys when her cell rang.

"Hi, Meg."

"Hi. I've got bad news and more bad news."

"Give me whichever is the least bad."

Meg blew out a breath. "Claire doesn't know much about that bar. Mr. Brannigan—your dad—doesn't talk about it."

"Not a big surprise. What's worse?" She jingled the keys in her hand.

"The one thing she did know was that your dad bought it for Keith."

The keys bobbled in the air and she missed them. They hit the floor with a clunk, as did her heart. "It's Keith's?"

"It's in your dad's name. You were right about that, but Claire is sure that he bought it after Keith brought it to him and convinced him to buy it."

"Okay, thanks."

"Do you want me to book your flight home?"

"No. Not yet. I'm not done here." She poked at the keys on the floor with her toe.

"But—"

"Don't worry about it. I'll deal with Keith and my dad." She disconnected, knowing she'd been rude to Meg. It wasn't as if she needed the reminder that Dad had made it clear long ago that she and Keith were not allowed to fight over any property. They'd mostly mended fences from the one time they fought. Since then, she'd been relegated to working after Keith put plans in place.

Except for this time. He'd had twelve years to do something, and as far as she could tell, he'd only made it worse. Elizabeth drove to IP and debated who she should call first. She shouldn't keep working toward turning this bar around without the green light from Keith or Dad, but it was obvious that neither of them cared much. It was a tax write-off and nothing more.

Armed with that knowledge, she decided to further assess the business before alerting anyone about what she was doing. She wanted to know how bad this situation was so that she could propose a plan to her dad, and by extension, Keith.

She unlocked the front door of the bar and was assaulted by a vile smell. Smoke, whiskey, and possibly vomit. She gagged and flipped on the light. The place didn't look any better with the lights on. Although she really wanted to leave the door open to air out the room, she locked up behind her. It would be just her luck to have a group of bikers come in while she was alone.

Moving toward the office, she tried not to touch anything. If Mitch left books out, she couldn't tell where. The office was a pile of papers and dirty coffee cups. She needed to find out how much they were paying Mitch. It was probably too much.

She sat at the desk and the chair wobbled and creaked. An old radio sat on the file cabinet behind her, so she turned it on and found a news station. The news anchor rattled on about the new mayor and what little he'd been doing for the city. She tuned it out as background noise to keep her company. The mayor was of little concern to her; she didn't plan on being in the city long enough to care.

She hung her jacket on the back of the chair and then set to work organizing the piles of paper. With the first stack clear, she uncovered an ancient laptop. It looked to weigh about ten pounds. She opened it and booted it up, hoping to find the books on there.

As the machine whirred and gurgled, she continued with the papers. Pages stuck together with an undetermined substance she was afraid to inspect too closely. How could Mitch find anything in this mess? She took the outstanding invoices and placed them in a folder to be paid. Random notes Mitch had made to himself she stuck in a brown bag she found in the corner of the room. Once the desk was reasonably clear, she sat again and attacked the computer.

The accounting was on the desktop and easy to find. Unfortunately, it wasn't easy to understand. It was a basic Excel spreadsheet, but nothing was marked or described adequately. She scrolled up and down the sheet trying to understand. She stared until the numbers began to blur.

Then she gave up. Mitch would have to find the time to explain his accounting system. This place was a disaster. No wonder it never saw a profit.

Pushing away from the desk, she craved another cup of coffee. Looking at the nasty, gunked-up cups around the room almost quashed her desire for caffeine, but not quite. She gathered those cups—eight in all—and took them back into the bar and dumped them in the sink. Something else for Mitch to take care of.

While in the bar area, she saw that the liquor license was up-to-date. Mitch at least had managed to get that much right. He wouldn't want to totally screw himself out of a job. She sighed and grabbed her purse from the office. She'd make a quick run to Starbucks and then return to finish clearing out the mess.

She stepped out into the clear morning and sucked in a deep breath of fresh air. Even in this mostly residential neighborhood, she had the sense of Chicago's beauty. She stood at the corner and looked up and down the street. A convenience store stood opposite her position, but everything else was apartment buildings. Behind her, down the side street, were single-family homes, mostly brick bungalows.

For the life of her she couldn't figure out what would possess someone to put a bar on this corner. It made no sense. There might be a good amount of foot traffic in the neighborhood overall, but how many of those people would stop in for a drink?

She got in her car and drove with the windows down to enjoy the air while she could. As she roamed through the neighborhood in search of decent coffee, her mind began to catalog the information gleaned from her barhopping last night. She made a mental checklist of things that needed to change at IP.

The creation of the list was slow going, though, because she was distracted by a sexy smile. Every time she pushed the bartender from O'Leary's out of her head, he muscled his way back in relentlessly.

Finally, she caved and allowed a brief fantasy to take over her tired brain.

A little fantasy never hurt anyone, right?

* * *

Colin O'Leary bounded down the back steps that led from his apartment to the bar. As he moved through the bar flipping on lights and prepping for the lunch crowd, he whistled a tune. As much as he enjoyed the crowds and the noise of the lively bar, this was his favorite part of the day. This was his time to be Colin O'Leary, bar owner. It didn't matter that the bar wasn't really his. Morning prep allowed him the time to pretend it was, that his father had left the bar to him. As if he hadn't screwed up everything.

Then the back door swung open and his bubble burst. He could tell by the sound of Ryan's steps that his brother was in a bad mood. Again.

"What's up?" Colin asked as he took chairs down and reset them where they belonged at each table.

"Don't ask. Did you get the inventory done?"

"Just about. I—"

Ryan spun from where he was making coffee. "What do you mean, just about? I told you I needed to get orders in today."

Colin let out a heavy breath. "As I tried to say, I got most of it done, but then we got slammed last night. By the time we got the crowd down to a manageable size, I was tired and didn't want to miscount."

Ryan shook his head. "Sorry I jumped on you. Things are a little crazy."

"Everything okay with Quinn? Any more problems?"

"Nothing more than usual. She's ready to pop and won't take it easy. You'd think that after spending most of the winter in bed, she'd know better. At this point, she just wants to have the baby. It doesn't help that Indy went into labor early. Indy's due date was a couple of weeks after Quinn's, so now she's really impatient."

Colin continued to work his way around the room. "Send her over to the house. Mom's so excited about the baby, she'll do nothing but fuss over her."

Ryan smiled. "I already tried. Quinn wouldn't fall for it."

"You look like shit. Aren't you sleeping?"

"Not much."

"Then take off. I can handle this."

Ryan raised a single eyebrow and Colin's shoulders tensed. After all these months, hadn't he proven enough yet? "It's inventory, not rocket science."

"How many times have you ordered?"

He shrugged. "Mary walked me through it while you were out of town. The distributors' numbers are in the Rolodex."

Ryan scrubbed a hand over his head. "No, I should check the numbers. I want to make sure we don't over-order."

Colin slammed a chair down harder than he'd intended. "When are you going to stop treating me like a fuckup? I've been here for a year, every day, doing exactly what you've asked. When are you going to stop punishing me for leaving?"

Ryan crossed his arms and stared at his feet. "You're right."

Silence.

At first Colin thought he'd imagined it. "What was that?"

A tired grin crossed Ryan's face. "You heard me. I said you're right. Something had to give. I thought I could keep doing it all with both bars even after getting married and having a baby."

"I told you I'm not going anywhere. You can depend on me. Let me take on more. Between Quinn and the baby and running Twilight, your hands are full. I'll ask if I have questions about anything before I make a move."

Ryan still didn't look sold on the idea.

"I'm ready for this."

"Fine." The acquiescence came quietly, but Ryan followed with a finger pointed at him. "But if you fuck up this time, Mom won't be able to save your ass."

"Like I'm afraid of you?" Maybe Ryan had forgotten who was the older brother.

As if he'd read Colin's mind, Ryan continued, "We're adults now, age is meaningless, except for the fact that your body has already taken an extra year of beating that mine hasn't, so I'm faster and stronger."

"Only in your dreams."

Ryan left on that note, and Colin felt the most at ease with his position in the family since his return. When their father died, Colin had taken off for three years. Everyone thought he'd done it out of anger because Dad gave O'Leary's to Ryan. He let them believe it because the truth was so much worse.

Now he finally had the chance to redeem himself. He no longer had to be the irresponsible, lazy O'Leary. He could finally become the man his father had expected him to be.

* * *

Elizabeth stood and stretched her back. She'd been hunched over the crippled desk for hours attempting to make the office usable. Mitch had come in and explained what he called accounting. She was on her fourth cup of coffee and she knew better than to keep drinking it, but without it she might fall asleep. Sleeping here would never be an option.

Although Mitch grunted at her when he left the office, she hadn't heard much noise coming from the bar. She wanted to see what his opening routine was, so she ventured out. She found Mitch sitting on a barstool with a beer in front of him watching a small TV.

"What are you doing?"

"Waiting for customers."

"Isn't there work that needs to be done while you're waiting?" This was a new business to her, so she pushed down the urge to fire him on the spot. He was the only one who knew what had been going on with the place for years.

He shrugged in response.

"The bar is filthy. It needs to be cleaned."

"Honey, the guys who come in here aren't staying for the décor."

She inhaled through her nose and bit down hard. This would take more than patience. "I understand that you're used to doing things, or not doing them, your way for a long time. Things need to change. That's my purpose for being here. I'm telling you, as your boss, that you cannot drink while on the job, and I expect you to clean the bar."

He picked up his glass, gulped the beer, and slammed the empty glass down on the bar. Turning the volume up on the TV, he grabbed a rag from the bar and pretended to wipe the surface.

"Hey, Mitch," a man called as he entered the bar.

Elizabeth turned to look at him. He stood in a smudged T-shirt and ragged jeans. He had a red bandana wrapped around his head.

"Hey, Rick." Mitch dropped the rag on the bar and shot a quick look at her.

Rick looked her up and down. “You lost?”

“No, I’m not.”

“Can I buy you a drink then?”

“No, thank you. I don’t drink while I’m working.”

“Rick, this is the new boss, Elizabeth.”

Rick laughed loudly and slipped onto a stool. Mitch had moved around to the other side of the bar and began pouring a beer. It was three in the afternoon. If these guys started drinking this early, how drunk would they be by nightfall?

She knew Mitch had to go. He wasn’t on board with the changes she would need to make. Unfortunately, she couldn’t afford to fire him just yet, but it was coming soon.

The idea of returning to that office was something she couldn’t stomach. “I’m going out. I’ll probably be back later.”

“We’ll be waiting.” Mitch tossed her a smile.

She stormed out, trying not to let him get to her. She’d been in worse situations with pigheaded men. This one, however, wasn’t something she was used to. Keith tended to hire the best he could find. She always had some trusted people to rely on, even when she had to fire the ones who didn’t work out.

If she got rid of Mitch, there was no one else. Her first order of business would be to find someone who could take over the daily operations of the bar. Back in her hotel room, she opened her computer and began placing ads. Mitch would be gone by the end of the week.

CHAPTER 2

Four days later, she'd conducted eleven interviews and hired two new managers. They were set to start the following day. Between the two people she'd hired, Gary and Mike, she'd be spending only slightly more than Mitch was being paid. Now all she had to do was fire Mitch. It was probably the worst part of her job.

She waited until closing, yet another endless night for her. When the last drunk left, she called him into the office. "We need to talk."

"About what?"

"I'm letting you go."

"What?"

"You're fired. The books don't add up, and while I believe you've been skimming, I have no proof. I'll give you two weeks' severance so you have time to find a new job."

He stood in the middle of the cramped office with his mouth hanging open. The creases on his face appeared to deepen. His eyes weren't quite focused, and she wondered how much he'd drunk.

"You can't fire me."

"I can and I did."

He wasn't the first person she'd had to fire, so this conversation was nothing new.

"Keith hired me. I'll call him and straighten this out." He pulled a phone from his dirty jeans.

She hadn't counted on that. She stood and held up a hand. The last thing she needed was Keith getting involved. She wasn't ready for him to know she was prying into his business. "First, he won't answer his phone at this hour. Florida is an hour later than here, and he's an early-to-bed kind of guy. Second, if you make that call in an attempt to go over my head, the severance is off the table. I will bring in a forensic accountant to find out exactly how much money you've stolen and I'll prosecute to the fullest extent of the law." She was totally talking out her ass, and she prayed he wouldn't call her on it. Given that he didn't seem too bright, it appeared her threat might work.

"Three weeks' pay."

Maybe he wasn't as dumb or drunk as he looked; he wanted to negotiate. "Two and a half and you don't try to collect unemployment."

"Fine. I'll have a job by tomorrow. You have no idea what you're getting into. My guess, you're gone inside a week."

He had no idea how tenacious she could be. There was no way she was leaving until she'd accomplished her goals. She pulled out the checkbook and wrote his check.

He snatched it from her hand, turned on his heel, and left.

"Nice doing business with you," she called after him. She dragged herself to the front door and locked up. Tomorrow would be a fresh start. Both of the men she had coming in were experienced bar managers. It had to be an improvement over Mitch.

She looked back over the darkened room and wondered what she was doing. She'd made employment decisions for other jobs, but this felt different. Doing it on her own made the difference. She really had no backup here, and preventing Mitch from calling her brother was the deciding moment. She was going to do this.

* * *

Early the next morning, her phone rang. Groggy, her blurry eyes attempted to focus on the screen. Dad. She'd known this call would come; she'd hoped it would've taken longer, though. She had to make a quick decision about what to tell him. She knew she wouldn't be able to disappear without being noticed.

"Hi, Dad."

"Hey, sweetheart. Where are you? I haven't seen you for days, and I don't remember sending you to a job."

"I'm in Chicago. I'm visiting with Janie. You remember her, don't you? I was feeling burned out from all the work travel, so I decided to take a break." It was only a partial lie. She was burned out; she really did want a break. Unfortunately, Dad never truly heard her desire to take over the company and stay at home. He was always more focused on her social life.

"Oh. Why didn't you say something?"

"It was spur-of-the-moment." She sat up and scrubbed her hand over her face and waited to be busted for that. Spontaneous wasn't her style. Dad didn't seem to notice her lapse.

"When do you plan to come home?"

"I'm not sure." She knew what was coming next, and her stomach turned.

"I have a new property I'm considering. If I get it, it'll be ready for takeover within two months."

Two months? Too bad this wasn't really a vacation. She didn't want to head to another job, in another city. "Can't Keith do this one?"

She heard fumbling on the other end. She'd caught him off guard since she'd never turned down a job before, but she had a feeling about this bar. This project would surprise her father. She would prove that she had the ambition and initiative to take over his spot. She could be him.

"Well, if that's what you want. But you know I try not to send him out of town for too long. The kids miss him. It's hard on a family."

She flopped back on her pillow. And there it was, the accusation beneath it all. Didn't she know how hard it was on a family to have a dad who traveled? She'd lived it. It was hard on her nieces when Keith was gone, which was why Dad leaned toward giving the company to Keith. But she shouldn't be knocked out of the running because she didn't have a family.

"We'll see how it goes. If you get the property, send me a timeline." She hesitated and then pushed forward. What was a little more truth stretching? "I'm actually looking into some options here myself."

"You are?" More shock.

"Yeah. I'm pretty tired, Dad. I was out late and I'm an hour earlier than you."

"Sure, honey, go back to sleep."

"Give Mom my love. I'll call you soon." She turned over with the intention of getting more sleep, but her mind wouldn't cooperate. She hated lying to her dad. That wasn't the kind of relationship they had. She picked up the phone again and brushed her fingers over the buttons, but didn't engage a call.

No, she'd started this and she'd see it through. If she hadn't made significant progress within a couple of weeks, she'd tell Dad the truth. All she had to do now was dodge Keith. He'd see right through her and ruin her plans.

With that settled, she rose and took a shower. Her brain was fuzzy, but she intended to use the extra time wisely. She needed to make improvements quickly.

* * *

Colin strode through the back door of O'Leary's to grab a cup of coffee before heading up to shower. He was getting a little old for this.

Mary sat at the bar drinking coffee and reading the Sunday *Tribune*. She looked over her shoulder as he got closer. "The walk of shame again, Colin?"

He shrugged and smiled. She didn't need to know that it was a poker game with the guys and not a woman that had kept him out all night. He enjoyed his reputation as a ladies' man. If he got half the action everyone thought he did, he'd be a very happy man. "What are you doing here so early?"

"I like the quiet here on a Sunday morning. Don't you have family dinner today?"

He nodded and poured a cup of coffee. O'Leary family Sunday dinner was early afternoon to accommodate the bar schedules. He checked his watch. "I have time for a nap before I go. You need anything down here before you open?"

"Nope. I'm good."

And she was. Ryan had totally lucked out in hiring Mary. She ran the place in Ryan's stead, a job Colin should've had years ago. He took his mug with him up to his apartment. This, too, used to be his brother's. When Ryan moved into his house with Quinn, Colin decided he'd rather live above the bar than with their mother.

He set his cup on the counter and lay across the couch his brother had left for him.

Hours later, Colin sat on the couch in his childhood home and felt the cushions sink and curve around his body. The nap hadn't done him any good. He needed a good night's sleep. Liam sat and handed him a beer.

"Mom know you grabbed these?"

"Hell, no. She's in the kitchen talking babies with the girls."

That had such a strange ring to it, but it fit. The girls Liam referred to weren't their sisters, but were family just the same. Ryan's wife, Quinn, waddled into the dining room carrying the basket of silverware. He jumped up to help.

"Go sit down," he suggested.

"If one more person tells me to take it easy, I'm going to hurt him. I'm fine. I want to move. I want this baby out of me."

Colin took a step back. The woman was downright scary. This hormonal version was worse than anything he'd experienced with his two younger sisters growing up. He didn't have a response. "I'll get the plates."

"Thank you."

In the kitchen, Quinn's sister, Indy, stood with a baby cradled in her arms. He leaned in and kissed her cheek. "Hey, good to see you. Where's Griff?"

"He went with Ryan to get dessert. Ryan forgot it was his turn, which pissed off Quinn because she would've made something. Bugged me too, because she probably would've made chocolate cake." The baby squirmed.

He reached out. "Let me have her."

Indy's brow furrowed. "You sure?"

"I'm the oldest of six. I spent most of my childhood with babies around." He scooped the tiny girl from her mother's arms. She weighed nothing, but then again, she was little more than a week old. She had that baby smell no one could resist. While he held Colleen against his chest, he said, "I need the plates for dinner before Quinn gets mad at me."

Indy brushed past him. "Don't mind her. She's mad at everyone right now. I'll get the plates."

He followed Indy back through the house and took Colleen into the living room with him. Holding her like a football, he returned to his spot next to Liam and drank from his beer.

Liam slapped Colin's free arm. "You look kind of natural holding a baby."

"Shut up." He took a drink from the bottle again. The truth was that he had been thinking about marriage and babies a lot lately. How could he not? Ryan had gotten married, then Michael. Griffin and Indy were engaged. He was surrounded by marriage and babies.

Colleen squirmed again, so Colin set his beer on the table and shifted her onto his shoulder. It did feel natural.

Some old cowboy movie played on TV in front of them. "What's going on at work?" he asked Liam.

"Nothing. I guess I don't have to ask how the bar is going. Ryan would've told us if there was a problem."

"Let me ask you something."

Liam shifted to face him. Of all of his brothers, Liam was by far the most serious and level-headed.

"Do you regret not getting involved in the bar?"

"What do you mean? We all grew up in that place. We all work St. Patty's Day. I'm involved."

"Not in the daily stuff, though. You never wanted to run it?" He smoothed a hand over Colleen's back.

"No. It always belonged to you and Ryan. It was your place with Dad. We all kind of knew it."

Liam said it with no animosity, but Colin wanted to know. "Did we push you out? Make you feel like you couldn't be there?"

"No. We all found our own things. You and Ryan, though, O'Leary's has always been yours." He finished his beer and stood.

Liam's assessment didn't fit. Eight years ago, sure. O'Leary's was his until he fucked it up. Now, he felt like a foreigner. Maybe not that bad, but he didn't fit. For a year now, he was pushing to find that fit, to make it feel like home, and it wasn't happening.

Of course, it didn't help that Ryan kept him at a distance either. He didn't know how many other ways to apologize. Maybe it was time to move on again.

Colleen fell asleep in his arms, and he laid her in the cradle his mother had bought for the grandbabies. She'd turned his old bedroom into a nursery. He watched the baby sleep and knew he wanted more than what he had.

Ryan and Griffin came into the living room holding a grocery-store coffee cake. "Before anyone bitches, Blackstone's was already closed. I did what I could."

Quinn's golden-brown eyes shot daggers at her husband, and Colin derived no small amount of pleasure from witnessing it. He moved to the table and took the seat that had always been his father's. When he came back to town last year, Colin had started sitting in the spot just to irritate Ryan. He'd succeeded, but he never felt right in the chair.

He was no more head of the family now than he could've been when his father died. Those were shoes he didn't know how to fill.

Mom and Moira carried the last of the plates of food to the table. Colin was struck by how much Moira looked like their mother. Red hair and pale blue eyes. His sister had become a woman when he wasn't looking. He was suddenly grateful Maggie wasn't there to make him feel even older. Ryan said grace. Colin looked around the house and saw subtle differences. The pictures on the wall had been updated with wedding photos of Ryan and Quinn and a family portrait with everyone but him.

One photo of him remained on the wall: His father stood with Ryan and Colin at his side in front of the bar at O'Leary's. One more piece of evidence that his life hadn't moved on but everyone else's had.

Moira nudged him with a bowl of potatoes. "Something wrong?"

He slid his easy smile into place to be the man everyone expected. "Nope."

* * *

Elizabeth's first day with the new managers went well. They agreed that the place needed to be cleaned up and that there was no excuse for the condition it was in. They both offered suggestions, and they talked about drink prices and schedules. When she left at six in the evening, she wanted to believe they had a handle on it. Gary was going to close tonight and Mike would open tomorrow afternoon.

She planned on getting some rest and then returning to watch Gary work. She was no fool. Leaving a new employee unsupervised on the first day could easily spell disaster. Back in her hotel room, sleep claimed her before she even thought about the list of things still hanging on her to-do list.

Elizabeth startled awake with the ringing phone. She shot into the air, while clearing her throat. "Hello?"

"Hey, Elizabeth. It's Gary. You'd better get back here. There was a fight. I had to call the cops and it's a mess."

"I'm on my way." She stood and smoothed a hand down her suit, then stopped. Absolutely no one involved was going to notice a few wrinkles. Of that, she was sure. She couldn't believe that there were problems already. She sped to the bar, hoping she wouldn't get pulled over. She was pretty sure she wouldn't be able to talk herself out of a ticket.

Outside the bar, the usual row of motorcycles leaned drunkenly against the building. That was the first problem. Red and blue flashing lights filled the street in front of her. Bar fight? It must've been an all-out brawl. She parked in front of the bikes and went inside. Two patrolmen were hauling out a man in cuffs and, from the looks of it, he hadn't been the only one.

She strode over to where Gary stood behind the bar, talking to a cop. He looked much younger than he had when she'd hired him. His inexperience showed as he shifted under the officer's questions. When his gaze met hers, he gestured to the cop. "Hi, Elizabeth. Officer, this is the owner, Elizabeth Brannigan."

"Ma'am."

"What happened?"

Gary shrugged. "I'm not sure. Two guys started getting loud, and I told them to take it outside. They laughed at me and started swinging on each other. Before I knew it, it was a free-for-all."

Elizabeth turned in a slow circle to survey the damage. She counted at least two tables and three chairs as casualties. The look on Gary's face let her know she was about to lose more than just furniture.

She tapped the officer on the arm. "This is the first time I've been at the bar for any length of time. My father bought it and let it run itself, so I know very little about what has been going on. Do you have any idea how often the police are called to this location?"

He smiled in a you-poor-thing way. "I don't have exact numbers, but we usually expect a few calls a month. I have to say, though, that this is the worst I've seen in years. Mitch used to keep it pretty quiet. There's always someone looking for trouble, and he was good at keeping it under control." He pointed at the damage and the few drunks still sitting around, enjoying the show. "You might want to close up for the night and think about getting a doorman or bouncer."

More things she hadn't thought of. Keith always had staff in place. Bouncers were never even on her radar.

Gary announced last call and the few men still drinking grumbled, but one look from the cops quelled that.

"Give us a holler if you need help," the officer called as he walked out the door.

Elizabeth leaned against the bar. Inside her head, she screamed, "Help," but nothing left her lips.

A few minutes later, Mitch strolled through the door.

"We're closed," Elizabeth said.

"Yeah, I heard you had some problems. I brought you a gift." From behind his back he produced a baseball bat.

Her stomach jumped and her heart beat double time. She took in his disheveled appearance—hair standing on end, stains on the front of his shirt—and he seemed to sway in place.

Mitch gently swung the bat in his right hand until it landed softly in his left palm. He neared and Gary said, "Do I need to call the cops back?"

Mitch shook his head. "Not for me. I thought you might want to keep this behind the bar. The crowd is a little rough sometimes."

He laid the bat across the bar with a sick little smile. "See ya 'round."

Gary sighed. "You know, Elizabeth, I really want this job, but I can't do this. I'm here all alone, and this could've gotten bad."

"I'm sorry, I had no idea. Mitch didn't tell me about problems, but I should've guessed, given the clientele."

"When you get new customers, give me a call, and I'd be more than happy to work for you. Until then, you're not paying me enough to risk my life."

She nodded. She wasn't even going to try to convince him. Maybe between herself and Mike, they'd be okay. Mike was a much bigger guy, so maybe he'd be more intimidating than Gary. When the cop mentioned getting a bouncer, she'd immediately thought of Mitch. The cops seemed to think he had some magic with this crowd, and being a bouncer didn't put him near the register. After his visit, though, her stomach turned again. No, she wouldn't go back to him. He'd had a decade to prove his worthiness.

Elizabeth locked the door behind the last customer. It was just after ten o'clock, but it felt like three in the morning. Gary helped her close and clean up the broken furniture. She pulled cash from the register for his one night of work. "If you know anyone who would make a good bouncer, please send them my way."

"I will. Thanks for the chance. I hate to leave you like this, but I have a family."

"I understand. I'll figure something out. Thanks."

Gary walked out the door, and Elizabeth sat in the silence, too wound up to go back to sleep, too defeated to attempt to tackle the problem at hand. She grabbed her purse and locked the door behind her.

Not wanting to be alone, she drove to O'Leary's. She probably wouldn't find any answers there, but she was sure to see a friendly face.

* * *

Colin poured another beer and checked the time. Still two hours until closing. It had been a quiet evening, which suited him, so he'd sent most of the staff home. He and Jenna could close by themselves. Someone kept playing some sad, sappy music on the jukebox, which didn't help his mood.

He wiped down the bar, thinking about his options if he left O'Leary's. The money he'd socked away wasn't enough for a business of his own. The few offers he'd made went nowhere. Ryan had made it abundantly clear that he would be no help. Colin would have to figure it out on his own.

He didn't get far with his tired brain when a soft scent tickled his nose. He looked over to see Legs. Of course, the woman had yet to introduce herself, but she had a great pair of legs, so in his imaginings of her, he called her Legs.

Even at midnight, she wore her usual power suit, albeit a little on the wrinkled side. Her dark hair was pinned tightly in place except for a few locks around her face. She sat on a bar stool and waited. Dark smudges marked under her eyes. She looked beat. "Hi there."

"Hi." The smile she offered stayed a little on the stiff side, neither genuine nor friendly.

"It's late. Are you still drinking Irish coffee?"

"Sure, why not. It's not like I'm going to be getting much sleep tonight." She shifted and propped her elbows on the bar.

"You know, when I think about staying up all night, it's usually because I'm having fun."

She shook her head. "No fun here."

"That's too bad. You look like you could use some." He turned to make her drink.

She wasn't the only one. He needed to find a spark, something interesting before this life swallowed him up.

He'd thought that coming home would fix things, that he'd find what he was looking for. It felt good to be home, around his family, but he still needed more. He just had no idea where to find the more.

Turning back to give Legs her drink, he thought he might like to have a night of something more with her. He put on his best fuck-me smile and leaned against the bar. "What do you say we get out of here?"

The drink in her hand bobbled and some whipped cream slipped down the side. Her face, however, showed no sign of nervousness.

"That's a tempting offer. More tempting than you can know, but I have too much work to deal with."

"What work needs to happen after midnight on a Sunday?"

"Everything that didn't happen earlier today and everything that did." She sighed and drank her coffee, leaving a mustache of cream on her upper lip.

He hoped to watch her lick the cream off, but she swiped at it with a napkin instead.

"A couple of hours off could work miracles for both of us."

She stared at her cup and he thought he had her.

"I have proven methods to get rid of that stress you're carrying." Her cheeks grew pink, and he wanted to stroke them to see if they were as warm as they looked.

"Thanks for the offer, but I have too much going on right now."

"No one can work twenty-four-seven. A little break, a little relaxation. Could be fun." He leaned forward and watched her throat work as she gulped her coffee. Then he made a rare suggestion. "I live really close. Like, within minutes."

She stirred the quickly melting whipped cream in her cup. "I really shouldn't. But thanks for the offer."

Shouldn't, not won't, not can't. Colin left her with her thoughts as he continued to clean up. She didn't run after he'd made his proposition, so maybe he had some hope yet.

CHAPTER 3

Elizabeth stared into her coffee cup. She'd had so much caffeine, she'd probably be riding high for a week. The sexy bartender had made her a hell of an offer. She hadn't had sex in a long time. Her job crippled every relationship she'd tried to have. Her life had become a series of short, monogamous flings. Like a sailor with a lover in every port.

She watched the man clean glasses like he was giving a woman a rubdown. Who knew soapy water could be so sexy? When he came by again, drying his hands on a towel, his brows furrowed.

"Something wrong with the coffee?"

She shook her head. "Not at all. I just decided that I've had a enough caffeine and this wasn't going to help me relax."

He took the cup, dumped the contents into the sink, and returned with a glass of red wine. "Try this."

She sipped and the rich flavor rolled across her tongue. Much better than coffee, but far from the expensive bottles her mother had gotten her used to. This was more like fresh-from-college-living-on-a-budget wine.

"Good?" he asked.

"It is. Thanks."

He walked away again. This time she noticed the way his jeans stretched across his ass. Very good. As if he felt her ogling, he spun around.

The obnoxious blush that always ruined her ability to hide anything rose again. She cleared her throat. "Where's the washroom?"

He pointed toward the back. She took one big gulp of her wine and slid from the stool. She knew exactly where the washroom was. She remembered from her last visit, but she hoped the question covered her irrational behavior.

She hadn't been so struck by a guy since college. Even then it was Janie and Lori who drew guys in. It's not that she was the ugly friend; on the contrary, she knew she was pretty, but she was also clumsy around guys. Spilling drinks and tripping on her own feet had been staples of her dating life.

In the bathroom she used the facilities and washed her hands. She felt a pleasant buzz hum through her bloodstream. She couldn't figure out, though, if it was the bartender's flirtation or the alcohol causing it.

The thought of his proposition warmed more than her blood. Her girlie parts started to tingle.

Oh, God. It had been way too long if she started thinking about girlie parts. She stared at herself in the mirror. Her life was pretty screwed up. She was in over her head working on a project that she didn't know how to fix. Her father wouldn't consider her as his replacement. Her brother . . . well, she hadn't known what to think of Keith for years.

She deserved a night of fun. The bartender was right. For tonight, she'd abandon thoughts of CEO and IP and focus on having a good time.

She went back to the bar and ordered another glass of wine. This time, she'd take it slow so she wouldn't be drunk. It would be just her luck to have a guy willing to take her to bed and then she'd be too drunk to enjoy it.

Other customers filed out slowly. The lone waitress wiped down tables.

"Can I get you anything else?" the bartender asked. "It's last call."

"No, I'm good with this." She shot a look over her shoulder to make sure the waitress couldn't hear. "About what you said before . . ."

He froze, reading her expression, and then leaned in against the bar. "What?"

"I think you're right. A night away from the chaos would do me good. Does your offer still stand?" She smiled enough for it to be an invitation.

The silence stretched for what seemed like an eternity, and she started to believe she'd imagined the entire conversation. Maybe he hadn't really been flirting with her. Maybe she had just wanted him to.

He shifted closer, slowly, almost unnoticeably. But then the smile slid across his face, brightening his navy eyes, and she knew she hadn't imagined any of it.

"You mean my offer for stress reduction?" His voice was low, barely above a whisper. It was a bedroom voice if she'd ever heard one.

Oh, yeah. She nodded, not trusting that words would come from her mouth. A moan was poised at the back of her throat seeking a reason for escape.

Without looking away from her eyes, he called out, "Hey, Jenna, you can go on home. I'll close up."

"You sure?"

"Yeah." He broke eye contact then and pointed over his shoulder as he addressed Elizabeth. "I need to finish up a few things."

The waitress called out a good-bye and he followed her to lock the front door. He dimmed the lights, and Elizabeth spun her stool to continue watching.

She couldn't believe she was doing this. She hadn't had anonymous sex in almost a decade. The thought gave her pause. Those one-night stands had been far from great. She'd been young and too timid to ask for what she wanted or needed in bed.

She watched this man move across the room efficiently and purposefully. Lust tugged low in her belly and hormones surged.

He stalked toward her, sure in his movements. He probably did this all the time. She'd seen women smiling at him across the bar. Flirting was no different from small talk for him. She hoped he bought condoms by the case because she didn't even have one.

"Second thoughts?" he asked.

"No."

He stepped closer, nudging her knees apart. The heat from his body brushed her thighs, and she wanted to pull him into her.

"Maybe we should at least exchange names. I'm—"

Elizabeth quickly put a finger on his lips to stop him. "No names."

Names would complicate their time together. No names meant no future, no way to track each other, just pleasurable anonymity.

His tongue darted out and wet her finger. He lowered his head, and her heart beat so loud she was sure he'd hear it. Lips made contact and the moan she'd withheld bubbled back up. His fingers skimmed down the side of her body sending shivers through her.

He took his time licking and nibbling across her jaw and down her neck. There was way too much fabric between them.

She pulled back. "Let's get out of here. You said you live close?"

"Right upstairs."

He stepped away and she hopped off the stool. She immediately lost her balance. *Not now, not again.* She hadn't felt a bit of nervousness this time and clumsiness still struck.

"Whoa." He reached out and grabbed her elbow to steady her.

She felt like a ten-year-old wearing her mother's heels for the first time. She straightened and ran a hand down her skirt. "I'm fine. Let's go."

He didn't answer, but took a moment to study her face. She smiled and nudged him.

"Are you sure you're okay?"

"I'm fine. Which way out?" God was she starting to sound desperate?

"You look a little drunk."

"I'm not drunk. Not even two glasses of wine. Who gets drunk off two glasses?" She spread her arm out and promptly knocked over the glass she'd left on the bar. "Oh, shit. I'm sorry."

She grabbed the towel he'd left on the counter and began to mop up the small puddle.

"Hey, it's okay." His hand landed on her shoulder. "Maybe I should call you a cab."

She spun quickly, rag in hand, to tell him no. Unfortunately, she misjudged how close he stood to her. The wine-soaked rag squished against his shirt.

His eyes darted north the way most men's did to control their anger, but he looked like he was attempting to control laughter.

Great. Now he was laughing at her. Blood rushed to her head from anger instead of lust. "I am not drunk."

He crossed his arms and continued to study her as if he were a visual Breathalyzer.

The moment was gone. The lust she'd felt dissipated. Embarrassment replaced passion. "This was a mistake."

She pushed past him and made her way to the door.

"Wait."

Elizabeth didn't. She unlocked the door and rush-walked to her car. She would've run, but she was afraid she'd fall on her face. She knew alcohol had nothing to do with it, but she had no way to convince him.

Once, just once, she'd like to have an encounter with a man that didn't involve her damaging property or causing bodily harm. She'd been a clumsy child, but after her father had found success, her mother had sent her to every dance class imaginable. Her mom figured dance would give Elizabeth the grace she so desperately needed. It didn't have the desired effect, not totally, anyway. Elizabeth had learned to dance, but her clumsiness had stayed. It reared its ugly head every time she moved too fast or felt nervous.

Intimacy with a man made her nervous. Good-nervous, but still. Once they really started she was fine, but getting there was the problem.

She thought back to the sexy bartender. She'd been so close to getting there with him. He wasn't the first guy to think she was drunk. That was the main reason she tried not to meet men in bars. Her clumsiness usually made them think she'd had too much to drink.

Being spontaneous didn't work for her. If she'd planned ahead, if she psyched herself up for a one-night stand, she would've fared better.

Elizabeth drove back to her hotel alone. Back to the drawing board. Maybe a good night's sleep would give her the relaxation she needed.

Yeah, that'll be so much better than a round of hot, sweaty sex.

* * *

Elizabeth had been in town for a week and she felt buried. IP wasn't just in the red, it bled profusely. She was desperate to turn this bar around, and her self-imposed deadline to make some kind of improvement was bearing down on her.

Two days had passed since almost having sex with a stranger. She knew how Keith and her father normally approached a job, but this one was so different, she thought she'd tackle it with a new method, one she prayed she wouldn't regret. Armed with the bit of research she could drag up, she entered O'Leary's Pub again before she lost her nerve.

She'd never tried a move so bold, and she wasn't sure she could pull it off. But it felt right.

She stood at the bar and waited to get the attention of the bartender. Of course, it would have to be the sexy one who'd offered her plenty of distraction and left her disappointed. She'd hoped that since it was early afternoon, he wouldn't be here.

The bar was slow, the only customers being a couple of old men at the end of the bar nursing their beers and watching a baseball game.

With a towel slung over his shoulder, the bartender approached, smile at the ready. Then his eyes focused on her, recognition changing his expression. "Hi."

She shoved unpleasant memories from her mind and pasted on her business smile and said, "Hi, I'm looking for Mr. O'Leary."

He slapped the towel against the bar. "You found him."

Oh, Christ. Why couldn't she catch a break? How was she supposed to negotiate with a guy who turned her on with a simple look?

She cleared her throat. "Mr. O'Leary, I'm Elizabeth Brannigan, and I have a proposition for you."

He leaned his forearms on the bar and lowered his voice. "As good as the proposition I made the other night?"

Although his jaw had been smooth the other night, it looked like he hadn't shaved since. His scruffiness added to his sex appeal, and she tried to block it. Her ears burned, and she wished she hadn't pulled her hair back. Before she could respond and make her intentions clear, a petite blonde sped around the corner.

"Hey, Colin, there's a problem in the kitchen."

Elizabeth straightened. "Colin? You're not Ryan O'Leary?"

Colin pressed his lips together. "Nope." He stuck a thumb over his shoulder. "He's in the back office."

She clenched her teeth and turned on her heel, anger burning in her chest. She'd done her homework. Why didn't she know there was a brother?

"A word of warning. He won't be as receptive to a proposition as I would, given he has a wife and a baby on the way." He tossed a grin over his shoulder as he headed into the kitchen.

She strode toward the office, practicing her speech again. She could do this. It was different from their usual approach. Keith would normally hire an all-new staff and then send her in to supervise them. Maybe it was because her dad had kept the bar for a dozen years and never said anything.

She wanted to make this work, not pay someone else to do it.

She knocked on the office door and waited.

"Come in."

She swung the door open into a small but tidy office. Of course, it was bigger than the one she'd been trying to work in. A leather couch sat in the corner and a huge oak desk dominated the other end of the room. The man behind the desk was a dead ringer for Colin. Even if she had known there was a brother, she could see where one could easily be mistaken for the other.

She cleared her throat and began her speech again. "Mr. O'Leary, I'm Elizabeth Brannigan, and I have a business proposition for you."

He stood and his eyebrows quirked up. He gestured to the chairs in front of the desk. "I'm not really looking to expand."

She took a seat, putting her briefcase at her feet. "I own a bar that is in desperate need of an overhaul. I've done research on the bars in the area, and yours is the most successful and closest to what I'm trying to build."

Sitting behind the desk, he steepled his fingers in front of his face. "You want me to help you build up my competition?"

"I'm not in direct competition with you. I would make it in your interest to help me succeed. I'm offering you a percentage of profits and a bonus when I sell." She'd spent hours running numbers to put together an attractive package. She laid the proposal in front of him. Even if she failed, which she wouldn't, she would be able to pay him from her own savings.

"I'll admit, it's an intriguing offer, but I have too much on my plate right now. I'm already running two bars and I'm about to become a father."

Her heart sank. "I wouldn't need you to run the bar. You would be more like a consultant. I'm in new territory with this business and could use some guidance from someone who's been there."

"Sorry. If you had caught me last year, I'd be all over this. I just don't have the time right now to devote to another business."

She swallowed hard past the lump in her throat. "I understand your position. Here's my card." She slid it onto the desk. "Give me a call if you change your mind."

She stood, willing her hand not to shake as she extended it. She'd known this was a long shot, and she really didn't like to lose. If Keith caught wind of this, he'd never let her hear the end of it. He'd call it good-natured teasing, but she'd end up grinding her teeth.

Ryan O'Leary shook her hand and she knew he wouldn't be calling her. Well, she'd tried. Now she'd go back to what had always worked in the past. She'd start making calls to people she knew. Someone would send a man her way who could do the job.

* * *

Moments after Elizabeth had left, Colin walked into the office, dying to hear her proposition. "What did Legs want?"

"Huh?" Ryan looked up from the computer screen.

"Long legs, power suit. Had a proposition?"

"Oh. Her name is Elizabeth Brannigan."

"I heard her name when she introduced herself, but she's a lot of leg. What was the proposition?"

"Get your mind out of the gutter. It was business. I just Googled her. Her father is some big investor in resorts in Florida. He buys them when they're run-down and fixes them."

"What does that have to do with you?"

"She bought a bar and wants help."

"And?"

"I told her no. I don't have time to add another business. Although, now that I'm looking at the money and power behind her dad . . . the profit might be worth it."

"I'll do it." The words left his mouth before he thought clearly about what he was suggesting.

"What?"

"Give me the information. I'll work with her."

Ryan shook his head. "She's not looking for a bed-buddy. She needs a business partner."

Colin's shoulders tightened. "I can do that. You just said that it would be profitable. Something like that would give me the money I need to open my own place."

Anger flashed in Ryan's eyes. "So much for being here. It hasn't even been a week since you swore you weren't going anywhere. That I could count on you."

Guilt sank into Colin. It was a feeling he knew too well. "You run two bars and have for a long time. It's a fact you've been shoving in my face for a year now. I can do what you do. I'm not an idiot."

They stared at each other like they had as children, each thinking he knew best, each knowing they worked better together than apart.

"Whatever." Ryan flung a business card at him. "Do what you want. That's something you excel at."

Colin scooped up the card and tucked it into his pocket. "I'll be at the bar if you need anything."

Ryan answered with a grunt. He'd get over it. At least Colin was pretty sure he would. He was ready for this. If that meant he had to prove it to Ryan first, he would.

Back at the bar, he pulled the card out. *Elizabeth Brannigan, VP Brannigan Enterprises.* Hmmm . . . VP explained the power suits she always wore. Also explained the stick up her ass when she'd introduced herself.

Completely different from the woman who was pliant and moaning in his arms. He knew he'd made the right choice by not sleeping with her. If he was going to get into bed with her, she was damn well going to be sober enough to remember it.

And enjoy it.

On the back of the card, neatly printed, *Sheraton Hotel Higgins.* Now he knew where to track her down.

Stick up her ass or not, Colin could make this happen. He'd help her make the bar a success, they'd sell with a nice profit, maybe have a little fun on the side, and then go their separate ways. How hard could it be?

* * *

Elizabeth sat in the conference room of the hotel and sipped from the glass of lukewarm water in front of her. She'd met with eight different men, each attempting to astound her with their business acumen. They all held MBAs and explained how they would increase profits and decrease loss.

She didn't like any of them. Profit-and-loss statements she understood. She didn't need help with that. Something else was missing, and she didn't even know the right questions to ask. Normally in this situation, she'd call Keith. Doing so now, though, would tip her hand. She still wasn't ready to let him know her plan.

She didn't know how long her vacation charade would last, but she hoped long enough to prove she was on the right track with the bar.

When a soft knock sounded at the door, she cringed before answering. She wasn't ready for Mr. MBA-Number-Nine, but she sighed and called, "Come in."

The door opened and Colin O'Leary strode into the room, wearing jeans and a T-shirt, and looking utterly delicious. She choked on her latest drink of water.

"Whoa. Are you all right?"

She cleared her throat and carefully sipped more water. "Fine, thank you. What can I do for you, Mr. O'Leary?"

The muscle in his jaw twitched and he said, "My dad's Mr. O'Leary. Call me Colin. And it's what I can do for you."

Her mind flashed to about ten different things that she'd like him do for her, and she felt heat creeping up her neck. She forced out, "What could that possibly be?"

"My brother said you were looking for a business partner. I'm here to apply for the job."

She looked him up and down. "That's how you show up for a job interview?"

He spread his arms wide and glanced down at his body. "A job at a bar? Yes. I didn't think this was so much a formal interview as a business negotiation."

Nothing like a bit of arrogance in the morning.

"Exactly why would I be negotiating with you?"

"Because I can help you turn your bar around."

She crossed her arms on the table and waited.

"I passed by the suits waiting out there. I'm assuming they're here for you. What bar needs more suits to run it? You need someone who knows people. If you don't have customers, you don't have a business."

"I'm aware of that." But he definitely held her attention.

"I'll admit that running the books isn't my strong suit. Ryan has always been better at that. But I grew up in a bar. I understand people. You've been to O'Leary's, different days, different times. I understand now that you were using us for research. You obviously liked what you found."

In so many ways. "It's a very successful bar."

"It's successful because people keep coming back."

"And you're telling me that you're the reason for that?"

"I'm part of the reason. It's the whole thing. It's atmosphere. I can help create that."

He was onto something. He was the first man to walk through the door who had offered her what she wanted. Unfortunately, she wasn't sure he could deliver. In the time since Ryan turned her down, she had done more digging. She was surprised at how much information people from the neighborhood had given her about the O'Leary brothers. The father founded the bar and Colin ran the bar for a while, but disappeared for years after his father died. She was sure there was more to that story, but no one seemed to have it. Everyone agreed, though, that Colin was the go-to man for a good time. Men and women alike all appeared to have a genuine fondness for him.

She could see why. But she and Colin had unresolved . . . issues.

"Tell me about the bar you bought," he said as he lowered himself into the seat across from her.

She slid a folder to him, the same one she had forwarded to all the other candidates.

He flipped it open and a bark of laughter shot from his mouth. "You bought The Irish?"

"No. Yes." His laughter flustered her, making her feel like she was mentally unstable for owning this particular bar.

He closed the folder. "Which is it? Do you or don't you own the bar?"

She cleared her throat. "I do. I personally didn't buy it; my father bought it twelve years ago."

"That explains a lot."

"What?"

"Ryan told me you're from Florida. Why would your father buy a bar in Chicago when he's not around to run it?"

"I've been wondering the same thing."

"You didn't ask him?"

"You don't have to worry about the reasons for ownership."

He closed the folder without reading anything she'd provided. "The Irish used to be a profitable bar. When the original owner died, things fell apart. Something like five owners came and went in as many years."

"I already know this. It's a matter of record. What would you do to change what it is now?"

"You have to close it and change everything. It's a total dive right now because that's what it's turned into. If you want it to be something different, you need to start from scratch so the current clientele won't want to return."

She'd been thinking the same thing. Closing the doors after the brawl had been a good idea. "When was the last time you were in there?"

"Years. But I don't need to go there to know what it is. Everyone in the area knows that The Irish is where you go if you want a brawl. The drunker and meaner, the better." He leaned back in the chair and forced it to recline. His long legs extended under the table, and she had a flash of those legs between hers. He looked smug as if she wouldn't be able to turn him down.

"You don't have the business management experience or education the other candidates have."

He smiled. "Neither does my brother, but you went to him."

"Like the saying goes, the proof is in the pudding. He's a success. Just because you share a branch of the family tree doesn't guarantee me anything."

"But you've seen me with people." He thunked the chair back down on all four legs. "I was good with you."

Between his intense blue eyes and his low bedroom voice, his words warmed her blood again.

"And that would be another reason to not work with you. I don't have time for someone who's more interested in flirting than working."

"Sweetheart, you flirted with me. I took your cues and acted on them. I'm completely capable of working with a partner without sleeping with her."

Part of Elizabeth felt relief at his statement. More of her felt another sting of disappointment.

His steely blue gaze bore into her. No sign of lust. Nothing to imply that he planned to kiss her again. Not even a hint of sexual attraction. If they pretended that night had never happened, a partnership could work.

She steadied herself for a strong negotiation. "I'll offer you twenty-five percent profits and a bonus twenty percent when I sell, assuming you hold up your end of the bargain and bring in the customers. I remain the manager and boss and all decisions go through me."

"Make it forty percent profits and thirty percent on sale."

"You bring personality to the table. No proven experience, and you expect me to give you almost half the business?" She leaned back in her chair.

"My personality is the one thing you need most. It can't be taught or bought."

"Thirty profits and twenty-five at sale."

He narrowed his eyes as if computing, then leaned forward. "Deal."

"One more thing. No flirting. Just business."

He sighed like she was being insufferable. "Contrary to popular belief, I am capable of being professional. When do we start?"

"It's locked up, so we can start tomorrow. I'll have the contract drawn up for you to sign when you get there. Nine a.m.?"

"I'm closing at O'Leary's tonight. Make it eleven. Even I need my beauty sleep."

"You plan to continue to work at O'Leary's?"

"It's my family's bar."

"I'm not a simpleton. There are only so many hours in a day. I won't have you thinking you can drop by The Irish just to collect a check."

His smile was disarming. "Sweetheart, simple isn't what anyone would call you. I'll prove my worth soon enough. Seems a lot of people expect that." He rose and extended his hand. "I'll sign your contract, but a handshake will do for me."

She shook his hand and tried to ignore its strength and warmth and the zing of her nerves. As he turned to leave, she enjoyed the view and immediately began to question her sanity. She'd just created a business partnership based on a man's charm. What the hell was she thinking?

CHAPTER 4

Colin left his meeting with Elizabeth feeling both optimistic and horny. As stiff and uptight as she looked, he saw a fire in her eyes when she began negotiating with him. His blood raced as she stipulated her terms, but when he touched her hand, he knew he was in trouble. He was half hard from a handshake.

Getting involved with someone like Elizabeth would be a mistake, if for no other reason than she thought she was better than him because she had money and a degree. She needed to remain a business partner, a means to an end.

His optimism outweighed everything else. This was the perfect position for him. A few months back, he'd made an offer on that exact bar and was told it wasn't for sale. Now he knew why. Elizabeth's plan suited him and his own plans.

On his way back to O'Leary's, he drove by The Irish. It was locked and a posted sign read UNDER NEW MANAGEMENT. The bar itself, if he remembered correctly, was less than half the size of O'Leary's. It would never be a nightclub or a hot spot. It would always be a neighborhood bar.

He let his mind wander over the possibilities of what to do to draw in crowds. It wasn't long before he knew what it had to be. A Chicago bar, on Addison, one short bus ride from Wrigley Field—a sports bar was the only thing that made sense.

Back at O'Leary's, Ryan stood behind the bar, talking to the old men who sat there every afternoon. He was dressed for Twilight, his other bar, so Colin knew he'd been waiting for him.

"You're not going to believe this."

"Huh?" Ryan asked.

"I went to see Elizabeth Brannigan. Guess what bar she owns?"

"Nothing around here has been for sale."

"That's because Daddy bought it a dozen years ago. She's the proud owner of The Irish."

His brother's jaw dropped. "No freakin' way. Did you tell her thanks, but no thanks?"

I wonder how hard he'd laugh if he knew I tried to buy it myself. Colin shrugged, not sure how Ryan would take the news. "No. I took the deal. Thirty percent of profits and a twenty-five-percent cut of the sale."

Ryan snorted. "She offered me thirty-five. And I would've gotten forty."

"I figured. She pointed out that I'm not you and, like with everyone else, I have to prove myself." He tried not to sound like a snotty teenager, but wasn't sure if he'd succeeded.

"You're crazy. That bar is never going to be what it used to be."

"You're right. That's why we're going to make it into something new. We're going to reinvent it."

"We, huh? Already chummy, I see."

Colin picked up a rag and wiped down the bar. "It's not like that. It's a business deal, nothing more."

Ryan patted him on the shoulder as he walked past. "You remember that every time you think about those legs you mentioned."

He'd been telling himself pretty much the same thing. Ryan seemed to accept the news as well as could be expected. Tension still clung to their every interaction, and Colin didn't know what to do about that. He couldn't afford to waste any more time trying to make Ryan happy. The past was the past and they all needed to move on.

Lucky for him, The Irish offered a great path for him to take.

The night was slow, so in between customers, Colin thought about changes he'd bring to Elizabeth. Figuring she'd want more than him talking to her, he began taking notes on cocktail napkins. By the end of the night, he had twelve napkins filled with his scribbles.

* * *

Elizabeth finally felt like she was making forward motion. She talked to Mike and informed him that the bar would be closed for renovations effective immediately. She told him that he still had a job, but to take a few days off so she could figure out where she needed his help.

She'd had an additional sign printed and posted on the doors of the bar letting customers know it was closed for renovations. Then she returned to the hotel to prep for her meeting with Colin the following day. She created a list and a basic spreadsheet of what she thought the budget would be.

Then she checked her appointment calendar. Her afternoon was booked with interior designers and vendors. With any luck, she could dump the vendors on Colin to handle. They needed to remove stock that wouldn't move and order what would. Which meant they'd better have a plan for a drink menu. She added that to the discussion list.

By the time she looked at her watch, she'd missed both lunch and dinner. Instead of room service, she decided to enjoy some fabulous food in one of Chicago's restaurants. She wished she knew more people in the city. Running solo constantly wore on her. Maybe instead of fine dining, she'd find a good pizza. She hadn't had Chicago-style pizza in forever, not since she was in college.

Thoughts of Northwestern reminded her that she did know people in the city. She hadn't visited in years, but she knew that Janie and Lori both still lived here. They spoke online at least every couple of months. And having dinner with them made her lie to her father less of a lie.

She scrolled through her address book and dialed.

"Hello?"

"Hi, Janie?"

"Yes."

"It's Elizabeth Brannigan. I'm in town and thought we could get together."

"Oh, my gosh. It's great to hear from you. When did you get in?"

"I've been here a little more than a week."

"And you're just calling me now?"

Her stomach sank. She'd believed their friendship was still good. "Well, I've been busy with work. I'm not here for pleasure."

"I'm just yanking your chain, Libby. Good to know it's still easy to do."

Elizabeth sighed. No one called her Libby anymore. "I know it's last minute, but are you free for dinner? I'm dying for some pizza."

"You're in luck. I'm just leaving the office now. Where are you staying? I'll come pick you up."

"I can meet you."

"Don't be ridiculous. It'll give us more time to catch up. Have you talked to Lori?"

"She was going to be my next call."

"I should feel special then, since you thought of me first."

Elizabeth didn't admit that she'd simply come across Janie's name first in the address book. "I'll give her a call while you're on your way."

"She won't be free to meet us. She's in *love*."

"I didn't think she was serious with anyone."

"Things change, babe. You haven't been around. You've been busy with your plans for world domination."

Elizabeth felt the chuckle in her chest. It had been too long since she'd spent time with friends. "I'll call Lori. You hurry up and get here. Pizza and drinks on me."

She gave Janie her hotel information and hung up. Lori's phone went straight to voice mail. After leaving a message, Elizabeth changed her clothes. She'd only packed work clothes, so she didn't have anything casual. She settled on slacks and a silk shell, opting for no jacket. On her mental list of things to do, she added shopping for new clothes.

Janie met her in the lobby with a strong hug. It had definitely been too long since they'd seen each other. E-mail chats didn't accomplish what a simple hug could.

"How are you?" Janie asked.

"Good, I guess."

"What are you doing here? I thought your dad was focusing his operations in the Southeast."

"He is. I found a failing business in his holdings and decided to come here to fix it."

Janie led the way to her car. "What kind of business?"

"A bar. A really crappy dive of a bar. Motorcycle riders and cancer-inducing smoke included. I hate every minute of being there. I'm so glad I decided to call you."

"So am I. How long do you think you'll be in town?"

"A month. Maybe a little longer."

"Good. Then we can hang out like old times. Maybe we can even talk Lori out of the guy she's into."

"Sounds like a story."

* * *

Morning sun glared through the windshield of her car as Elizabeth nursed her coffee. She definitely should've stopped drinking earlier in the evening. Three in the morning came faster than she had remembered. But it had been fun to talk, really talk, with a good friend. They'd managed to discuss jobs, family, and everything in between. They'd overindulged in drinks and food. Elizabeth had loved every minute of it.

She was paying for every enjoyable moment now. She should've said no to the last drink. Hell, she should've refused the last three drinks. It was good that Colin had pushed their meeting to eleven. At least she had time to grab a coffee on the way. The coffee burned a path down her throat and splashed into her stomach as she parked in front of IP. The sight of the ugly building made her ill. Her stomach roiled and she swallowed hard.

Stepping from the car, she shaded her eyes and willed the throbbing in her head to go away. Hopefully, the caffeine would help and she'd be more like herself before Colin arrived. She let herself into the bar and flipped on all the lights. The stench was even worse than the last time she'd been here in the morning.

She propped open the front door for fresh air. She moved the CLOSED sign into plain view so people wouldn't take the open door as an invitation. Staring at the disgusting floor and the bar that wasn't much better, she shook her head. Her stomach heaved again, so she pressed her hand to her abdomen. Although she'd never been much of a drinker, she'd never gotten sick from it either.

"It's not that bad," a voice said behind her and she jolted.

Colin stood in the doorway holding a box of doughnuts.

"Good morning," she said.

"Same to you." He lowered his sunglasses and stared at her. "Are you feeling okay?"

"I'm fine." She turned back to the bar and swung her arm wide.

"As you can see, the place needs a lot of work. I'm not sure it was even cleaned nightly. The smell makes me want to vomit, so I think we need to get rid of that first."

He put the box on the bar and ran his fingers over the wood. "The bar looks to be in good shape. I can't tell much about the floor with this crappy lighting. Do you have brighter bulbs we can put in?"

She shrugged. "I have no idea what's here. I haven't looked at any of the inventory. In fact, I was hoping that would be one of the things you could handle. I have decorators coming in later as well as a slew of vendors."

"Like to move fast, don't you?"

She was suddenly grateful for the dim lights as she felt heat creep up her neck again. "What's that supposed to mean?"

"Do you know what you want to do with this place yet? How are you going to have decorators in here if you don't have a plan?"

"My plan is to get rid of the crap and start new."

"You don't need decorators to get rid of crap. They're going to charge you for stuff we can do ourselves. That doesn't make sense." He fished into his pocket and pulled out a pile of napkins. "I have ideas."

She took a napkin and used it to wipe down one of the stools to take a seat.

"Hey, those are my notes."

She looked at the crumpled paper. "You took notes on cocktail napkins?"

"I used what I had handy." He snatched it from her.

After shuffling through the pile, he looked up. "I think this bar has a lot of potential."

"As what, a dump?"

"You said that you wanted to turn this bar into a profitable business." He looked at her like she was a child playing a game. "I thought you were serious."

She hopped off the stool. Serious? Everything in her life was serious. Everything she did was to advance her career. How dare he question her work ethic? "You think because I'm not impressed by your pile of napkins that I'm not serious?"

Before he could answer, a dull pain shot through her stomach. She clenched her midsection and rubbed it with a flat palm as if she could will the pain away.

Colin moved closer. "What's wrong?"

The pain passed and she straightened. "Nothing. I'm fine. Slight upset stomach."

"Maybe you should sit back down."

As much as she wanted to argue with him—he had no business telling her what to do—she really wanted to sit down. She eased back on the stool. As quick as the pain arrived, it seemed to disappear. In the back of her mind she feared the ulcers had returned, but she brushed the thought aside. She'd been fine for years, able to live and eat and drink normally. Last night's alcohol was just taking its toll.

Colin's gaze followed her every movement. She didn't like being scrutinized by him, so she pointed at his mess on the bar. "Go on."

He hesitated, but continued, "This bar is in an excellent location. You're right on Addison."

"So?"

He shook his head. "One quick bus trip and you're at Wrigley Field."

She had no idea where he was going with this.

"The Cubs? Baseball?" He sighed heavily. "I'm suggesting we make this a sports bar. Chicago has great teams and even better fans. Instead of letting this place flounder as some Irish pub imitation, we make it something new, like you said."

His enthusiasm caught her off guard. She knew less about sports than she did about bars, but he was excited. He thought he was really onto something.

"All of the research I did on bars in the area was on Irish pubs. I didn't look into sports bars at all."

"In Chicago, Irish pubs are a dime a dozen. You have North-Side Irish, South-Side Irish, and plenty of fakes in between."

"And sports bars?"

"Also a dime a dozen."

He'd lost it. Worse, so had she to think that bringing him on board was a good idea.

"Don't give me that look. Sports bars are everywhere. Chicago is a sports town. What you have here is a neighborhood bar. It's never going to be more than that. Take a look outside."

She glanced through the open door. As she had on her first visit, she noticed the residential neighborhood.

"We have to give people a reason to come here to drink instead of sitting on their couches. We need to offer something better than what they have at home."

He began to make more sense than she'd expected, but she held her hope in check. "How do you suggest we do that?"

"Bring in big-screen TVs. Get quality satellite in here with all of the sports channels. Offer bus rides and tickets to some of the Cubs games."

"Where would I get a bus?"

He shook his head at her again. "You rent it. You buy a block of tickets and sell them. Like a field trip. They get drunk to and from the game and don't have to drive. Once the place is cleaned up, people will come to check it out. Neighbors will be nosy. They'll want to know what we've done. Once we get them in, we need to entice them to stay and come back again."

She sipped at her coffee, now cooled. Her nerves had calmed and her stomach seemed to settle. She wasn't sure she liked the idea of a sports bar, but she had nothing else. Colin was right; the location restricted what she could expect. "Okay."

* * *

With that one simple word, Colin relaxed. He'd thought for sure Elizabeth wouldn't agree to any of his ideas. She looked completely lost over the concept of a sports bar. He didn't understand why she wanted to make this thing work instead of selling it when she had no idea what she was doing. He doubted she'd ever even stepped foot in a bar, except for doing *research*.

"Awesome." He scooped up his napkins and balled them up. One by one he shot them into the trash can behind the bar. He only missed twice.

"Are you done playing now? We have a lot of work to do. I have decorators coming in to look around and offer bids on fixing this mess. I also have vendors coming in. Before we can know what to order, I think we need to determine our drink menu." She reached into her briefcase and pulled out the legal pad. "Beer will be our biggest seller, don't you think? But like you said, this is a neighborhood bar, so I'm thinking we stick with mostly domestic and a few popular imports. What else?"

"Liquor. No girlie drinks."

"Well, that ruins my plan for an upscale wine tasting."

Colin froze and stared at her. She hadn't moved, but her cheek twitched. He asked, "Did you just make a joke?"

"Obviously not a very good one."

He smiled. "It wasn't bad. You caught me off guard. I didn't know you could joke."

Her gaze left her list and met his eyes. "There's a lot about me you don't know."

Even in the dim light, her hard stare shot into him. He had to remind himself that they were on the same side. Something about her made him feel as if they were opponents. He didn't know much about her, but he'd like to peel away that guarded layer that made them rivals. Like when she'd sat at his bar, tipsy on wine.

"I'll head into the storeroom to do inventory."

She nodded. "I'll be in the office going through the mess there. How long do you think you'll need? The vendors and decorators will be here around four."

He looked at the clock and realized that it was broken, so he shrugged. "That should be fine."

He headed to the back, looking for a door to the basement like they had at O'Leary's. He found it and opened it to a stench worse than death.

"The inventory is in the storeroom. Next door down," Elizabeth said from behind him.

"What the fuck is that smell?" He pulled his shirt collar up over his nose to block the odor.

"I don't know. I've never been down there. Smells like a job for you."

He slammed the door. "You're not paying me enough to dispose of corpses. Talk to your decorators."

"Before I can hire someone to fix it, I need to know what the problem is."

He turned to look at her. She stood with her arms crossed, waiting for an argument. "I'll check it out after I finish with the inventory."

She stared at him like she couldn't believe he'd agreed. Well, neither could he. He opened the next door and flipped a switch for lights. The storeroom was small, about the size of the supply closet at O'Leary's. Two metal shelving units held beer; a third held hard liquor. On the opposite wall sat an assortment of things that didn't look well used: paper towel rolls, a case of toilet paper, various bottles of cleaners. The wall to his right had a long, beat-up counter running the length of the space. On it was a tabletop pizza oven, a microwave, and a coffeemaker.

It dawned on him that the place had no kitchen. It was almost unheard of for a bar not to have a kitchen. They should see if they could get something going here. Check the plumbing lines and gas lines to see if they could turn this into a kitchen and move the inventory to the basement.

He was getting ahead of himself. Elizabeth wanted to make changes to turn a profit. Neither of them was in this for the long haul. Building a kitchen would be too much. But if he could sell her on his ideas, the bar would be what he wanted when he bought it. Using her budget figures, he had an idea of what she'd be looking for when she was ready to sell. With the twenty-five percent promised in their contract, he could do this.

His grin spread as excitement rose. He'd be able to get his own bar and it wouldn't cost him anywhere near the money or sweat equity because Elizabeth would bear the brunt of making the changes. All he had to do was bide his time and make sure the bar was profitable enough for her to want to sell.

Grabbing a clipboard that Elizabeth had left on the counter, he began counting cases of beer and bottles of alcohol. Tucked away in the corner between shelving units, he found a box of stale pretzels. He dragged it out the back door and tossed it in the Dumpster.

An identical metal door stood eight feet to the left of him. It was for the adjoining business. Faded lettering on the door couldn't be read. He scanned his memory for what used to be there and came up empty. He walked around the other side of the building. This side had a few more windows than The Irish had, but they were all soaped and boarded up. The other half of the building was bigger than the bar and it had a parking lot attached.

He wondered if Elizabeth had looked into who owned it. Did her father own the entire building and The Irish just happened to come with it?

There were a lot of questions crowding his brain. He shouldn't care. He had a deal. Make a profit and get her out. He circled back to the door he'd exited, leaving it open behind him for a cross breeze.

From the back hall, he heard Elizabeth's voice. They weren't expecting anyone for a few hours yet. A voice rose, but it wasn't hers. Colin headed into the bar to see what was going on.

Elizabeth stood near the door. The sunlight was blocked by the behemoth of a man she was talking to.

"We're closed. Not just now, but indefinitely."

"Mitch always lets me come in early." He stepped toward Elizabeth, and Colin moved in.

Before he had a chance to say anything, Elizabeth put her hands on her hips. "Take another step into my bar and I'll call the police."

Not a smart move. Colin could see the guy was already half in the bag. Calling the cops would just piss him off.

"Fuck you." He looked over Elizabeth's head and called, "Mitch. Get this bitch out of my way before I move her."

"Mitch is gone. Fired. He won't be back."

Colin stood beside Elizabeth. "Excuse me, I'm Colin, Mitch's replacement. Can I help with something?"

Elizabeth glared at him and pressed her lips together tightly.

"I just want a drink. And she"—he stuck his thumb at Elizabeth—"won't let me in."

"We're not open for business right now. She's a stickler for the rules. You know how some people are." The man cracked a smile, and Colin knew he had him. "I don't think one small drink could hurt. You are alone, right?"

The man furrowed his eyebrows.

"I don't want to tell you to come in for a drink and have you bring fifty of your closest friends."

"Just me."

"Come on in, then. But only one and then you have to leave. We're trying to fix the place up."

The hulk of a man brushed past Elizabeth, and she stormed off into the back. "Feisty one, ain't she?"

Colin didn't respond. He knew he was already going to pay for letting this guy have a drink. The man plopped onto a stool while Colin moved around the bar. "What's your poison?"

"Shot of whiskey and a beer."

Colin quickly poured both. "I'll be right back."

The man grunted and swallowed the shot. Colin went to the office.

As soon as she saw him, Elizabeth opened her mouth. "You have—"

He cut her off. "You can yell at me later. Call the non-emergency line for the police and let them know we have a guy who plans to leave here and drive drunk. He won't get far."

He left the room with her mouth still hanging open. Back at the bar, the man was nearly finished with the beer. "You're gonna need a new place to hang out for a while. We really are closed for remodeling."

"No shit?"

"No shit. The boss back there wants to turn this place around."

The man stood and looked across the room. "What's wrong with it?"

Colin shrugged. This was one conversation he didn't need to have.

The man slapped a five on the bar. "Keep the change. Thanks for the drink."

He stumbled out the door. Colin moved to the corner of the bar to see what car the man was in. He threw his leg over a motorcycle. As the drunk fished for his keys, a squad car came down the street. Colin returned his attention to the rows of alcohol behind the bar.

As soon as he'd poured the shot, he knew the whiskey had been watered. He started with that bottle and went to the sink. The liquid splashed and glugged down the drain. He turned to the next bottle and poured a bit into a semi-clean glass. The cheap tequila had been watered too.

He worked his way down the line, taking a taste and pouring everything out. If the manager was watering drinks, the bar should have been showing more of a profit. It was a good thing Elizabeth had fired Mitch. Her manager had probably been lining his own pockets. He sipped from the next bottle.

* * *

"What the hell do you think you're doing?"

Anger burned in her stomach. Colin had only been here a few short hours and he was turning her life upside down. She didn't need this kind of stress.

He stared at her while holding a shot glass. "I'm doing inventory like you asked."

"Somehow, drinking the inventory is how you decide what we need to buy?"

"I'm tasting it to see if it's good. It's not." He poured the contents of the bottle into the sink.

"Pouring alcohol down the drain isn't going to make this place profitable."

He raised an eyebrow at her. "The alcohol has all been watered down. If that's the way you plan to do business, let me know now and we can terminate our contract. I'm not in the habit of cheating people."

Her face flushed. He'd done it again. At every turn he was embarrassing her. "I have no intention of cheating anyone. I didn't know the alcohol had been diluted."

He shook his head and turned back to the row of bottles. "It would just kill you, wouldn't it?"

"What?"

"To trust me. We're supposed to be on the same side. You know, a team, but you walk around like you're expecting me to screw you over." He shifted again to face her.

"I don't know you. I'm not looking to be on a team. We have a partnership, a limited one at that. I need to make sure this works. I can't afford to waste time or energy." He didn't need to know how close he was to guessing the truth. Her brother had taught her early on not to count on anything or anyone.

"Fine. I'm going to dump all this liquor. Do you have a problem with that?"

Of course she had a problem with losing hundreds of dollars' worth of alcohol. But he was right. Again. "Go ahead and dump it, but I did tell you that I expected all decisions to go through me."

"Excuse me for showing initiative. It won't happen again."

She turned and went back to the office, closing herself in the silence. This would never work. She couldn't even have a conversation with Colin without it turning into a power struggle. She should've known better than to partner with a man like him. He wanted to be the boss just like every other man.

She opened the bottle of antacids she'd brought with her and chewed on one. Her stomach was still upset. She wasn't just hungover; she knew that feeling. Maybe her stomach was upset because she'd skipped breakfast. It was past lunchtime and she hadn't even eaten a doughnut.

Her thoughts ran back to Colin. Strange that while on the topic of pain she had thought of him. She shouldn't have snapped at him. She felt crappy because she hadn't gotten enough sleep and she was hungry.

Maybe she'd invite Colin to lunch. She had to be able to work with him. He hadn't done anything to make her think he wasn't trustworthy. He'd done nothing wrong. In fact, he'd come up with some good ideas.

She grabbed her purse and headed back into the bar. He stiffened at the sight of her. Oh, yeah, this was going well. "We missed lunch. I thought maybe you might want to grab something to eat before we have to meet with people."

His shoulders relaxed and his mouth quirked. "Is that an invitation?"

"Yes. I'm sorry I snapped at you."

"That's all?"

What else did he want? She raised her brows, waiting for an explanation.

"No 'thank you'?"

"Why should I thank you for doing your job?"

He walked around the bar and stood much too close for her comfort. "I think you owe me a thank-you for rescuing you from the biker."

She rolled her eyes. "You did not rescue me. I handled myself fine."

His smile broadened. "From where I stood, he was about to handle you."

"I didn't ask for your help."

"What would you have done if I wasn't here?"

She debated telling him that the door wouldn't have been open. The clientele of this establishment made her uneasy, but she wasn't about to give him that fuel. "I would've called the police."

"Wrong choice. You need me more than you thought, Legs." He walked past her toward the door.

"What did you call me?"

"Legs." He tilted his head and his gaze ran down the length of her. "As in you're all leg."

"My name is Elizabeth."

He smiled, and her heart jumped. A smile should not have that effect.

He continued, oblivious to her condition. "Anyway, if you'd made that call to the cops, he would've gone into a rage. You have to be able to read people."

"That's why I hired you. So we're back to you just doing your job and no thanks are necessary." She turned to the door with her car keys in hand. His laugh echoed in the empty bar behind her and she couldn't hold her smile back.

She pressed the alarm button for her car, and Colin stopped her. "I'll drive."

"I'm capable of driving."

"But I know the area and I don't want to be seen in your ritzy car. I have a reputation to protect."

She let her mind wander to what kind of reputation he had. "Fine. Where are you parked?"

He pointed to the Jeep in front of them. He had to be kidding. It was one of those off-road things with no top.

CHAPTER 5

Colin barely kept his laughter in check. She stood in front of him trying not to be insulted that he'd checked out her legs, and now she stared openly at his Jeep in fear. "I'm a safe driver. No worries."

She ran a hand over her neatly tied-up hair and tugged at the hem of her jacket. Could she possibly be more buttoned up? At the rate she was going, she'd need surgery to remove the stick up her ass. No one was always that tense. "Are you worried about your hair? Seriously?"

"No," she snapped. "My hair is fine. Let's go."

"How about Jimmy's? Good hot dogs and burgers."

"Whatever you want. I don't live here."

As if he needed the reminder that their partnership was temporary. He drove to Jimmy's and pulled into the lot. They didn't speak on the short trip. At the counter, Elizabeth ordered a salad and a side of fries, then stepped aside for him to order. He pulled out his wallet to pay.

She nudged in front of him. "I invited you to lunch."

"I never let a beautiful woman pay my way." He shoved bills into the hand of the cashier, who was clearly amused by their conversation.

"So if I were homely, you'd allow me to pay." She stood behind him with her arms crossed, ready for a fight.

He knew there was no correct way to answer that question. The woman obviously didn't accept compliments well. "My mother raised me to pay when I'm with a woman."

That was diplomatic.

"That's sexist. I make plenty of money. I certainly don't need a man to pay for my lunch."

He couldn't win. "I'll let you buy me dinner then."

She smiled. "What makes you think we'll be eating dinner together?"

He couldn't answer. Her smile was amazing. It totally opened up her face and made her so much more than beautiful. Unfortunately, it only lasted a brief moment because then she scowled.

She waved her hand in front of his face.

He lifted a shoulder. "We have a lot of work to do. Long days and nights. We'll be eating plenty of meals together."

She picked up the tray with their food and walked toward a table. His mouth went dry at the thought of long nights with Legs. He gave himself a mental shake and walked to the counter to get some ketchup and napkins.

Legs could not be a conquest. He needed to keep it professional. Starting with calling her Elizabeth instead of Legs.

Besides, he didn't think she even liked him.

He sat across from her. "Is the salad supposed to balance out the fries for a healthy meal?"

"No. My stomach was upset earlier and so I wanted something bland, but I love french fries."

He took a big bite out of his burger and moaned to let her know what she was missing. Her face became stone. After swallowing, he held the sloppy burger out to her. "Want a bite?"

She looked at him like he'd asked her to swallow a flaming sword. Maybe she was afraid of germs. It would explain why she wanted to pay someone to clean the bar when they could easily do it themselves.

He sank his teeth into the burger again. She picked at the salad. This was going to be a long meal.

"Why did you come to see me about the bar?"

Her question caught him off guard, and he choked a little while trying to swallow. He heard his mother's voice echo in his head: *If you chewed your food, you wouldn't choke*. When his airway was clear, he said, "Ryan told me about the offer you made him. He already has two bars, so his plate is full. But it sounded like a good business move to me. Of course, that was before I found out it was The Irish you owned."

"But if you have O'Leary's, why this?"

The tension crept back into his shoulders. "I don't have O'Leary's. Ryan does. I help run it, but he's the owner."

She chewed on some fries. He felt like he'd just passed a test.

"What about you? Why are you doing this? It's obvious you don't particularly like bars."

"This is what I do. I take something that isn't working, that isn't profitable, and I turn it around. Sometimes we sell, and sometimes we hold on to the property."

"I know that much. You're not in the bar business. You do resorts. Why this?"

She shifted and stared at her plate. He had hit on something.

When she lifted her face, she was nothing but business. "Let's just say this is a pet project."

He knew that was all he was going to get out of her. She could call it whatever she wanted as long as they made a profit. She could keep her secrets as long as they didn't interfere with the business at hand. It wasn't like he didn't have some of his own.

They finished eating without conversation. Elizabeth pushed her salad away. "We'd better get back to the bar. People are going to start showing up. Do you have the inventory ready to talk with vendors?"

"All set, boss."

"Do you need me to sit in on those meetings?"

"No. I think I can handle ordering beer and liquor."

She stood. "I figured you could. What's your schedule look like for the rest of the week?"

He led the way to the Jeep. "I'll be around plenty. We need to clean the bar before we can get anything else done."

"We?"

"If you pay people to do what we can do ourselves, you lose money for other things we need, like some kick-ass high-def TVs."

She buckled in as he started the engine. "That's a need?"

"For a sports bar it is. You can't call yourself a sports bar and then set up some crappy thirty-six-inch TV." He pulled into traffic not hiding his smile as he caught sight of her death grip on the door.

Hours later Colin was dog-ass tired and he still needed to work at O'Leary's. If he didn't at least make an appearance after only one day at The Irish, Ryan would never let him hear the end of it. He rapped on the office door.

"Come in."

He swung the door open and saw Elizabeth sitting behind a cluttered desk, looking completely out of place. "I'm heading out. The inventory is done and ordered. Information's on the bar. There are some good promotions coming up I think we should do. That's on the bar too."

She twirled her pen. "About what you said earlier."

Shit. What'd he do now? He waited, but she didn't continue. "I talked a lot today."

"When you said we could handle the cleaning ourselves. Did you mean it?"

"Yeah. Afraid of a little dirt?" Maybe germs did freak her out.

"It just seems overwhelming."

"Nah. Once you scrape off the first layer of scum, the rest will be easy."

"Okay then. I'll get cleaning supplies tonight and we'll start scrubbing tomorrow."

"See you then." He walked out of the bar knowing that she took him seriously and liked his ideas, but he was too tired to celebrate. Now he'd talked himself into cleaning a bar that hadn't seen a mop in years. It was time to call in reinforcements.

* * *

Elizabeth opened the bar early the next morning. Colin hadn't said what time he'd be in, but since he had worked at O'Leary's last night, she didn't think it'd be any time soon. She hauled the box of supplies she'd purchased into the bar and tried to figure out where to start. The tables were as good as any other spot. She took a bucket and went to the back to fill it with hot water.

As she hefted it to the front, the door opened, flooding the room with sunlight. Shit. She knew she should've locked it. She squinted against the glare. Although she couldn't make out any features, she knew it was Colin.

"I didn't expect you here so early. Aren't you tired?"

"I'm fine. Cleaning was my idea, and I'm not about to have you accuse me of slacking off." He propped the door open and she was grateful for the fresh air.

"I'm starting with the tables. They all look salvageable if they come clean." She turned away from him and began scrubbing with the soapy sponge. She heard no movement behind her, so she turned back to see Colin staring at her. "Is there a problem?"

"Yeah. You don't want me to call you Legs, but then you show up wearing a pair of jeans that show just how long your legs are."

"Did you expect me to wear a suit to clean the scum?"

"I thought that's all you owned."

She wasn't about to admit that she'd made a special trip to buy some T-shirts and jeans. Although she owned some in her regular wardrobe, she hadn't packed them. "I'm a regular person. I wear business attire when conducting business and casual wear when I'm not."

He still didn't move, so she swung her arm out. "Get to work. We have a lot to do."

She turned back to scrubbing and watched the white, soapy bubbles turn gray after only a few swipes. Part of her was tempted to get rid of all the tables and buy new ones, but it wouldn't be fiscally responsible. She needed to watch the bottom line on this site closer than any other.

Music suddenly blared from the bar and she jumped at the noise. She looked over her shoulder to see Colin grinning. He'd brought a stereo with him. "Better, don't you think?"

"Keep it down. We'll talk about music selection later."

He tuned to a classic rock station and she didn't argue. When he began singing along, slightly off-key, she almost did. He wasn't horrible, though. She moved on to the next table and she saw him drag a large trash can toward the bar.

"I'm going to throw out all the crap. Is that all right?"

"Yes." She sighed, but knew she had it coming. She'd said she wanted all decisions to go through her. They worked to the sounds of the radio for the next half hour and didn't talk.

She went back to refill her bucket for the third time. When she returned, four people were standing in the middle of the bar, staring. "I'm sorry. We're not open for business. We're in the middle of renovations."

A short, busty redhead snorted. “You might want to start with a wrecking ball.”

The tall blonde standing next to her elbowed her. “I’m sorry for Moira’s rudeness. Colin asked us to come help today. I’m Indy, Colin’s sister-in-law, and this is my fiancé, Griffin. This is Moira, Colin’s sister, and his brother Michael.”

She couldn’t have been more shocked. She quickly recovered, wiped her hand hurriedly on her jeans, and extended it. “I’m Elizabeth.”

“I know. We’ve heard about you.”

They shook briefly, and Elizabeth did her best to hide the fact that not only did she not know they were coming, she knew nothing about them.

“Hey, you made it,” Colin called from behind her.

“Of course we did,” Griffin said, leaning forward to slap Colin on the shoulder.

Colin looked at Elizabeth. “Did you meet everyone?”

She nodded.

Colin continued talking. “Where’s Colleen?”

Indy answered, “With your mom. She can’t get enough of being a surrogate grandma.”

Griffin looked at Indy. “You’d better learn to drop the surrogate. It’ll piss her off.”

Elizabeth watched the exchange with fascination. They were all so at ease with one another. That feeling was something missing from her childhood.

Indy turned to her. “Where do you want us to start?”

She shrugged. “Everything needs to be done, so—”

Colin interrupted, “The basement really needs work. Take Griffin with you. There might be some animals or something down there.”

Once her mind had a chance to clear, she looked at the man standing next to Colin. Griffin, was it? There was something familiar about him, but she couldn’t put her finger on it. They’d never met, of that much she was sure.

Griffin smiled. “How about you take the basement and I’ll do the bar.”

“Consider this payback for taking Indy from me.”

Indy laughed. “As if you had a chance.”

Indy and Griffin turned toward the back. Elizabeth couldn’t believe Colin had convinced them to do the basement. She stood staring for a moment, taking it all in. Colin and Indy? Now she was with Griffin . . . Griffin Walker. Holy cow. That's where she knew him from. Her mother read the society pages religiously. Elizabeth paid little attention, seeing them as tabloids. She had better things to do than gossip.

Her mother, however, had thrust the paper under her nose at least once a month to point out someone else she thought would be the perfect bachelor for her to snag. Now she knew why Mom hadn't mentioned Griffin Walker. He was engaged and had a baby.

Colin nudged her. "I didn't think you'd mind me calling for help. If you have a big family, you might as well use it."

So much for getting this done themselves. At least they would be cheaper than professional cleaners.

As if reading her mind, he leaned closer and whispered, "They work for beer and pizza."

Moira heard him and said rather loudly, "Now that I've seen the place, I think you need to offer me something better than pizza and beer."

"A deal's a deal. Besides, you owe me."

"I've never owed you this much."

"Ha. You've moved twice in the last year and I helped both times. If you don't want to owe me, you better get yourself a big, strong boyfriend for the next move."

Moira moved toward Elizabeth's bucket of water and dipped her hands in. "Believe me, after this, I will."

When Colin and Michael went back behind the bar, Moira mumbled, "And when I find him, I'll keep him hidden from you."

Elizabeth grabbed another sponge and set to work. "Why would you have to hide your boyfriend from Colin?"

"You don't have a big brother, do you?" She began scrubbing the table beside Elizabeth.

"Actually, I do."

Moira stopped, midswipe. "Do you introduce him to every guy you date?"

There really hadn't been that many men in her life, especially of late. "Sometimes."

Moira shook her head. "My brothers have a tendency to scare off any guy that wants to date me. They're even worse with our younger sister, Maggie. She had to go all the way to Europe to escape the protective bubble."

Elizabeth finished the table she was working on. "Having someone look out for you can't be all bad."

"Not at all, as long as you never expect to get laid."

"I heard that," Colin called from the bar. "As far as I'm concerned, you're a virgin until your wedding day."

Moira laughed. "Kind of hard to find a husband if I can't sample the wares first."

"Gross. I don't want to hear."

Moira threw the sponge into the bucket, causing bubbles to fly. "Are you going to tell me that you would marry a woman that you'd never slept with? Have you ever even dated a woman without sleeping with her?"

Colin stood in stunned silence.

"I thought so."

Michael, who had been working silently, pushed Colin. "She's got you there."

Elizabeth's face warmed. She couldn't imagine having such a frank discussion with anyone in her family. Janie and Lori, yes, but Keith?

"How about you, Elizabeth?"

"Huh?" Elizabeth returned to scrubbing furiously at the table in front of her.

"You wouldn't get married without having sex with the guy first, right? I mean, what if he was really bad in bed?"

Without looking up from her soapy sponge, Elizabeth said, "I don't know. In my experience, a kiss can tell you a lot about someone. If the chemistry is there to make your toes curl from a kiss, sex won't be an issue."

"I guess I've been kissing the wrong guys. Toes curling I've had happen, but never from a kiss with my clothes on."

"What's that about toes curling?" Colin asked.

Elizabeth's ears burned and she couldn't look up. She'd spent too many hours thinking about Colin's smiling mouth coming toward hers and how much fun it could be.

"Elizabeth's had some great orgasmic kisses, that's what. I think I need to hang out with her."

Colin strode across the room. "Are you trying to ruin my little sister?"

Elizabeth straightened from over the table. "We were having a conversation that didn't include you. Besides, your little sister is an adult. Maybe it's time you treat her like one."

Moira swooped in and stood on tiptoe to wrap an arm around Elizabeth, startling her.

"I like her, Colin. You need to spend more time with her. She'll be a good influence on you."

Colin slung a towel over his shoulder. "Not likely."

Which? Spending time with her or her being a good influence? "Aren't you supposed to be working on the bar?"

He grumbled something and returned to his spot on the other side of the room.

Moira stepped back. "Let him go sulk. He doesn't like being told what to do."

"Too bad. I'm the boss."

Moira swished her sponge in the water again. "I'm liking you more and more."

Elizabeth found she liked Moira as well.

* * *

Colin watched Elizabeth work alongside Moira and a twinge of jealousy bit into him. Sure, it had been his call to get his family involved, but he hadn't imagined Moira becoming friends with Elizabeth. He'd been looking forward to having time to work with her and on her. He believed they'd hit it off if given the opportunity.

And here was Moira stealing that opportunity.

He strained to hear their conversation, but their tones became too muted. Instead, he focused on the task at hand, clearing off the bar and everything beneath it. He'd already tossed most of the bottles of alcohol. Filthy rags and dusty bowls collected on the shelf underneath the bar. He threw them all away. If Elizabeth wanted to save a few pennies, she could rescue them and waste her time cleaning them.

Michael looked up from his position squatting at the lower shelf behind the bar. "How come Ryan's not here?"

"I didn't ask him to come."

Michael grabbed some old mousetraps and flung them into the trash can. "He's too good for grunt work?"

"He wouldn't have shown if I did ask. You know that. He thinks this is a stupid idea, and he's just waiting for me to fuck it up so he can say, 'Told you so.' " Colin scrubbed with renewed ferocity thinking about Ryan.

Michael stood. "That's not true. It was hard while you were gone. Ryan felt responsible for everything."

"He blames me for everything."

Michael shook his head. "He resents you for doing what he never could. He couldn't walk away to grab a chance at his own life. You did."

Colin bit back his response. He hadn't been grabbing at life; he'd been running from it. "He's still pissed off. Every time I think we're okay, he accuses me of screwing up."

"He's mellowed out. Wait till the baby's born. He's just worried about Quinn."

"Doesn't matter. There's nothing more I can do. Maybe if I'm successful here, he'll get it. I'm home for good."

Michael punched his shoulder. "We're glad about that. Especially Mom."

They both turned back to the job at hand. Colin had been home for a year now and he was still trying to reconnect with everyone and everything.

After a half hour, Indy and Griffin returned from the basement. They'd lasted longer than Colin had expected.

Indy wiped her hands on her jeans. Her ponytail was crooked and strands of her long blond hair dangled in her face. "Your basement is repulsive."

"Thanks. I think I knew that."

Griffin stood behind her. "You need to call an animal-control-and-disposal unit. You have some dead creatures down there, and we're not taking any chances with whatever diseases they might have."

Colin laughed. "It took you that long to figure it out? I think Elizabeth and I came to that conclusion about thirty seconds after we opened the door."

"We gave it a few seconds more. We actually went down the stairs to investigate."

"Then where—" Colin stopped himself when he realized that the two had found a dark corner to be alone. He eased forward. "Please tell me you didn't screw on Elizabeth's desk. She'll blame me."

Indy giggled. "Give me some credit. I just had a baby. But Colleen is up every few hours. We don't get a lot of alone time."

Griffin put an arm around Indy's shoulders. "We're going to clean out the storeroom for you. Got a broom?"

Colin pointed to the corner. "The room's pretty small. It'll be a tight fit for both of you to work in there."

"That's the way we like it," Griffin answered and they made their way into the back again.

He watched them disappear down the short hall, jealousy burning him. He'd never had a shot with Indy, although he liked to tease them about it. It wasn't Indy he was jealous of, it was what Griffin had found with her.

Colin shook his head. Sappy thoughts would get him nowhere. Finding some holy grail of a woman wouldn't fix his life either.

With the bar complete, he pulled out his phone to call for pizza and animal control. Elizabeth and Moira had finished up the tables and chairs while he made the calls. Indy emerged from the back and was talking with Elizabeth about décor.

"You know, Elizabeth," he started. Her full name felt weird rolling off his tongue. "Indy is a decorator. She'd probably give me the family discount."

Indy smiled at him. "I'd work for free in exchange for babysitting duty."

Elizabeth snorted. A very unladylike and unbusinesslike snort.

"What?" he asked.

She faced Indy. "Are you really thinking of entrusting your baby to Colin?"

"Don't be so fast to judge. He's actually very good with her. So yes, if that means I get a few hours alone with Griffin, I'm all over that." She turned to survey the walls. "What do you have in mind?"

"Sports bar," Colin answered. "We need some sports memorabilia for the walls, which obviously need to be painted first."

Indy stretched an arm out in front of them. "I'm thinking a dark blue. Broken up in sections for each sport. How many TVs do you think you're going to get?"

"Four, maybe five."

"Five TVs?" Elizabeth asked with wide eyes.

He moved closer and threw an arm around her shoulder, an immediate mistake, but he didn't stop. He pointed to areas on the walls where he wanted TVs. "I think we need to do some field trips so you can see what a sports bar looks like."

Her usual cinnamon scent tickled his nose, and he wanted to sniff her hair. She pulled away as if she had just realized he was touching her.

"I'll tell you what. If you beat the other bids I have and get this place decorated for under my budget, you can get all five TVs."

He clapped his hands. "Done." He had faith in Indy being able to do the job. What's more, now that Elizabeth had put the decorating in his hands, the bar would have his stamp on it. His chest tightened with the thought. She was making it easier every moment for him to reach his goals, and she did it unknowingly.

And Ryan thought he didn't have any business sense.

* * *

Colin didn't think he could be more exhausted. They'd been working what felt like forty-hour days. He'd had to carry his own weight at both O'Leary's and The Irish, but it was worth it. After that initial day of cleaning, Elizabeth seemed to be warming up to him.

As warm as she seemed to ever get, anyway.

She still insisted on wearing business suits, stiff and pristine, every day while he wore his usual jeans and T-shirts. They talked, mostly about bar business. Every time he broke through her defenses, she'd relax and smile until she caught herself having a good time. Then sometimes he'd catch her watching him. Of course, when caught, she'd scowl. He didn't know what to make of the woman or their mutual attraction, so he focused on the bar.

The place was almost finished. The best part was that the basement was cleared out. Animal control and exterminators had forced them from the building for a couple of days and they'd been playing catch-up. Final deliveries were set for tomorrow.

They were ready.

He moved around the bar to really check out the basement, to see the layout and how they could best utilize it for storage. As he neared the hall, Elizabeth poked her head out of the office.

"Can you handle finishing up here?"

"I'm about to go into the basement to have a look now that it's all clean and fresh-smelling. Want to join me?"

"As tempting as that is, I'll pass. I have plans tonight, and I'd prefer not to smell death before I leave."

"Plans?"

"Yes, plans. I do have a life outside this place."

"Probably a video conference with Tokyo," he mumbled. He didn't think the woman knew what fun was.

"I'll see you tomorrow morning."

"Yep." He watched her walk to the back door, her heels clicking on the hardwood floor, making his eyes focus on the definition of her calf muscles. Which then led him to follow that trail up the line of her long legs to the curve of her ass.

The sound of the door banging shut forced him from his fantasy. He shook his head. He needed to get laid. He'd been spending too much time with Elizabeth and not enough finding recreation.

He turned and went to the basement. The lighting wasn't great, only a few bare bulbs, but what they exposed was amazing. The basement ran the entire length of the building, not just under The Irish. The basement encompassed both sides of the building upstairs. Elizabeth must own all of it. He strode to the opposite end of the room and found a staircase leading into the other business.

His stomach sank. If the two businesses were connected, she would expect to sell the entire building, not just The Irish. He could never afford to buy the entire building.

Maybe if he talked to Mom about a loan.

No, that's exactly what Ryan would expect and then he'd never hear the end of it. Elizabeth had never made any mention of the other half of the building. He'd have to talk to her and feel her out. Which led him to the idea of feeling her up.

Shit, he really needed to get laid.

* * *

After leaving The Irish, Colin made a quick stop at home to clean up and change. It was a Saturday night, the perfect night to pick someone up. Moira had told him about a club he should check out that was hosting ladies' night, so he headed deeper into the city. It would be packed both with women looking to drink cheap or free and men looking to pick up those women.

He walked into the club and paid his ten-dollar cover charge. The place wasn't as packed as he thought it would be, but it was early yet. People milled around, bumping into one another, and music blared from the other end of the room, something with a thumping beat. He bought a beer and moved through the crowd to reach the dance floor.

Dancing meant women shaking their asses and getting thirsty while doing it. The best hunting grounds. On the dance floor, bodies clashed and ground against one another, people already paired off. He scanned the crowd to find the single women.

His gaze found its mark. A table with three women. Two blondes and one brunette. One blonde was short but stacked and drank an imported beer. The other blonde, with her hair cut short and spiky, was sipping on a pink drink, probably a Cosmo. Either blonde would be a good bet. They were both pretty and scantily clad. Spaghetti straps revealed smooth shoulders looking to be stroked.

The brunette, however, grabbed his attention as he made his way toward the group. Her back was to him and her hair trailed down, brushing the top of her rounded ass. She wore jeans and a T-shirt, and the jeans did amazing things for her legs. As he closed in, the brunette released a bark of laughter that was loud, just shy of obnoxious.

The pixie-haired blonde caught his eye and smiled. He sidled up to the brunette and said to no one in particular, "Can I buy you ladies a drink?"

The brunette turned and, with a swish of her hair, his heart stopped. The face staring back at him was none other than Elizabeth's. The glass in her hand wobbled and spilled over her hand. "Shit," she mumbled.

"Do you always spill so much?" he managed to ask, keeping his tone light.

She quirked one eyebrow up and his heart began again, now beating double time. The businesswoman was no business and all woman tonight, and while he thought he'd find someone to get her off his mind, these new images of her weren't going to help.

"Hello." Her voice was friendly, her eyes not so much. She dabbed at her wet hand with a napkin from the table.

"What are you doing here?"

"You know each other?" the short blonde asked.

"Yes," Elizabeth answered. "Colin, my business partner."

"Hi," she said as she nudged Elizabeth aside. "I'm Janie. This is Lori."

He nodded to each of them and shook their hands. He turned back to Elizabeth and said quietly, "What are you doing here?"

"Dancing. Hanging out with friends. I told you I had plans."

"Yeah, but—"

"The question is, what are you doing here? Did you follow me?"

Before he could answer her, Janie grabbed his hand. "Come on, let's dance."

He allowed her to lead him to the dance floor. Dancing wasn't something he did often, but it was a great way to meet a woman and flirt without words. As he turned, he saw that Elizabeth and her friend, Lori, had followed them to the floor.

Daggers shot from Elizabeth's eyes and he tried to ignore them. Janie made it a little easier as she started to shake her ass in front of him. The press of bodies made him hot, or maybe it was the bump and grind going on everywhere. He lost sight of Elizabeth and focused on the woman with him. When the man to his right collided with him, Colin turned and froze.

Elizabeth was doing a bump and grind of her own in between two men. He swallowed hard. His fingers itched to touch her long hair, and his jeans felt too tight. All thoughts of the blonde in his arms disappeared as he watched Elizabeth's hips wiggle and other men's arms surround her. Gone was the woman who stumbled and spilled drinks. She had great rhythm; she moved like someone who liked to dance.

The music stopped and the next song began, a slower beat, and Elizabeth extracted herself from the men. As she turned toward the table, Colin wrapped his fingers around her wrist and pulled her close. "What are you doing?"

She tugged her arm. "Let go of me."

Her pulse raced at the base of her hand. His fingers stroked the beat. "Let's dance."

He definitely wasn't thinking clearly, but after watching her in other men's arms, he wanted to know the feel of her. Surprisingly, she allowed him to pull her closer.

She sighed and held his hand as his other settled on her waist. Their bodies didn't touch, but heat filled the air between them. He suddenly felt like a sixth grader at his first school dance. "So how did you hear about this place?"

"Moira."

Of course. Moira and her big mouth.

Her gaze locked on his. She stepped closer. "If you want to dance, then let's do it right."

Their bodies aligned perfectly because of the heels that added to her height. Like her legs needed lengthening. She wrapped her arms around his neck and his arms wrapped around her hips. Her hair tickled his forearms and he pulled her into him. Like a heat-seeking missile, his dick twitched with the close proximity of her body.

They said nothing at first; the shock of having her in his arms blocked clear thought. They swayed to the beat, and she relaxed. Her body found its rhythm. Her face was close. Her breath quickened. Her tongue darted out and licked her lips. Dancing required all of his concentration at that point.

Elizabeth averted her gaze and broke the silence. "You never answered my question. Did you follow me?"

"No."

"Then why are you here?"

He sighed, knowing she wouldn't let him just enjoy holding her. The song ended and he leaned close to her ear. "I'm here for the same reason everyone else is: I'm looking to get laid."

CHAPTER 6

Elizabeth couldn't believe he'd said that. She pushed out of his arms, tripping and stomping on his foot accidentally. She was not here to get laid. She was visiting with friends and having fun.

Not that her body believed that one bit. Her blood still thrummed from his touch. Her hips were warm from where he'd gripped her, and she shoved away thoughts of those hands on her naked body.

She'd given up on the idea of picking up a guy at a bar since the last time had ended in disaster, with Colin at the center.

She watched Colin walk back to the table to chat with Janie and Lori. He wouldn't sleep with one of her friends, would he? Their interaction was smooth and friendly. Lori's face lit up as she laughed at something Colin said. He had a way with people. It was the reason she'd hired him.

In that moment, she knew he would sleep with anyone he wanted. He had that innate ability to literally charm the pants off a woman. The realization also made it clear that she needed to tighten her belt to prevent the effect of his charming ways.

She joined the group, determined to be social but not friendly with Colin. As soon as she arrived, Colin walked away. "Was it something I said?"

Janie answered, "He went to get us fresh drinks. You never said your new business partner was so sexy."

"I didn't think it was relevant, but about that . . . don't sleep with him."

"Why not? Are you calling dibs?"

"God, no." She swallowed a drink of water, hoping her answer came across as believable. "It would complicate my life if you decided to hook up with my partner."

"Mmm-hmm."

Janie wasn't buying it. Elizabeth looked to Lori for support.

"Don't look at me. I've got a boyfriend. He should be here any minute." She looked around the room, then added, "But I totally wouldn't blame you for calling dibs on Colin. Sexy and funny. Dangerous combo."

"Tell me about it." From the corner of her eye, she saw Colin making his way back through the crowd, smiling and chatting with every woman within grinning distance. If he thought the smile would work, he threw it out there. Dangerous indeed.

He handed her a glass. "Water, huh? I thought you were trying to have fun."

"I don't need to get drunk to have a good time." Alcohol would only aggravate any developing ulcers, but she didn't want him to know about her stomach problems.

"A little alcohol might loosen you up."

"I'm plenty loose, thanks."

He handed drinks to Lori and Janie, then turned back to Elizabeth. "So, you want to dance?"

"I do, just not with you." Dancing with him would work against the belt-tightening she intended. She walked away from Colin and hit the dance floor. As soon as she started, she was joined by men, who hoped, like Colin, to get laid. Glancing over her shoulder at the table, she saw Colin leading Janie to the floor again. His expression was stern, almost irritated.

She didn't want to upset him by not taking him up on his offer to dance, but she knew she would have a harder time holding her resolve if she allowed him to touch her again. They had to remain platonic.

Janie started rubbing her body against Colin's, and Elizabeth's jaw dropped. The irritation on his face disappeared and was replaced by lust.

She watched their bodies clash in rhythm. The movements of his hips held no grace, only sexuality. Elizabeth lost her own rhythm and left the dance floor. Watching him dance with her friend made fighting her own attraction more difficult. Being social with Colin would prove to be too hard.

Back at the table, she grabbed her purse. She looked at Lori. "Tell Janie I said good-bye. I'm heading home. I have an early day tomorrow."

"Are you okay?"

"I'm fine. Just tired." She turned and headed toward the door. Outside the cool night air brushed against her heated skin as she dug through her bag for her car keys.

"Hey."

She didn't have to turn to know it was Colin.

"What?"

"Why are you leaving?"

"I'm tired. We have a lot to do tomorrow." She pulled her keys out and allowed her purse to hang on her shoulder.

He wrapped his fingers around her wrist again and her pulse jumped. She turned to face him.

"I thought you wanted to have a good time."

"I was until you showed up."

"Really? I think your life vastly improved the moment I entered it."

"Don't flatter yourself."

"Why are you running away?"

"I'm not running anywhere."

He stepped closer, the heat from his body pressing against her, the scent of his cologne calling her close. She took a step back, afraid the air would run out and she wouldn't be able to breathe. It was a ridiculous thought; they were outside.

"See?"

"See what?"

"You're afraid of being attracted to me."

"How much have you had to drink?" She'd thought she had managed to not reveal anything to him.

"Not enough to stop me from doing this." He tugged her arm until her body collided with his. He lowered his head and his lips brushed hers. The moist heat of his mouth made her gasp and as soon as she did, his tongue moved in, stroking the inside of her mouth.

He wasn't rushed. Like everything Colin did, he moved slowly, drawing out every minute shift and swipe. His arms held her in place, as if he knew she would run. The strength in them made her lean in.

He felt so damn good. Smelled even better. Her blood warmed, but like Colin's movements, it didn't race. Muscles grew heavy and relaxed. The man's mouth was pure bliss.

A moan escaped her throat, and the sound helped her regain her senses.

As much as she didn't want to, she pushed him away. "What do you think you're doing?"

"Something we've both wanted to do for a long time."

She swiped a finger across her lip, as if she could remove the effect he had on her. "This is not going to happen. Good night, Colin."

His eyes stared widely, then he shrugged as though her rejection meant nothing, and he stepped away. His reaction affirmed her belief that she couldn't get involved with him.

She turned too quickly and lost her grasp on her keys. He bent to pick them up.

"See you tomorrow," he said and placed the keys firmly in her palm.

She backed up a step and stumbled on her heel. She would not let him make her nervous. She didn't have to be nervous around Colin because they weren't going to sleep together.

* * *

The following morning, Elizabeth pushed through the door of the bar and sniffed. The nasty smell had finally been eradicated. The place was clean and the finishing touches had been added to the décor. Bears jerseys on one wall, hockey stick and puck on another; a basketball net and framed picture of Michael Jordan hung near the door.

She flipped on the lights and looked around. A little more than a week and it was a brand-new place. Hope surged in her chest. This would work. Behind the bar, bottles of alcohol glinted in the lights. The smooth surface of the bar gleamed.

Who wouldn't want to come in here to drink?

Colin had had his five TVs installed yesterday along with whatever satellite system he needed to get the sports channels. It had felt good to relinquish that to him. They had been working somewhat like a team, which was a strange experience for her. She hadn't worked that closely with anyone since she and Keith had stopped turning properties together.

If she could only get past Colin's constant flirting. It had been hard to refuse his advances, and their kiss last night would only make it more difficult. Her body desperately wanted to say yes to sleeping with him, but she knew better. Regardless of his careless attitude, everything about Colin O'Leary screamed permanence. He had a stable, close-knit family.

She didn't want to get roped into that.

Right now, her only priority was to turn a profit and get back to Florida. She made a pot of coffee and tapped her fingers on the counter while it brewed. Why she didn't grab a coffee on her way in, she didn't know. Her stomach grumbled, and she considered her options for breakfast. They had cleared out all the stale snacks, but she had a delivery of fresh stuff coming in today.

In the meantime, however, it looked like coffee would be her meal. Her stomach hadn't gotten better, and she feared if she didn't get it under control, she'd land in bed again. One cup. She could afford one cup to get moving.

Tomorrow. For sure, I will cut back on the caffeine tomorrow.

As she sipped the first bit of coffee, someone began pounding on the front door. She glanced up. It wasn't Colin; she'd given him a key. She hesitated to answer because although they hadn't had any more issues with bikers showing up and wanting to drink, that first time put enough of a scare into her.

The pounding got louder, then her phone rang. Keith. Crap. She moved toward the back and answered the phone. "Hi, Keith. What's up?"

"You changed the lock on my bar. Open up."

Crapcrapcrap. She wasn't ready for this. Her stomach clenched and her muscles followed suit. She'd known this confrontation would happen; why didn't she prepare for it?

She set her coffee down and moved to the front door. She unlocked it and stared at Keith. He didn't look as mad as he'd sounded.

"You broke the rules," he said and pushed past her into the bar.

She closed the door behind him and leaned against it. "No, I didn't. I did an audit of Dad's properties and this one stuck out. I came to Chicago to check it out and found a mess."

"If this is on the up-and-up, why lie about being here on vacation?"

She crossed her arms. "I didn't lie. I told Dad I was visiting Janie and that I was feeling burned out. It's all true. I just didn't tell him that I had begun working on this. I wanted to surprise him. I took some initiative. So sue me." Christ, now she was sounding like Colin.

"I could. This is my bar and you know it."

He continued as if he wanted to fight, but his heart wasn't in it. There was something there she couldn't catch.

"The bar is Dad's."

"Which you know he bought for me."

"How would I know that?"

"I know you. You always do your homework." His voice held no anger. He walked the room, running his hand along the bar, and then eyed the TVs mounted on the walls. "I have to admit, it looks good."

Her cheeks grew warm. "Thanks. I think so too."

He slid onto a stool. "So what was your plan? Turn this into a moneymaker and then what? Convince Dad you should take over the company?"

She shrugged. "More or less."

"Not gonna happen."

The tension in her muscles and the burning in her gut returned full force. "Just because you have a Y chromosome doesn't make you the best candidate for the job. I'm every bit as qualified as you to run the company."

He narrowed his eyes and pressed his lips together for a moment, and she thought he would actually argue the point, which would be ridiculous. "You're right, in theory. But Dad wants you to have more than a name on the door or a title. You'll let this consume you, and we all know it. You already do."

She snorted, which felt juvenile. Keith always managed to make her feel that way. "So now you're telling me what? Dad thinks I can't run the company because I don't have a hobby?"

Keith's sigh was heavy as he shook his head. "He said you wouldn't get it."

"Get what?"

"Nothing. When do you reopen?"

The tension in her head forced her brows down. "Tomorrow."

"Good luck. I'll stop by and check it out."

"You're going to let me finish?" She couldn't hide her shock.

"Regardless of what you think, I really only want you to be happy. If turning this bar will make you happy, go for it." He cocked an eyebrow, and that unsettled feeling returned. Keith was hiding something, but right now she didn't care. She no longer had to worry about Keith's or her father's interference on this job. She had the green light to create her own success.

"Thank you. It means a lot that you won't try to stop this. It's going to be really good. I can feel it. You know what I mean, how sometimes, you just know?"

His smile spread slowly. "Yeah, I know. Those are the best jobs to work. Anything I can do to help?"

She shook her head. It was a nice offer, but she couldn't accept even if she wanted to. It might blur the lines of whose success it would be. "How long are you going to be in town?"

"A few days, I think. I want to see what happens here."

"I'll call you later. Maybe we can have dinner together. How's Melissa?"

"She can't wait for summer break. A few weeks and school's out. Maybe she can come visit you."

"I'll be home by then."

"Sure?" His skepticism fueled the uncertainty.

"I don't see why not. Everything's right on target here."

His eyes shifted and he wouldn't meet her gaze. "I'll call you later about dinner."

She nodded and he walked out the door. Elizabeth sat, stunned. The confrontation that she thought would explode hadn't, but Keith had left her with a feeling that was much worse. He was up to something, but she had no idea what.

An hour later, she had received the last of the deliveries they had been expecting, and Colin still hadn't shown up. Her frustration grew. Although she'd been glad he wasn't there to witness Keith's arrival, she had expected him to come in. They still had quite a bit of work to accomplish before they opened.

A different kind of burn swam in her stomach. She popped another antacid. He'd said he was looking to get laid last night. Maybe he did after she left. She thought of Janie and Lori, but she knew they wouldn't after she'd asked them not to. Golden rule of girlfriends. But it's not like Colin would have a problem finding someone else.

She sighed. It shouldn't matter. It didn't matter. His personal life was his business, unless it interfered with work. This was interfering, all right.

She continued to bustle around, setting up the new, freshly washed drink ware, lining up the bottles of alcohol to draw the eye to the most expensive liquor, while constantly watching the clock. Lunchtime came and went with not so much as a phone call from Colin letting her know when he'd be arriving.

She finally gave in and dialed his cell phone. It rang four times then went to voice mail. Her teeth clicked while she listened to his snappy little message. "Colin, Elizabeth. We have a lot to accomplish before we reopen in approximately twenty-four hours. Where are you?"

Leaving the message didn't ease her anxiety. She had two new waitresses coming in to get used to things before tomorrow. Colin had hired them, and he'd assured her that they were experienced.

The bar hadn't been this quiet since her first morning there. And even then she had the crappy, staticky radio as background noise. She realized part of her unease was the silence. She'd become not only accustomed to Colin's rambling and random singing, but she'd begun to rely on it as part of the atmosphere.

Determined to move forward without Colin's help, she grabbed a remote and turned on a TV. The volume blared and she jabbed at buttons to lower it. "Who the hell needs the volume that loud?"

"It won't seem so loud when there are fifty people milling around and talking."

Colin's voice startled her. The volume of the TV must've drowned out him opening the back door. "Where the hell have you been? I've been here all morning trying to get everything together."

"I had an important errand to take care of. It wasn't ready, so I had to wait." He dropped a box on the nearest table. "I hope you like it. I know I didn't run it past you first, but I figured at this point you could trust me to show a little initiative."

He opened the flaps on the nondescript brown box and grabbed what was inside. T-shirts.

"That was your all-important mission that took more than half the day?"

"Yeah. One of the things that helps the employees at O'Leary's stand out is that they all wear bar T-shirts." He paused with one shirt balled in his hand. "I know we didn't talk about this, but I know how much you dislike the name The Irish Pub, and really, if we're reinventing the bar, it should have a new name."

"What did you do?" Suspicion crept back up her spine.

"I just ordered a few, so if you don't like it, it's no big deal." He grasped the shirt in both hands and opened it. Bright orange letters on the left breast read BRANNIGAN'S SPORTS BAR.

An uncharacteristic surge of pride filled her chest. "Brannigan's, huh?"

"Well, I figured you'd really flip if I called it O'Leary's, especially since the name is already taken." He turned and dug through the box.

A litany of problems rose in her brain. There had been no legal name change, the business license and everything was listed as The Irish Pub. No advertising with a new name had been done.

Even with the problems that this would cause, part of her didn't care. She liked seeing her name on the business. She'd never experienced that pride before and it felt good.

"When I sell, the new owner might not like my name all over the place. Not to mention that paperwork has to be done to make it official. And the sign outside still says The Irish." She shook her head. "Now was probably not the best time for a name change."

"Don't stress. You worry about the paperwork crap, and I've got the word of mouth covered. While I got the shirts, I ordered a temporary banner we can hang outside until we decide on a permanent sign."

Word of mouth? How was he going to make that happen in less than a day? While she realistically planned for a slow build of customers throughout the week, she didn't want their opening day to be a flop.

Their Web presence was still being built. She began to tick off a mental list of what needed to be changed: Facebook, Web site . . . had they set up a Twitter account yet?

Something smacked into her face, and she blinked and looked to see what had hit her. A black T-shirt sat on her shoes.

"Wake up. We have work to do."

"I'm plenty awake. I've been here for hours. If I had known about your planned name change, I could've gotten other things taken care of, things that I'm now adding to my to-do list." She grabbed the shirt from the floor and tossed it back to him.

He caught it in his left hand. "This is yours. You can't possibly plan on wearing a suit to our grand opening."

"What is wrong with my suit? I'm the owner, not a barmaid."

He slung the shirt on his shoulder. "If you want to be successful here, you either need to blend in or be gone. People in this neighborhood are middle class, blue collar. They don't want to look at a suit when they're trying to enjoy some downtime."

"And by putting on a T-shirt, I'll blend in?"

He walked closer and slid the shirt from his shoulder and placed it on hers. "Not a chance, but you can at least fake it. You also need to get rid of the Benz."

"What's wrong with my car?"

"The only Mercedes these people come across is in a Janis Joplin song. Rent something more inconspicuous. Like a regular person."

"You're awfully bossy today. Any other demands?" She yanked the T-shirt from her shoulder and gripped it tightly in her fist.

His gaze didn't return to hers. He continued to dig through the box, sorting shirts. "I'm sure you'll do whatever you want, but you brought me in because I know people. Jeans and that T-shirt. Although you look really hot in heels, I would suggest gym shoes. The floors will get slippery, and I'd hate to see you fall and break your neck."

A little jolt of pleasure ran through her. He thought she looked hot in heels. His opinion shouldn't matter, she reminded herself. "Fine. I'll dress to fit in with regular people."

She turned to go into the office, but stopped. It bothered her that he assumed she'd always had money. Before she could stop herself, she said, "I'll have you know that just because I have money now, I didn't grow up that way. I am a regular person."

His head whipped up and his gaze bore into her. "Sweetheart, there's nothing regular about you."

"Shows what you know," she mumbled and turned back to the office.

* * *

Colin couldn't remember a time when he'd ever been this nervous. They had less than an hour until their official reopening. Elizabeth had been scarce all day. Although she'd agreed to dump the stuffy suit, she arrived in dark gray pinstripes, like any other day. He didn't comment, knowing it wouldn't matter. Every time he looked at her, he no longer saw the stiff businesswoman. He only thought of the pliant, sensual woman pressed against his body during their kiss.

His mind continued to wander back to the other night. After he'd kissed Elizabeth, he wanted more, but knew she wouldn't go for it. He probably shouldn't have touched her at all, but he wanted to know. Needed to have another taste of her, especially after seeing her dance with all those strangers.

He had no claim to her, and his fantasies were getting out of hand. The previous day, he'd intentionally come to the bar late, knowing he couldn't ignore their kiss. He made sure he'd had other things to occupy his brain when he did arrive. He shook his head now to force himself to focus on the work at hand.

The new waitresses had experience and quickly learned the lay of the land. Now he just had to hope that Moira's big mouth worked. She had an extensive network both professionally and socially that he hoped to use to his advantage.

As he stood in the quiet front room, peace settled over him. He turned in a circle and liked what he saw. This was his place. He'd done it. Now he just needed to make it a success. He ticked off the last few items in his head and realized that he hadn't talked to Elizabeth about the basement. He strode to her office and swung the door open without knocking.

Air whooshed from his lungs as her bare back faced him. Only the black strap of her bra interrupted the smooth skin. She slid the bar T-shirt over her head and tugged it down. She hadn't noticed his presence, so he cleared his throat and tried to avert his gaze. Sort of.

She flinched. "You didn't knock."

He ignored her reprimand and thoughts of her bare skin and said, "What do you think of the shirt?"

"Hell, no."

When she turned, he couldn't believe his eyes. She was beyond sexy in the scoop-neck shirt that dipped low, showing just enough cleavage to make his mouth water. The shirt hugged every feminine curve.

"Hey, eyes up here." Her hands rose above her chest to her face.

His gaze wandered up, drinking in every inch of her. "What?"

"Give me a shirt like yours. I'm not wearing this in public."

"How about in private?" He smiled at her, but she didn't budge. "It looks good. And it'll help sell beer."

"I repeat, I am not wearing this. I get that you don't want me in my business suit, but this is unacceptable." She shifted from foot to foot and her hands fisted.

She was uncomfortable. Nervous? The thought niggled in the back of his head. Why would she be nervous? "What's wrong with it?"

"I don't see you baring your chest for all to see." She crossed her arms, which only distracted him further because it pushed her breasts higher, like an invitation.

"Would it make you feel better if I did?" He tugged at the hem of his own shirt.

Quickly uncrossing her arms, she pointed at him. "That's not what I mean. I am a businesswoman, the owner of this bar. Not a sexual object to be ogled."

She was right and he knew it, but he couldn't help but ogle her. She was hot, standing there angry and flushed. Pink crept across the expanse of skin exposed above the black neckline of the shirt. He wondered if the same blush would streak her skin after an orgasm.

He cleared his throat. "You're right. I'm sorry. I'll get you a different shirt. I actually came in here because we need to talk about the basement."

"Now? We open in less than an hour."

"Yeah, but there's something not right about the basement. It's too big." He shoved his hands in his pockets to stop himself from reaching out and stroking her skin.

"The size of the basement is irrelevant. As long as there are no more dead critters down there, I don't care. Now get me a shirt. I can't go out to the front looking like this."

He smiled again. "Sure you can. The other girls are wearing the same thing." Not that they could hold a candle to her.

"That's your first problem. I'm not one of the girls. I'm a woman."

Oh, yes, she was. He turned and left to get her the shirt. Seeing her stiff and irritated should've helped ease the lust, but it didn't. Memories of the other night flooded back and he was feeling like a horny teenager again. Elizabeth was not the first sexy woman he'd kissed.

She didn't even like him, but the chemistry they shared wasn't something they could deny.

He tossed a shirt through her open office door without so much as a glance. He needed to keep his head in the game. Marissa and Erin, the new waitresses, were chatting at the bar. He glanced at the clock. Fifteen minutes until open. What harm could it do to unlock the doors now?

His fingers itched to flip the lock, but what if no one showed? It was a Monday night, after all. What if, after all this work, only the bikers showed?

His heart beat faster at the thought. No, they'd come too far. He'd given Moira the go-ahead to tell everyone. The girl liked to gossip like nobody's business. People would probably show just to see what the fuss was about. Luckily, both the Sox and Cubs had night games, so they could utilize the TVs.

As he moved across the floor, he felt like he slid in slow motion. This was ridiculous. He reached out, unlocked the door, and swung it open. A cool breeze swept in, but no customers followed. Part of him imagined a line running down the block.

The same part of him that clashed with Ryan on a regular basis.

This was one dream that he was going to make work. He grabbed a remote and turned on the radio. Music was a sure sign of a good time.

Luckily, he didn't have to wait long. As he stood at his post behind the bar, customers began trickling in, couples and small groups, and not a biker among them.

Tables filled and the waitresses served. When he pulled the first beer from the new tap, he slid it in front of the customer and said, "Enjoy it on the house. The first beer poured."

Elizabeth would be pissed if she knew, but it felt right. Giving away that one beer allowed his first customer to share in some of his happiness.

Success felt good.

CHAPTER 7

They were a success. Elizabeth couldn't believe her eyes. She'd waited in her office for more than an hour after opening, afraid of being disappointed. When noise crept past her door, she needed to investigate.

She walked toward the front of the bar and stared at a crowd. Not a few people standing around, but an actual crowd. Tables and stools were filled. Waitresses delivered trays full of drinks.

She couldn't believe it. It was only their first night.

Making her way to the bar, she scanned the area, wondering if Keith had come in yet. A loud laugh caught her attention and she turned. There was Colin, pouring a beer and laughing so hard she couldn't understand how he didn't spill.

"You're making that up," he said as he slid the beer in front of a patron.

"No, really. She couldn't help herself," the man responded.

Elizabeth moved closer, drawn in by Colin's easy smile. He leaned on the edge of the bar.

"Tell me your secret," he said.

The man drank from his beer, giving Elizabeth her opening. "Hey, how's it going?"

Colin straightened and his already-too-big smile broadened. "Do you need to ask? We're a hit."

His smile was contagious, and she tried to rein hers in, but couldn't.

She shouldn't think that an hour of being busy made them a success, but it at least set the tone, right? She could enjoy this.

"How?" she asked.

"I told you, when you have a big family, use them. Moira loves to talk. She's a gossip queen. I set her loose on social networks and this is the result." He swept his long arm out toward the room.

"I hope she knows how much you owe her."

He swung and smacked a towel against Elizabeth's leg. "I owe her nothing. She did it because she loves me."

"Hey, Colin," a coy voice sang across the bar.

Elizabeth turned in time to see a woman and her friend both wagging fingers at him. "Looks like everybody loves you."

"What can I say?" He walked away to continue pouring drinks.

She'd known Colin was a huge flirt. It shouldn't surprise her that he had a following. Elizabeth watched everyone come and go and realized that she didn't have a purpose. She didn't know how to mix drinks. She could probably take some orders and deliver them, but she'd never been a waitress.

Her relative uselessness took the wind out of her sails. She should be used to it by now. It was the same with every business. She didn't know why she thought this one would be different. Just because she dressed differently didn't change the outcome.

She was still the boss. She was just doing it in jeans and a T-shirt. At least in her suit, she knew how to behave. It was the equivalent of a uniform, like armor. People viewed her as the boss. Dressed like this, she wasn't sure what people saw or expected. She wasn't sure herself.

She quietly walked back to her office. This was where she belonged, but she itched to be out front.

It was an odd feeling; she normally didn't enjoy the interactions that came with running a business. She messed with papers on her desk and paced in the small area, looking for a reason to go back to the customers.

Alternating between pacing and wandering, Elizabeth wasted time. She greeted customers as they took their seats and introduced herself. She worked the room. It wasn't the kind of social interaction she enjoyed, but at least she felt like she was part of something. As the hours passed, both her feet and her cheeks began to ache, but she pushed through.

Colin moved ceaselessly. She didn't think he took a break all night, but he seemed to be having the time of his life. He was definitely in his element.

After ten o'clock, the crowd began to thin, and the pace slowed. Colin had said he wouldn't need the waitresses to stay past eleven, and it looked like he knew what he was talking about. The girls counted their tips and checked to see what else needed to be done before heading out.

Irritation pricked at her because they should've checked with her, not Colin. She was the boss. It was the one thing she did well. She tamped the feeling down, knowing Colin wasn't trying to take control. He'd hired them, so it was natural that they would report to him. She even forced a smile as they made their way to the door.

Colin poured another round for a couple of guys sitting at the bar and then his gaze found her.

"You can go home. I can close up."

"No. I should be here."

"You look beat."

She straightened her back. They'd been there the same number of hours. Was he implying she couldn't hack it? "I'm fine."

In truth, she wasn't fine. Her feet throbbed and her stomach burned. She'd avoided coffee all night to save her stomach, but it cost her wakefulness. The small sandwich she ate hours earlier had helped momentarily, but her stomach wouldn't settle for any length of time. She knew she'd need to go to the doctor again.

On her way to the back to grab a rag for wiping down tables, she stopped in her office for some antacids. She chomped on the chalky tablets as she ran hot water over the rag and then went to clean.

Most of the tables were in good shape. The waitresses had stayed on top of that as the night wore on. The quiet conversation between Colin and the customers centered on sports, but she wasn't sure which sport they were talking about. She half listened as she straightened chairs. She was disappointed Keith had missed their opening. The turnout would've impressed him.

She didn't know why it should matter. Impressing Keith wouldn't change how their father viewed things. She needed to amaze her dad. Doubt crept into her. Would turning a profit in this rinky-dink bar be enough? She'd already created million-dollar businesses for him, and he obviously didn't care about this place.

A hand landed on her shoulder. She twitched and turned to find Colin looming beside her.

"Are you okay?"

She blinked rapidly. How long had she been standing in the same spot? "I'm fine. Just thinking. And you're right, I am tired."

"You can go. I'll handle this."

The temptation tugged at her, but she didn't respond.

"You've put in a shitload of hours over the past couple of weeks. Give yourself a break and get a good night's sleep." He stroked the back of his hand over her cheek.

The gentle gesture took her by surprise. His strong, capable hands drew her attention. A surge of desire to have those hands roam her body zinged her. "I'll be fine," she croaked out.

"At least take a break. Have a seat at the bar and talk to us." He tilted his head toward the bar and grabbed her hand.

The warmth and strength of his grasp blurred her focus. Damn, she must be really tired if holding hands turned her on. She stumbled and hoped he didn't notice. Unfortunately, he did. He tightened his grip and waited until her butt was planted on a bar stool before he let go.

The bar was immaculate. She didn't know how he managed to keep it clean and organized while serving all of the customers. She wished she could've done more to help.

The idea struck like a flash. He could teach her.

Colin moved to the other side of the bar carrying a stool for himself. He eased onto it and a look of relief crossed his face. He must've been every bit as exhausted as she was; he was just better at hiding it.

"You have a strange smile on your face."

She felt her sore cheeks widen. "Teach me to bartend."

"What?"

"I was pretty useless tonight. I want to take a more active role here."

His laugh rang out, drawing attention from the men at the other end of the bar.

Her smile disappeared as the tension in her jaw returned. "You don't think I can handle it?"

"I'm sure you can handle whatever comes your way."

His gaze darkened for a flicker, and the heat pooling in her stomach had nothing to do with acid. She wasn't so sure she could handle Colin if he came her way.

"Then what's so funny?"

"That you think you need a more active role. You've been busting your ass getting everything in line. You handle the paperwork and organization and bills. Why the hell would you want to bartend too?"

She shrugged. "It seemed like a good idea." She began to question her sanity. Maybe the exhaustion was affecting her thought process. Bartending wasn't a skill she'd need as CEO.

He leaned forward on the bar, like she'd seen him do multiple times throughout the evening. "Maybe you're onto something."

The two remaining customers pushed off their stools.

Colin rose. "Have a good one, guys. Thanks for coming in."

They waved him off and headed out the door. He took their empty glasses and put them in the sink. He swiped the dollar bills they'd left and tucked them into an overflowing glass beside the register. She'd thought the waitresses made out in tips, but it looked like they had nothing on Colin.

When he returned to the stool across from her, she said, "You were saying?"

"We make a pretty good team."

Her cheeks warmed as she nodded.

"But we're divided in our jobs. I have mine and you have yours. I think it would be smart for us to have some experience doing the other's jobs."

She narrowed her eyes. What was he getting at?

"I'll teach you the basics of bartending and you teach me the basics of office crap."

The smile returned to her face. One thing she liked about Colin was that he didn't hide how he felt. "Office crap? Is that how you view my job?"

"Kind of, yeah."

"Then why would you want to learn it?"

"I plan to have my own bar someday, and I'll have to handle the office as well as the bartending to succeed."

"Didn't you learn it working with your brother?"

A flash of something crossed his face. He masked it quickly, but it was unpleasant.

"Ryan likes to keep me in the front. I'm a better draw for the ladies than he is, especially now that he's married." He gave her the best flirty smile in his arsenal. When did she become adept at distinguishing his smiles?

"You should know by now that your seductive smiles don't work on me." Her voice was steady, and she hoped she sounded convincing. He'd never leave her alone if he knew the truth.

"I beg to differ. I haven't been using my full charm on you. No female can resist."

Her pulse spiked. If this wasn't already his full charm, she was in trouble.

He tilted his head, examining her. He pushed back from the bar. "Let's get started."

* * *

Colin slid off the stool, hoping to conceal his hard-on.

"Wh-what?"

Her stammer caught him off guard. Elizabeth never stuttered. "Come over to this side and I'll give you your first lesson."

The prettiest shade of pink swept across her cheeks. Her wide-eyed gaze slammed into him. His throat worked, swallowing nothing as he tried to find his voice. This was a mistake. "What do you want to learn first?"

Her chest lowered as she expelled a breath. "Oh. Now?"

"Why not? We're open for another hour, unless you want to close early?"

"No, but shouldn't we have customers if I'm going to pour drinks?"

"It'll be fine. Come on. We'll start with beer." He followed her trek around the bar. Her movements were hesitant. Seeing Elizabeth unsure of something tilted the room. She never lacked confidence. He softened his smile. "No worries. It's just beer."

She returned a smile as she joined him. "Okay. Let's do this."

Nerves fluttered in his stomach. He knew his job, but he'd never had to teach it to anyone. He strode to the taps. "On the left, we have imports, on the right, domestic."

Her eyebrow shot up. "I know how to read."

"I'm giving you the tour so you know where to find everything. I've set it up the way I like it."

She swung her arm out for him to continue. As he pointed out which glasses were used for which kind of drink and explained the organization of the liquor, his stomach eased. She listened intently, and he imagined that she really wanted to take notes.

He stood to the side of the tap. "Grab a glass."

She pulled one from the green rubber mat where it had been drying and turned it right side up.

"Pull the handle, on. Flip it up, off."

The pink returned to her flesh, and once again he found himself wanting to stroke it to see if it was as warm as it looked. She cleared her throat and yanked the tap.

"Whoa." He grabbed the handle and thrust it back in place. Obviously, she'd never even watched someone pull a beer.

She looked at the beer in her hand, more than half foam. He took the glass and set it down. "No one wants a glass of foam. Let's try again."

He handed her a fresh glass and she stood in front of the tap, but made no move to pour.

"It doesn't bite." Against his better judgment, he stood behind her and wrapped his arms around her body, doing his best to limit contact. He helped her tilt the glass with one hand and his other rested on top of hers on the handle.

"Easy," he said as he moved their hands to pull the tap. "You tilt the glass to keep the head small."

Her back was mere inches from him and her hair tickled his nose. She'd worn it up again, exposing her long neck. Cinnamon scent drifted up. If he dipped his head just a little, he could taste the soft skin. His mouth watered and he thought her breath quickened.

Suddenly, his hand was wet as she yelped, "Hey."

He jerked the handle to stop the tap. He'd forgotten about the beer and the glass had overflowed. "Sorry," he mumbled.

Turning away to grab a towel, he checked his thoughts. Elizabeth was not a piece of ass for a one-night stand. She was his business partner, and she'd made it clear they would never be anything more.

"Here." He thrust a dry towel into her hand.

"Thanks," she said, but she didn't look pissed off. She looked . . . amused. "Can I pour you one?"

"Huh?"

"A beer. I think we should celebrate. We had a great night, it's time to close, and I learned how to pour a beer." She paused, a grin lighting her face. "Not very successfully mind you, but I poured."

"I'll have a pop. Sorry about the spill. I got distracted." His gaze wandered down the length of her.

He scooped ice into a glass and turned toward the pop spigot. Once the glass was filled, he faced Elizabeth with his raised glass. "To success."

She clinked her glass against his and took a gulp of beer. Her nose crinkled and she set the glass down. "I hate beer."

"Then why drink it?"

"Because I poured it. It was my first, and it seemed like I should."

"Do you always do what you're supposed to?"

"Pretty much." She took another sip of beer.

He grabbed the glass and poured it down the drain. "Life's too short to do what you hate."

"Hey, buddy, you owe me three fifty for that."

He laughed. "Put it on my tab. Can I get you a glass of wine or something else?"

"No, it's late and we have clean-up to do." She turned and began wiping down his already clean bar.

"I have these last few glasses to wash and the floor to sweep. Everything else is done."

"Oh. Then I'll grab the broom." She shifted her body and angled to move around him.

His arm reached out and landed on her hip. Her chest rose and fell in rapid succession.

"What are you doing?"

He didn't respond with his voice. He let his body answer. Pulling her close, he tasted her lips, the tang of beer lingering. He angled his head and licked, hoping she would open her mouth. She complied, and he slid inside her slick warmth.

One of her hands rested on his at her hip, the other fisted in his shirt. She rocked against him with a slight moan. He turned them so that she backed up to the bar. Trailing kisses down her neck, he tasted the skin at her pulse. She threw her head back to give him more access and in doing so thrust her hips into his groin.

As if he wasn't turned on enough, his dick hardened and strained against his jeans, looking for release. He tugged at her shirt, and his hands caressed the warm skin of her torso and glided up to find her full breasts.

God, he wanted to get her naked.

A sound trilled from behind her and she jerked, smacking her shoulder into his head. He pulled away and rubbed the sore spot. Getting involved with this woman was definitely dangerous.

Her eyes stared, darkened with desire, and he knew the blush on her skin was because of lust. Her chest heaved as she straightened from the bar. Reaching behind her, she pulled out a phone. She scanned the screen and inhaled deeply.

"I have to take this." Seriousness returned to her face.

"I'm sure whoever it is can wait." He wasn't sure he could.

The phone stopped.

"No, I have to call him back." She slid along the bar to get out of his reach.

Him? Maybe she wasn't just serious, maybe she felt guilty. "Are you married?"

"What?" She shook her head. "No." The grip on the phone tightened.

"Then what is so important you have to interrupt what we were doing?"

The muscle in her jaw twitched, and he knew he'd fucked up. Again.

"What we were doing was wrong. It shouldn't have happened. It will complicate things. You should be grateful you were saved by the bell. Literally."

"Do you really believe I was the one who was saved?"

The phone rang again. She pressed the button and began talking as she walked away.

He snatched the towel from the bar and wiped everything down again. *Nice going, asshole. Way to control your dick.* Elizabeth was right. They shouldn't have been making out. How many times had she told him that they were business partners and that was all?

But she didn't push me away.

That thought had him adjusting his crotch again. She was every bit as attracted to him as he was to her. They were both adults. Why couldn't they enjoy each other's company?

He wasn't looking for another one-night stand, but Elizabeth wouldn't be a permanent fixture either. She would be a nice distraction while he worked on getting his life in order. Besides, if he showed her a really good time, she might even cut him a deal when he asked to buy the bar.

* * *

"Hi, Keith. I thought you were coming in tonight." She forced the words out slowly in an effort to sound natural instead of like a lust-crazed teenager.

"I had to take care of something for Dad. Surprisingly, he didn't want to interrupt your vacation."

"Did you tell him?" Her stomach fluttered.

"Nope. I'll leave that up to you. How did tonight go?"

She leaned a hip on her desk. "Great. We had a crowd. A real crowd."

"That's good. I'm glad it's working out."

"Thanks."

"I'm tired, Elizabeth. I just wanted to let you know that I didn't forget about you tonight. I'll stop by tomorrow morning and you can tell me all about it."

He sounded beat, and she wondered what had happened that Keith needed to handle. Her brain scanned the few properties they owned in Chicago. Nothing popped. "Thanks for checking in. We'll talk later."

"Definitely tomorrow. I want all the details."

She clicked off the phone. Keith had sounded really interested in her success. Like when they'd first started working with Dad. She took a deep breath. Suspicion crept back in. Keith had something up his sleeve. He was a great brother, but he hadn't been supportive of her jobs in years. He was always afraid she'd get the upper hand.

Standing at her desk, she stared at her closed door. The nervous flutters returned, and she popped another antacid. How was she going to get out of here? She didn't think she could face Colin again.

This time, she was every bit as involved in the kiss. She couldn't pretend she didn't enjoy it or that it wouldn't have gone further if the phone hadn't rung. Keith had saved her from making a fool of herself. That would've gone over well with Dad. *Make me CEO. Ignore that I slept with my business partner.*

She hung her head.

Turning back to her desk, she reached for the bottle of antacids. Damn, only the green ones were left. They should really sell a bottle with only the pink ones. She grabbed a green and chewed. She could handle this. She and Colin were adults who happened to let things get a little out of hand.

They could control their hormones.

She swung her office door open and strode back into the bar. Colin looked up from where he was sweeping the floor.

"Sorry about that." *My mind more so than my body.* "That was my brother."

"Something wrong?"

"No." She hesitated, searching for the right words. "Look, I'm not sure what's going on between us, but we need to keep it in check. It's unethical and unprofessional for us to be doing . . . that."

"We're adults, and it's not like you're my superior. I promise not to sue you for sexual harassment."

"I'm sure you wouldn't. But I think it would be best if we kept everything platonic."

"I think you're wrong."

"Sorry you feel that way. I like you, I really do, but I don't have time to start something here. I need to keep moving forward to get the work done."

He leaned against the broom handle, bending the bristles to the floor. "You know what they say about all work and no play."

"I'll take my chances. Do you need any help here?"

"No, I'll lock up. What time do you want me here tomorrow?"

Keith had said he'd stop by in the morning. She debated whether she wanted them to meet. "We don't open until four, but I'd like you to work with Mike to make sure he knows what he's doing."

"Okay, see you in the afternoon."

Elizabeth grabbed her keys and purse from the office and left, turning over Colin's words in her head. They were both adults, and she hadn't had any kind of companionship at all lately. She shoved the illicit thought from her mind. It would be too complicated for her to get involved with Colin, even short-term. Risking her career wasn't worth it.

She drove back to her hotel and smiled at the smooth ride. Colin had talked her into trading her business suit for a T-shirt, but she'd kept the Mercedes. No one paid any attention to the car she drove. And even if they did, so what? She owned the bar. She didn't need to fit in.

Her phone rang as she pulled into the hotel parking lot. Mom? She never called this late. It would interfere with her beauty sleep. "Hi, Mom. What's wrong?"

"Is that any way to greet me? Who said anything was wrong?" Her mother's voice was strained.

"You never call this late. It's the middle of the night."

A quiet sigh eased across the line. "It's your father."

Elizabeth slammed the car into park. "Is he okay?"

"Yes. No. He promised he'd retire by the end of the year, but he keeps acquiring more buildings and businesses. You need to talk to him."

Elizabeth rested her head on the steering wheel. For a moment, she'd thought something bad had happened, and now she realized it was just her mom's usual high-strung nature. "Even if he does retire, the business will continue. He keeps acquiring so that everyone who works for him continues to have a job. Have you talked to him? Did he say that he wouldn't retire?"

"Well, no, but shouldn't he be easing away from the business? I expected that by this time he'd be spending more time with me."

Cue the woe-is-me speech. Elizabeth was too tired to listen today. "Talk to him, Mom. Keith and I are more than ready to take over."

"You? I thought we decided that Keith would run the business. He has a family to support after all."

"And how does that make him more qualified? I have more time in the field than he does. I've brokered as many deals as he has. I'm every bit as qualified to take over the company, and I'm really tired of you thinking I'm not, simply because I'm female."

Silence met her. She barely heard her mother's breathing on the other end, but Elizabeth knew her mother hadn't hung up. That would be rude and her mother was nothing if not totally polite.

"I never said you were unable to take over. I just think that Keith is a more appropriate choice."

"I know what you think. You've made it abundantly clear. I'm tired of this conversation. I'll talk to you later." She clicked off before her mother could say anything more. She began to think that running the family business wouldn't be all she'd thought it would be. Maybe branching out on her own would be the way to go.

CHAPTER 8

Colin swept the floor and prayed his hard-on would go away. He couldn't get Elizabeth out of there fast enough. Smelling her scent as she walked out made his blood pound south. Sleeping with her might not be the brightest idea, but it sure as hell wasn't the dumbest. Their chemistry was scorching if just kissing her made him hard.

He gave the bar another once-over and made sure all the glasses were clean. Not bad for a first night. If they could keep this up, the weekends would be fabulous. He'd have to check the sports schedules to see what kind of games were going on over the weekend. Maybe some fights for Saturday night.

He locked the door and headed to his car. He was beat and grateful that he didn't have to work at O'Leary's for a couple of days. Although Ryan hadn't been too supportive of the new bar idea, he knew opening night would be hectic. Colin drove on autopilot to get back to his apartment. As he pulled his keys from the ignition, his phone rang. Late-night calls weren't that unusual for him, but everyone knew he'd be busy with Brannigan's. He smiled, liking the sound of the new name.

Colin glanced at the phone. Moira? "Hi."

"Come to the hospital."

His stomach twisted and every muscle in his body knotted. The last time he got a phone call like that his father had died. "Who?"

He death-gripped the steering wheel, waiting to hear the response, afraid he'd lose his mother when he'd just gotten back into life with the family.

"Quinn. She's having the baby."

His heart lifted. Not bad news. Good. Excellent, in fact. His lungs finally refilled with air. "I'll be there soon. How long?"

"Who knows? She went into labor about an hour ago."

"Why am I just getting the call now?"

"Ryan said you'd be busy and it'll probably be a while yet."

After disconnecting, he sat, slowly releasing his fingers from the steering wheel, waiting for the dread to completely leave his stomach. The high of his evening had disappeared immediately with the thought of someone in the hospital, but the fear dissipated at a much slower rate. There was probably some psychological reason for that. He'd chalk it up to exhaustion.

When his hands and stomach were steady again, he pulled out and went to the hospital. He didn't want to miss the arrival of his first nephew. He smiled. He was going to be an uncle. Uncle Colin. Had a nice ring to it.

"Dad" would sound better. He pushed the thought deeper. It just wasn't his time yet. The streets were empty on his drive to the hospital, so he stopped for some decent coffee on his way. If he remembered nothing from his time in the hospital with his father, it was the terrible coffee.

Juggling the box of coffee, creamer and sweetener packets, and cups, he kicked the car door shut and headed into the hospital. He had to look at the directory to know where to go. Labor and delivery had never been a stop for him.

He got off the elevator and saw a waiting room filled with O'Learys. This was the biggest thing he'd missed while he was gone. The unconditional support. Whether you wanted it or not. He thought of his sister-in-law, Quinn, and was pretty sure that she wouldn't want them all there, but she'd deal with them for Ryan's sake.

Quinn and Ryan had been together for a year, but she was still getting used to the idea of a big family. He scanned the room.

"Where's Ryan?"

Moira took the box of coffee and looked at him like he was stupid. "With Quinn, of course. He and Indy have been back and forth. They'll both be as grateful as I am for the coffee."

"If Indy's here, where's Griffin?"

"He's at home with Colleen. You can't bring a baby here."

Now he did feel stupid. This was where babies arrived, but they couldn't come back to visit? Where was the logic in that?

He knew he'd get another you're-an-idiot look, so he opted not to ask.

His family sat in silence, waiting to hear something. All worried about Quinn, who'd had complications earlier in the pregnancy. All afraid to speak the worries for fear they'd come true.

His mother whispered the prayers of the rosary.

Moira texted someone; Liam and Michael focused on the TV in the room that was tuned to an infomercial for cleaning supplies. Michael's wife, Brianna, sat with her arm around Mom's shoulders.

He grabbed a cup of coffee and sat next to his brothers. Fatigue sank deep into every muscle. After his success at the bar, he'd thought of being able to tell his family, make them proud. He couldn't bring it up now. It would pale in comparison to a new family member.

After sitting for two hours, Indy poked her head in and said, "She's finally ready and is starting to push. Hopefully, it won't be too much longer."

Then she was gone again. Colin wondered how Ryan was holding up.

Colin must've dozed because the sudden noise of cheering startled him. He scrubbed a hand over his face and checked his watch. Nine-thirty? He'd been here all night and half the morning. Moira stood on tiptoe, bouncing back and forth. Liam and Michael were standing behind Ryan as Mom hugged him.

Standing in the back, Colin waited.

"He's perfect," Ryan said. "Totally healthy."

His voice wobbled and his eyes became watery.

Colin moved forward with his hand extended. "Congrats, man."

Ryan pulled him into a surprising hug and whispered, "I'm glad you're here. I want to talk to you."

"Sure."

Ryan nodded to the rest of the family and led the way a little farther down the hall. Colin began to feel a bit like he was headed for the firing squad. He hadn't done anything to piss off Ryan this week that he could remember, so he tried to prepare to be blindsided with something stupid.

"So," Ryan started. Then stopped.

Colin shoved his hands into his pockets. "So?"

"I wanted to talk to you about the baby's name." Ryan stared at him as though Colin should read his mind. "We want to name him Patrick."

Colin's gut clenched at the sound of their father's name. He said nothing.

"I didn't want to just use the name without talking to you first." Something in his eyes shifted.

"Really?"

Ryan blew out a quiet breath. "No, Quinn said I should talk to you because you're the oldest and you might want to use the name. I didn't think you'd care."

Wrong. He did care. He'd always wanted to name his own son Patrick. He still said nothing.

"It's okay, right? I mean, it's not like you even have a girlfriend right now, much less a wife."

Something primal in Colin wanted to scream no, it wasn't okay, but he knew Ryan was right. Once again, Ryan had what Colin wanted. He'd been more together and quicker to get it.

Telling Ryan no would only deepen the rift between them.

He hugged Ryan hard and tempered his voice. "Of course it's okay. I want you to be happy."

"Thanks."

They separated and stood awkwardly staring at the floor. Colin forced out lighthearted words. "You're a dad, huh?"

"Yep, Uncle Colin."

They walked back to their family, both smiling, a tentative peace settling over them.

Yeah, Uncle Colin definitely had a nice ring to it.

* * *

Elizabeth walked through the bar with a smile on her face. She'd spent the morning totaling the receipts from the night before. Their first day open had been a success. If they kept this up, she'd be back in Florida in no time. Three weeks, tops.

It was near noon and she hadn't heard from Keith yet. He'd said he'd come by in the morning, but he hadn't called. Even if he'd slept in, she should've heard something by now. She wanted to talk with him before Colin showed up.

She knew it was ridiculous, but she didn't want Keith to know about Colin. In business, they hired outside help all the time, but somehow she felt if Keith knew about Colin, it would take away from her success here.

Without Colin, this success wouldn't have happened.

The thought hit her hard. Colin had done more than she had originally thought. He'd pulled his weight and then some. He'd been a good pick as a partner.

She'd have to remember to tell him that.

Two hours later, Mike showed up as promised to make sure he knew where to find everything and get a feel for the new setup. Unfortunately, since Colin had done the setting up, she couldn't direct much.

"I'm expecting someone for a meeting soon; maybe you can look around until Colin gets here?"

"Sure. The place isn't that big. I think I can manage." He settled his large frame behind the counter and surveyed the setup.

The front door opened, and Elizabeth turned to let the customer know they weren't open yet, but it was Keith. Finally. She glanced at the clock. Maybe she could still get him out of here before Colin showed.

"Hey. It's about time. You said you were coming this morning. Where have you been?"

"Sorry. I got hung up with calls." He pointed over his shoulder toward the door. "Brannigan's, huh?"

Shit. She'd forgotten about that change. "Yeah. Since we changed the entire concept, it only made sense to change the name. Take on a whole new identity. The old one wasn't exactly working."

"I like it." He looked at her from head to toe. "You look pleased."

"I am. Come to my office and I'll show you the numbers from last night."

"I don't need to see the numbers. I have no doubt you did well."

She crossed her arms. "Then why did you want to come by? I thought you wanted to see the success."

"I'll take your word for it. I wanted to see you to see how *you* were doing. To see if you were enjoying yourself as much as it sounded like you were." He tucked his hands into his pants pockets. The smile on his face was odd.

A noise from behind caught her attention. Mike was bringing

more glasses to the bar. "Hey, Mike, this is my brother, Keith. Keith, this is Mike, one of my managers."

As they exchanged greetings, Elizabeth started toward the back, hoping Keith would follow. She thought about his question. Was she having fun? Her immediate reaction was that it was a job like any other. But in reality, it was more. Maybe it was the sneaking behind Keith's and her dad's backs, maybe it was the unusual challenge. Over the past weeks, she had been enjoying herself.

A hand touched her shoulder. "So?" Keith asked.

"What?"

"That smile tells me either you know a good joke, or I was right and you've been having fun with this project."

"Okay, I admit that I've had more fun doing this one than most."

The tender look on his face startled her. "What is it?"

He shifted again. "I have something to show you."

"Okay." She looked over her shoulder. Still no sign of Colin, but Mike would be okay until he showed. "Where are we going?"

"Close." He grabbed her hand and pushed through the back door. "I didn't want to tell you before. I figured you'd get discouraged. But this was the real reason I had Dad buy the place."

He pulled her around the corner to the front of the building again. He jingled keys and stopped in front of the boarded-up door. He unlocked the door to the business that adjoined the bar and her stomach sank.

This couldn't be good.

His enthusiasm swirled around like a strange aura. Keith didn't act this way. She followed him through the door into the dark room. With the soap on the windows, sunlight battled to illuminate the space, but failed. Her eyes tried to adjust as Keith dropped her hand.

"What's going on, Keith? I don't like surprises."

"Trust me. You'll like this surprise."

Her stomach went from flopping to burning. Fluorescent lights flickered and buzzed to life. She squinted against the sudden light and blinked. What the hell?

Keith rushed back to her side. "What do you think?"

"About what?" She stared at the space. Racks covered in plastic and layers of dust and rows of lanes, equally as dusty.

A bowling alley?

"This is the other half of the bar."

"What?" Her voice squeaked, and she spun to face him. "No other business was listed as part of the holding."

He smirked. "Ah, Libby didn't do her homework after all. How unlike you."

The burn raced up toward her chest. "I did my homework. The business is listed only as The Irish Pub."

"The lanes are part of the pub. When the business began to fail, I closed off this part and left the bar open."

She forced air into her lungs. "You mean you left the bar to run into the ground, and now you dump this on me? How dare you? You could've mentioned this before. You said nothing."

"Like you said nothing about your real reason for being in Chicago?" He crossed his arms. He only did that when he was looking for a fight.

"You're just determined to see me fail. I really thought you were happy for me." She spun and walked toward the door. What the hell was she supposed to do with this?

"Wait. Elizabeth."

She stopped, but didn't turn around.

"I didn't tell you before because I didn't want you to get discouraged. When we talked, you were happy. I could hear it in your voice. I didn't want to ruin it."

"So you waited until now to point out that all my success means nothing. I have to start over to prove myself. That's just like you."

"You don't need to prove yourself. That's what I keep saying."

Tears burned behind her eyelids. She faced Keith and said in a low voice, "You're wrong. I have to prove myself every day."

She turned back and walked calmly away. In the bar, she nodded at Mike. She cleared her throat and hoped her voice would stay steady. "No Colin yet?"

"Nope."

"Do you need anything?"

"I'm good." He looked at her like he might want to say more, but stopped.

The front door opened again, and they both turned. She was sure Keith had followed her back, but one of the waitresses entered. They opened in less than an hour and still no Colin. Damn him. He was always coming in late.

She pulled her phone out and called him. No answer. Straight to voice mail. She stormed back into her office to get his address. She'd make damn well sure he knew that this was unacceptable.

Then she remembered that he lived above O'Leary's. That made it easy for him to show up to work there. No travel. Well, he needed to get it into his head that when he was supposed to work at Brannigan's, she expected him to not only show up but to be on time.

With her keys in hand, she waved at Mike. "I have to run out. If Colin comes in, let him know I need to speak with him. I should be back soon. My cell number is by the register if you need to reach me."

"No problem."

She drove to O'Leary's on a mission. The burn in her stomach splashed around and even the antacids didn't help. She couldn't do much about Keith and his underhandedness, but she could do something about Colin.

As she drove, images of the beat-up bowling alley flashed in her head. Her hands shook. She wasn't sure if it was out of anger or frustration or nervous energy.

Nervous? Why should she be nervous?

She threw the car into park and walked around the exterior of the building to locate Colin's apartment. At the back, stairs led up to apartments above the bar. Her heels clicked on the wooden steps. After pressing the doorbell, she felt her teeth grind.

The door swung open and a sexily rumpled, shirtless Colin stood before her. She swallowed hard. Damn hormones. She wouldn't let them distract her.

"Elizabeth?"

God, even his voice was sexy.

"Unbelievable. Do you have any idea what time it is?"

He scratched his stomach, and her gaze followed his hand on its path. His jeans were unsnapped.

She cleared her throat and looked up.

"Uh, you want to come in?"

He stepped in, so she followed. Why he bothered to ask what she wanted bewildered her, since he'd obviously planned to go in anyway.

Colin led the way down a dark hall toward an open door.

She called after him, "You were supposed to come in early today. You said you'd tell Mike what he needed to know."

Inside his apartment, he turned to face her. "Sorry, I'm running late. I was up all night—"

"I told you when we signed the contract that I wouldn't put up with any games." She thought back to what he'd said to her the night he found her with Lori and Janie. "If you want to go out and get laid, I don't care. But I expect you to take this business seriously."

Anger suddenly flashed into his eyes. The bright blue turned steely. Something she'd said struck a chord. He reached out and slammed the door shut behind her, putting his body within inches of hers.

"First of all, I've been busting my ass taking the bar seriously. Second, I wasn't out getting laid. I couldn't even tell you the last time I had a date, much less got laid."

"I bet it hasn't been as long as it has for me." Shit, she really hadn't meant to say that out loud. She shook her head and added quickly, "That's not the point. You said you were going to be there. I waited and I called and you didn't show."

She was rambling and knew she wasn't making sense. She'd needed Colin after seeing Keith and he hadn't been there. She'd wanted to lean on him and now she was lashing out at him. What was worse, she felt her emotions getting the better of her. They were going to spill out and she fought to contain them. She hated sounding desperate.

* * *

Fuck. He shouldn't have yelled at her. Her body trembled. Elizabeth was about to have a meltdown. What the hell was he supposed to do if she became hysterical?

The muscle in her jaw twitched and her hands clenched into fists.

"Elizabeth."

Her right hand flicked up. "Just don't."

Her voice was weak, but he knew she fought to make it sound strong. He wasn't sure what to do with an emotional woman. He'd never had one around long enough to see her get emotional. Except his sisters.

A hug always worked with Maggie and Moira. He stepped closer and wrapped his arms around Elizabeth. Immediately, he questioned the move. Excitement stirred when he saw the fiery anger on her face, but actually holding her in his arms was a mistake. His hard-on raged against his jeans.

Her back stiffened and she resisted for a minute. Once she realized what he was doing, she gave in and let him hold her.

When he spoke, his voice was gruff. "Elizabeth, I was coming into work. I just overslept. I was at the hospital all night."

She jerked, but he held tight. "What happened?"

She was concerned about him. Hmm. "Nothing bad. My sister-in-law went into labor. Healthy baby boy Patrick O'Leary was born this morning."

"Oh. Congratulations. I'm sorry I came in screaming at you." The words rushed from her mouth, like it was painful to have to apologize.

As he talked, her body softened against him. Cinnamon tickled his nose, and he felt her breath quiet against his shoulder.

"I'm sorry I yelled at you."

Her lips curved against his skin. "It wasn't that."

"What was it then?"

"Nothing. Don't worry about it." She closed off the conversation, but didn't move away from him.

His jeans grew uncomfortably tight. Minutes dragged. He didn't want to push her away, but he needed to adjust his cock. She finally turned her head, which made her lips brush across his collar, and his dick twitched.

She lifted her face and whispered, "Thanks."

Again, he moved without thought. His mouth captured hers. Ryan was right; he didn't have a wife or a girlfriend. He excelled at casual relationships.

Elizabeth's mouth opened for his tongue. She tasted good and her body fit nicely against his. He angled his head, and she raised her arms and wrapped them around his back. She wasn't pushing him away this time.

He tugged her hair free from the knot at the back of her head. The silky softness fell over his hands. He pushed his fingers through it to her scalp and walked her backward toward the breakfast bar. His dick throbbed, seeking release.

A moan slipped from Elizabeth, and it was the only green light he needed. He pushed at her blazer and yanked it off. He trailed kisses down her neck as he unbuttoned the blouse. Warm cinnamon greeted him as he licked her neck.

She arched her back, pushing her chest toward him and her hips into his groin. Just as he loosened her blouse and glimpsed a lacy bra, her long fingers were tugging at his pants.

The only sounds in the room were their heavy breathing and the hiss of the zipper. Her wide eyes looked into his.

"Stop now unless you're sure about this." His voice was raspy with need, and he really hoped she didn't want to stop.

She answered with her eyes instead of her voice. She quirked one eyebrow up and pulled his fly open. Before she could use her hand to make him any crazier, he lowered his head to kiss across her bare chest, licking slowly under the edge of the lace bra. Her hands fell away from his waist and grasped his head, urging him on.

He felt her heart thump under his lips, and he slid his hands up her thighs, bunching her skirt on the way.

"Wait," she gasped.

Fuck, no, he wasn't going to wait. Not now. He pulled away reluctantly to see if he could talk her into continuing.

Her gaze held his as her fingers undid the clasp of her skirt. She stepped out of it. "It's a bitch with wrinkles."

She laid the skirt on the counter, and he stood confused for a moment. She wasn't backing off—she just wanted to take off her skirt?

When he didn't move, she ran a hand across his chest. Her cool fingers soothed his heated skin. A moment later, her lips followed the same path. She definitely wasn't stopping. He grabbed her hips and eased her onto one of the stools. As soon as he began to kiss her neck again, she moaned.

With one hand, he reached around and flipped the clasp on her bra open, and his other hand felt for the silk of her panties. Moist heat radiated into his fingertips. He stroked her through the soft material until her hips began to wiggle.

He pulled away again long enough to remove both the bra and her blouse. God, she was gorgeous, all flush with passion. Her breasts were slightly more than a handful and his tongue wanted to play with the stiff peaks jutting out at him. As he took one in his mouth, she grabbed his hand and brought it back to her crotch. This time, he slid inside her panties and felt how wet she was.

He used his teeth to tug at her nipple and slid a finger into her wet warmth. Moving to the other breast, he added a finger inside her and stroked her clit with his thumb. Her nails bit into his shoulders and her entire body vibrated with need.

"Now, Colin. For once, move fast."

For years he'd heard how women enjoyed going slow, and he liked to think himself a considerate lover, but her command had him donning a condom faster than he'd ever done. His jeans were low on his hips as he stripped away her underpants.

Without another word, he slid his cock into her, and her sexy, long legs wrapped around him. It was heaven, and he thought for a moment his legs would buckle under the pleasure. He gripped the counter behind Elizabeth for security and drove into her.

Her head lolled back and he kissed her neck. Her hips bucked and she moaned and gasped. He could feel her tightening around him. He grabbed her leg and hoisted it higher so he could go deeper.

"Oh, God!" Her eyes drifted closed. She bit down on her lower lip, still holding back.

He leaned close to her ear and whispered, "Let go. Let it all out. It'll be so much better."

Dropping her leg back to his hip, he moved his hand between their bodies and brushed against her clit. Her eyes flew open and she was gone.

"Oh, Colin, oh. Don't. Stop." Her words were gasps, and she tightened around his cock.

He loved the sound of his name in her mouth. He buried his face in her hair, breathing in her scent, riding her orgasm. Everything about her felt so damn good. He didn't want to finish, not yet, but the aftershocks of her orgasm caused trembling in her body that pulled him deeper.

A few more thrusts and he came with hard spurts that emptied his balls and made him weak. He held her close, afraid to move.

Afraid to look into her face.

Afraid that he'd see regret.

She stroked his bare shoulders as their breathing returned to normal. "I think I left marks. Sorry about that."

He pulled back and turned his head to look at her hands. Sure enough, crescent shapes marked his skin from her nails. "We're even, then. I think my whiskers did at least as much to you."

He ran a finger across her chest where he'd burned her skin with his kisses.

"It's getting late. Mike is going to wonder where we are."

He sighed. Elizabeth the businesswoman had returned. He pulled out of her and went to dispose of the condom.

She cleared her throat. "Can I use your bathroom to freshen up?"

"Sure. Down the hall on the left."

She picked up her clothes that he'd tossed carelessly on the floor and her skirt that lay neatly on the counter. He liked that she didn't seem shy about walking through his apartment naked. He'd always found it odd that he could do all sorts of things to a woman's body, but then she'd want to cover it up to go into another room. As if he hadn't seen, touched, and tasted it all.

Tasted. He hadn't tasted nearly enough of Elizabeth. He shouldn't have listened to her. Going fast had a time and a place, but this shouldn't have been it.

A fully clothed Elizabeth emerged from the bathroom, every hair tucked back, not a wrinkle to show what they'd done.

"I'm heading back to the bar. When do you think you'll be in?"

"I'll get dressed now."

"Okay. I'll see you there." She turned to pick up her keys.

He circled her waist and pulled her into him, planting a kiss on her that she wouldn't likely forget. "This isn't over."

She sighed. "We can't do this. We're business partners. Getting romantically involved will cause problems."

"Only if we let it."

"I need to stay focused on the bar. I have a huge mess on my hands and I need to fix it." She stroked his jaw. "This was a fabulous release. I had a really good time here, but it can't happen again."

"The bar is in good shape. It's not a mess. I understand that you live in Florida and you're going back. I'm just saying that we're both too busy to start a relationship, so why not enjoy each other? Have fun while you're here."

She sighed and melted into him a little.

"Besides, you haven't even had me at my best."

She belted out a laugh, full and obnoxious, like she did that night at the club. *Laugh* didn't really describe the sound. He'd have to look up a new word that would fit. Her hand immediately flew to cover her mouth.

He peeled her fingers away. "Don't. I like it when you laugh like that. It's real."

A soft smile crossed her face and she looked like a different woman. "It really is getting late. I don't think we should leave the employees alone on the second night of being open."

"Isn't that the point of having employees? So you don't have to do it all?"

"Yes, but that place was left unsupervised for far too long." She moved out of his embrace and turned toward the door.

"I'll be at the bar soon and then you can fill me in on the problems."

She nodded and left. Colin ran his hands through his hair. He couldn't believe it. He'd just had sex with Legs. It was every bit as good as he'd thought it would be. And he'd managed to escape bodily injury. His crappy day had finally taken a turn for the better. He whistled as he went to his bedroom to get dressed. Things were definitely looking up.

CHAPTER 9

Elizabeth walked to her car in a daze. What the hell did she just do? Not only did she throw herself at Colin to get a great orgasm, but by not disagreeing with him, it could happen again. It would happen again.

Her mind knew it was a mistake. The rest of her body, however, was humming with pleasure and the anticipation of it getting better. She couldn't stop smiling. The muscles that had been bunched in tight knots since she'd left Keith were now loose and limber. She drove back to the bar and prayed that Mike wouldn't question her absence.

As she entered the bar, she took note of the small crowd. Not as big as the night before, but not bad for before-dinner customers. She waved at Mike as she headed to her office. Heat crept up her neck and embarrassment swamped her. She felt like everyone knew what she'd been doing less than a half hour ago.

Back at her desk, she thought about the bowling alley next door. She knew nothing about bowling alleys. She hadn't stepped foot in one in at least twenty-five years. Not since Dad had made it big in construction and Mom decided that ballet and opera were more appropriate than bowling and having fun.

Her eyes fluttered closed and her mind wandered back to the birthday party she'd gone to when she was eight. It was the first time she'd gone to a bowling alley and she'd been completely overwhelmed. The cracking of ball against pin, people cheering, and the powdery smell of chalk dust shocked her, but within minutes, she was in love.

Some bowlers were superstitious in their routines and in how they approached the lanes. Others just ran straight ahead with little or no forethought. Everyone jumped and yelled and danced when they got a strike. So many people were wild and uninhibited.

Then, during the party, they switched to cosmic bowling and turned on black lights. She and her friends had so much fun playing. It was magical.

"I hope I'm the reason for that smile."

Startled at the sound of Colin's voice, Elizabeth jolted in her chair. She blinked rapidly to clear her vision and her brain. How long had he been standing in the doorway? "Hi."

"I checked with Mike and he has everything under control, so I thought I'd come back here and see why you think we have a huge mess. We have customers. How bad can it be?" He closed the door and leaned against it.

She studied his casual stance and tried not to drool. He was so damn sexy she wanted to get naked with him again. Now. She cleared her throat. "I should've listened to you when you tried to tell me about the basement."

He pushed away from the door and took the rickety seat in front of her desk. "Why?"

"My brother stopped by today. As it turns out, the other half of this building is also part of the business. With our success last night, we've only scratched the surface."

"Expanding into the other half of the building shouldn't be too difficult. Add a dance floor, a pool table, more TVs."

Her brain suddenly weighed too much. "It's not more bar space."

"What is it then?"

Her stomach began to burn again. She reached into her desk drawer and grabbed her bottle of antacids. Damn. She'd forgotten to buy more. Dumping two green ones into her hand, she stood. "It's better if I just show you."

He pointed at the bottle. "Are you okay?"

"Yes. Just an upset stomach." Although she was back to chomping antacids almost constantly, she wanted to believe that. She wanted to trust that the added stress wouldn't get any worse than what the small tablets could fix.

The chalky lime-tasting powder clung to the tops of her molars, and she grabbed the keys Keith had left. "Let's go out back and I'll show you."

She took Colin to the back door of the bowling alley. Shoving aside pretty memories of a birthday party, she focused on reality. She knew nothing about how to run a bowling alley. She knew even less about that than she did about running a bar. Part of her believed Keith had done this on purpose, like he'd known she'd come here and be completely overwhelmed. Logic told her otherwise, but the sibling rivalry always reared its ugly little head.

Inside the building, she flipped on lights. "Here it is. A bowling alley."

Colin said nothing in response. He turned in a circle and then walked down the length of the room.

His silence unnerved her all over again. "See, a mess."

"If it's been closed down this long, why not just leave it? We have a good thing going with the bar. Why not sell this half as is?"

"No—" She stopped herself from saying that it would be cheating. He knew nothing about her battle with Keith for the company. "I need to have the whole thing turned around."

He scrubbed his hands over his face. He was going to leave. She could see it. He'd bail, and she'd be back to square one. Well, not square one, because the bar was looking pretty good. "I know you didn't sign on for this. If you want out, that's fine."

He put his fists on his hips and narrowed his eyes. "I don't scare that easily. And you're not getting out of our contract. If I don't get my bonus until the whole thing sells, then we'll get the whole thing ready to sell. You're not cutting me out now."

A pain shot through her chest. "I wasn't trying to cheat you out of anything. I meant that we would figure out a decent split."

Although his face remained hard, his shoulders relaxed a fraction. "Well, I'm not going anywhere."

A deep breath worked its way from her lungs. Relief swamped her in a way she hadn't expected. She didn't want him to go. She enjoyed working with him. They made a good team. "Okay."

They stood staring at each other for another long moment. Finally, she cleared her throat. "What do you know about bowling?"

* * *

Not a fucking thing. That's what he knew about bowling. The muscles in his jaw were so tight he thought they'd crack. "Not much."

"That's what I was afraid of."

She looked defeated. Not quite as bad as her near breakdown in his apartment, but pretty bad. How did she handle working when she took everything so personally? Like this was a personal failure? "We'll figure it out. All we need is to find someone who's willing to teach us. There are plenty of bowling alleys in the city."

"And?"

"I can't believe I'm about to say this, but we'll do some research. I'm thinking if we can sway one good manager to join us, we'll be golden."

She crossed her arms. "Have someone in mind?"

"No, but I was just thinking that Ryan has his manager, Mary, trained so well that she could run the bar without him, so it would probably work the same way with a bowling alley." For someone who thought on the fly, he sounded pretty good, even to himself, and he knew he was full of shit.

"Okay. I'll go back to my office and start the search again. Will you be able to check some out tomorrow with me?"

He did his best to hide his grimace. He needed to put in time at O'Leary's, especially with Ryan being gone for Quinn and the baby. "Probably." He'd have to figure out how to squeeze a few more hours into the day.

Following Elizabeth back to the bar, he couldn't help but stare at the sway of her hips. Had they really had sex just hours ago? She showed no sign of afterglow, but he knew she'd enjoyed herself.

He shook his head again. He needed to keep thoughts of her naked body out of his head. The business needed his full focus. There was no way he'd be able to afford to buy both businesses from her. If he couldn't talk her into separating the bar from the alley, he'd at least have the bonus he'd get from selling. It should be more than enough to buy something else.

Especially if he helped her figure out the bowling alley.

Back at the bar, Elizabeth disappeared into her office, and Colin checked on the front. A decent-sized crowd had filtered in while he and Elizabeth were at the bowling alley. Mike didn't need his help.

Colin didn't know why Elizabeth had been so worried. If Mike kept this up, they would have plenty of time to investigate other alleys and begin work on this one without feeling too much of a strain.

Maybe Elizabeth was worried about money. Ryan had said that her family had deep pockets, but what if her budget couldn't accommodate the bowling alley? Maybe that's why she took it all so personally.

He needed to stop worrying about the whys of it all. None of it mattered. He and Elizabeth had a contract that stipulated she was the money end and he was the experience. If he was going to continue to hold up his end, he needed to learn about running a bowling alley. How hard could it be?

His brother Michael used to bowl on a league with the other firefighters. He'd give him a call and find out where they'd bowled. It was a starting place. He checked his watch. He needed to go back to O'Leary's and make sure everything was okay there.

Ryan was counting on him. He'd let Ryan down enough over the years that he didn't want to add to the stress of new parenthood by not keeping up with everything. Ryan's hands had always been full with work and now he had Quinn and Patrick.

Thinking the name of his nephew was difficult. He had no right to be jealous. He knew that, but he couldn't prevent the feeling. He knocked on Elizabeth's office door, but didn't wait for an answer. He swung the door open and saw her glaring at her computer screen.

"Hey, I'm going to step out for a bit. Mike has everything under control. I'll be back before closing."

She tore her gaze from the screen to face him. "Okay. Is everything all right?"

"Yeah. I just want to check in at O'Leary's. I'll be back. Then maybe we can go over to the bowling alley and see what we have and what we need."

She smiled sweetly. "Sounds good."

"See you." He tapped the door frame.

"Colin."

He turned back.

"Thanks. For everything."

"Everything, huh?"

Her neck and cheeks grew pink.

"I meant the help with the bar and bowling alley."

He entered the office and leaned over the top of her desk. "Does that mean you didn't appreciate the orgasm you had this afternoon?"

She lifted one eyebrow. "Oh, I appreciated the hell out of that. But it shouldn't continue. You need to stop flirting with me."

"Why? If you have such determination to not sleep with me again, then my flirtation shouldn't make an impact whatsoever."

"It just makes things harder."

He couldn't stop the chuckle at her double entendre.

She pushed away from the desk, putting distance between them as if she thought he might try to take her right there. "It would just make things easier if you didn't waste your time flirting. Plus, you could focus that energy on more productive things."

He straightened and offered her a half-assed salute. "Yes, boss."

He left her office letting her feel like she'd won. He had no intention of backing off. They'd be spending way too many hours alone together for him to give up the idea of having her legs wrapped around him again.

Driving to O'Leary's, he thought of what they could do with the space if they didn't want to keep it as a bowling alley but came up empty. At least a bowling alley loosely fit their design. Bowling was a sport, right?

They could do their own league and offer birthday parties for kids. If they made the alley a family place, it could grow a lot of their business. Mom and Dad could have drinks and watch a game on TV while the kids tried to bowl. Maybe they could get a small arcade going. He pictured the place in his head, but didn't have a strong sense of it. He couldn't even imagine how they could connect the two businesses. He needed more time there.

"Hi, Mary," he called as he walked through O'Leary's. "Everything okay?"

"Everything's right as rain. Did you see pictures of that adorable baby?"

"I saw the real deal this morning."

"Ryan called, and I let him know you were here earlier, but that I would close up. How are things going at your bar?" She wiped the bar down as she talked, simultaneously scanning the glasses to see who might need a refill.

"We hit a small glitch, but we're headed in the right direction.

What's the schedule like here for the rest of the week? I'm guessing Ryan won't be around much."

Mary moved to pour a beer, and as he watched her pull the handle of the tap, he remembered what it was like to have his arms around Elizabeth, teaching her to do the same. He shook his head.

"Ryan has all the shifts covered. He figured Quinn would be going in any day, so he planned for this."

Figures. Ryan didn't trust that he could rely on Colin. Colin had told him he'd be here, and he had been. Maybe he hadn't put in as much time since getting involved with Elizabeth, but he hadn't walked away either. He banked the automatic anger so he wouldn't take it out on Mary. "Give me a call if you need anything. I'm going to go upstairs and have a nap. Last night went on forever, and I have to work tonight."

"Okay. See you later."

He wasn't needed here. He never had been. How could he not feel resentment toward Ryan because of that? Ryan had made sure of it. For a year Colin had been trying to prove himself worthy while hoping for Ryan's forgiveness.

It looked like that would never happen. Maybe it was time to move on. If Ryan wanted to keep doing it all alone, Colin would let him. The rest of the family had welcomed Colin back with open arms. He was tired of trying to please Ryan.

Ryan wasn't Dad. Colin didn't need his approval. He'd build Brannigan's into something to be proud of. Then he'd move on to have his own place.

He'd be a success in spite of Ryan's disbelief.

* * *

Elizabeth stared at the list of bowling alleys in her hand. This was all too much. Keith's betrayal was reminiscent of their past. She couldn't believe he'd done this to her again.

Was winning that important to him?

Of course it was. It was important to her too. The difference was that she didn't cheat to win.

A bowling alley.

What would have possessed Keith to buy a bowling alley?

Interest stirred in her blood. The memories of that long-ago birthday party danced in her head. She wondered if anything was operational next door. She hadn't played the game since she was a kid, and she had a whole alley all to herself.

Why not? The worst that would happen was that she'd go over there and find out that nothing worked.

She pushed away from her desk before she lost her nerve. She stopped in the front and was surprised to see another crowd. Still not quite as big as the night before, but steady enough to suggest success. She smiled and waved at Mike. He seemed to be handling everything. The bar looked clean and the customers satisfied.

"I'll be next door if you need me. Call my cell. I'll be back in a while."

He looked a little confused about her going next door, but nodded. Inside the bowling alley, she turned on every light switch she could find. The place was a mess. Inches of dust and dirt coated every surface.

She yanked a tarp from a rack. The cloud of dust made her cough, but once she regained her ability to breathe normally, she saw that the rack was still filled with bowling balls. She ran her hand along a shiny, smooth ball. The cool surface made her fingers itch to pick it up. She spun the ball until the three holes were faceup.

Sliding two fingers and her thumb in, she hefted the ball. It was too heavy for her to use, but she liked the feel of it. Setting the ball back in its spot, she shook her head. She was being childish. She didn't have time for games.

Behind the shoe counter, she found some more switches and flipped them. Fortunately, there were no shoes. She didn't think she could bear the stench of shoes that had been sitting for a decade. The shelves held a few cans of spray, probably for the shoes. If she wanted to make this work, they would need to order all new shoes. The balls seemed to be in good shape. She picked up a mini-pencil from the shelf and sifted around for a sheet of paper.

Making a list was something she was good at. Just looking around, she was able to see many things they'd have to order. Little pencils, scorecards . . . unless they upgraded to all electronic scoring. That would probably be the way to go.

She'd never imagined that being the first one to take on a business would be so hard. She always came in after Dad or Keith had things in place. She was expected to run the staff and make sure they'd hired the right people, but Dad and Keith were the idea people. Maybe that's why they thought she couldn't handle being in charge.

They never trusted her to come up with the ideas. In fact, they'd never even asked for her input. Sure, she was good enough to maintain the books and follow their plans, but they'd never thought to invite her into the development phase.

Well, she would show them. She would take this alley and turn it around, just as she had the bar.

Upgrades of this nature would be more expensive than anything else she'd done. If she wanted access to company funds of this proportion, she'd have to explain to her father. No, for this, she'd use her own money to keep flying under the radar.

First, before ordering anything, she needed to find a repairman to make sure the equipment was operational. She didn't know if she could afford to replace the pin setters. It was too late in the day to make calls now. Tomorrow would come soon enough.

In the meantime, she'd start the cleaning process all over. She wondered if Moira was free. She could use the company. Unfortunately, she didn't have Moira's number. She dialed Colin again, but it went to voice mail.

"Hi, Colin. It's Elizabeth. I'm in the bowling alley, and I figured I'd get a jump start on cleaning and was wondering if you'd give Moira a call and see if she'd be interested in helping. Just a thought. See you later."

She disconnected and went back to her office to change into jeans and a T-shirt and get cleaning supplies. She bet her father and Keith never got this hands-on during a takeover. It was definitely a new experience.

The Brannigan's T-shirt she put on was the one Colin had given her that revealed too much skin. She wore it because she hadn't gotten an extra one from him and she wouldn't be with customers. In the mirror, she caught sight of the red marks just above the neckline of the shirt.

Colin's whiskers had done that. The skin was a little raw, but the memory flooded her with pleasure. She filled a bucket with soap and hot water and trudged out the back door and swung into the alley. She hoped to find the water still connected on that side or this was going to be a real pain in the ass.

She worked in silence, scraping away layers of dirt and scum, beginning the next phase in the project that was truly hers.

* * *

The bleep of a voice mail woke Colin from sleep. He jolted awake, more well rested than he'd felt in days, maybe even weeks. He listened to the message from Elizabeth. Where did that woman get her energy? She'd already been at the bar all night last night, found out about the bowling alley, fought with him, had sex, and now she was back at work, attempting to tackle the cleaning of the bowling alley. He rolled out of bed, knowing he needed to go help.

He checked the time. He could call Moira, but part of him preferred to have Elizabeth to himself. If Mike was handling the bar without a problem, there was no reason they couldn't work together to put a dent in the cleaning of the alley.

And maybe if he was really lucky, he could talk Elizabeth into coming back home with him.

He took a quick shower, checked in with Mary down at O'Leary's, and headed out. He began to question exactly how Ryan had managed to run both bars for so long by himself. Sure, he had Mary, but he still put time in at both places on a daily basis. He guessed Ryan hadn't had much of a personal life over the past few years.

Ryan had almost lost Quinn because he was so used to doing everything alone. Colin had convinced Ryan that he wasn't alone, that they'd work together to take care of their family. Now Colin felt the pressure of that commitment.

He pulled up behind the bar and parked in a spot on the bowling alley side. The back door was propped open. He walked in and saw Elizabeth scrubbing a long counter. The noise from the bar next door seeped through the wall. Before announcing his presence, he took a look around with fresh eyes.

The room was a mess, but it wasn't destroyed. Elizabeth had pulled tarps off the racks to reveal rows of bowling balls. The hardwood flooring of the alleys appeared to be in good shape.

Maybe this wasn't as bad as he'd originally thought. The place had been closed for a decade. That meant that it hadn't suffered the wear and tear the bar had been through. This was just neglected space.

"Hey," he called out to get Elizabeth's attention.

She jumped a little at the sound of his voice. "Hi. I guess you got my message."

She turned and tossed a rag into a bucket of water. She wore the T-shirt he had given her, the one that showed a nice bit of cleavage. Her soft skin was still red where his jaw had rubbed against it.

"I'm here to help. Mike will be fine at the bar." He moved closer. He stroked the sensitive skin below her collarbone. "Sorry about this."

She swatted his hand away. "It's fine. Collateral damage. Usually I'm the one inflicting the pain."

"I should consider myself lucky that I got away unscathed, huh?"

"Definitely." She reached back into the bucket and wrung out the rag. "This place is disgusting. I'm on my third bucket of water just to clean this counter."

"Where do you want me to start?"

She shook her head and looked around. "Pick a spot. At this rate, we'll be here all night."

He went to the backroom of the bar to grab more cleaning supplies, and while he was there, he snagged a bottle of wine. He rarely drank anymore, but if he had to suffer through more cleaning, he might as well enjoy himself. It also had to help loosen Elizabeth up.

They worked for hours scrubbing and listening to some classic rock station on a battered radio. Colin made a mental note to get the stereo hooked up in here as well. Elizabeth sipped at the first glass he'd poured for her.

"Do you know if both businesses ran together?"

"Huh?" she asked, clearly caught up in her own thoughts.

"Is there a way for the bar and bowling alley to connect up here?"

"I have no idea. I just know that Keith said they closed down the alley because it was too much work."

"Keith?"

Her face froze like she'd said something she shouldn't have. "My brother."

"Oh." Why would she be worried about talking about her brother? "I'm starving. Aren't you hungry?"

She shrugged.

"It would be nice if we had a real kitchen here like we do at O'Leary's. Then we could just yell out an order and eat." He planted the seed in her mind. Having a fully functioning kitchen would increase the value of the business. "I'm going to order pizza. What do you like on it?"

He prayed she wouldn't say something weird like fruit. Fruit did not belong on a pizza.

"I'm fine with whatever you get."

She seemed distant. He wanted to get her to interact. Respond. Something. He whipped out his phone and ordered a pizza with everything and had it delivered to the bar. He propped the front door open so he could keep an eye out for the delivery guy.

By the time the pizza arrived, the counter area was practically sparkling. He'd managed to get the tables at each alley clean. The floors were a different matter altogether. He wasn't sure if the ratty carpet was worth salvaging.

Colin reentered the bowling alley carrying the pizza. "Do you want to eat here or go next door and eat in your office?"

Elizabeth tossed the dirty rag back in the bucket. "We might as well eat here. My office is a little cramped."

He set the pizza on the counter and pulled over a couple of stools. He brushed the worst of the dirt off them and offered one to Elizabeth. She looked exhausted. Too bad she hadn't taken a nap like he had.

She took the smallest piece of pizza from the box and nibbled at it.

"Please don't tell me you're one of *those* women."

"*Those* women?"

"The kind that pretends not to eat."

"No. I love to eat. You've seen me eat."

"Yeah. A salad and fries."

"I'm just really tired and I still have an upset stomach."

"Your stomach is upset a lot. Are you okay?"

"I'm fine."

He wasn't buying it. She was holding back, but he didn't want to push her. He still had hopes for spending the night with her.

"Are you and your brother close? You never talk about him."

Elizabeth studied the pizza in her hand. "We get along. I live in the coach house on his property. But I wouldn't say we're close."

"Is he in the family business too?"

She nodded.

"Why isn't he here helping you then?"

"He's got other projects." She tossed her pizza down. "How's your family? I mean with the new baby and all?"

She obviously wanted to change the topic. Why was her family off limits, but his wasn't? "They're great. First grandbaby and all."

They sat in silence, but lustful images filled his head. "Why don't you head out? We can get back to this tomorrow when we're fresh and can think straight."

She shook her head. "We have to close the bar."

"I'll close up with Mike. I'm used to these hours. You aren't." He brushed a thumb down her cheek.

"I'm fine. I need the receipts anyway."

"The receipts can wait until tomorrow. I'll lock them up in your office."

He wanted to persuade her. She looked exhausted and she wasn't feeling well, no matter what she said. "I'll bring the receipts to you after I close."

Her eyes widened at his offer. "Why would you want to drive all the way to my hotel when your apartment is so much closer?"

"Good point. Why don't you go back to my apartment to sleep, and I'll bring the receipts home with me?"

He smiled, knowing he'd caught her off guard.

CHAPTER 10

Elizabeth's mouth dropped open. "Are you asking me to spend the night with you?"

"Sure."

She immediately wanted to say no, but she stopped herself. Why would it be bad? He'd made a hell of an argument earlier. They were both too busy to meet other people. She'd done this before. The only difference here was that he was her business partner.

As if reading her mind, he said, "We're partners and we make a good team. I get that sleeping together could complicate things, but we're both adults. We can handle it."

She laughed. "I'm an adult. I'm not quite sure about you."

"Did you just make another joke? Better be careful. It might become a habit." He leaned in and gave her a quick kiss. "So what do you say?"

"We don't know each other that well. And although I was fine with the idea of anonymous sex when we first met, things have changed. We are partners, and in my experience, men tend to think that once they've slept with a woman, they have the upper hand."

"What? You don't understand men at all, sweetheart. We talk a good game, but once we have sex, the woman holds all the cards."

She didn't believe him for a second, but he was so damn cute, she wanted to be convinced. "Then we need rules."

"Rules?"

He looked like the word alone would give him a coronary.

"Yes, ground rules. First, no hanky-panky at work. I'm the boss, the owner, and I need all of the employees to see me that way."

He scooted his stool closer to hers. "You might find it hard to keep your hands off me. What else?"

"We tell no one about this. It's just between us."

He shifted away from her. "I can't tell my family?"

"No one. It's friendly sex, not a lifelong commitment."

"I can agree to that, but you can't blame me if they figure it out. Moira's a reporter and the nosiest thing on two legs."

"Third, I expect monogamy for as long as I'm in town. When I head home, we go our separate ways, no harm, no foul." She waited for his reaction.

"Long-term booty calls. I like the way you think."

He grabbed the back of her neck and drew her close for a kiss, but she resisted.

"We're at work. You're already breaking Rule One."

"No one's here, so no one can find out."

She slid from her stool and out of his reach. "Looking for loopholes won't help you. Do we have a deal?"

He stepped beside her and took her hand. "Are you going to my apartment for the night?"

"Maybe. If we can agree on terms."

"I agree." He fished his keys from his pocket. "Make sure you take a nap before I get home. We'll be up for a while. I don't like to be rushed."

She accepted the keys, but her knees felt weak. She was afraid to move, knowing chances were good that she'd stumble. His body invaded her space again, causing her skin to warm.

"I don't have any clothes to wear."

"You can borrow something of mine and go back to your hotel tomorrow."

She backed away again to gather her thoughts. It all sounded too intimate. "How will you get in?"

"I have a spare set of keys at the bar. Go get some rest."

He turned away from her and busied himself with cleaning up their dinner. The thought of sleep sounded so good—the image of being awoken by him for sex, even better.

She wasn't sure about this, but it couldn't possibly make her life any worse than it had been. She'd been in over her head for weeks. What was a little deeper?

Elizabeth drove to O'Leary's and parked on the street so she wouldn't draw any attention to her car being there overnight. She'd never known a man to be so open with his house. She and Colin had only known each other for a few weeks, and he had not only invited her to spend the night, but he'd allowed her to go to his apartment without him.

She let herself into the apartment and tossed his keys on the counter where they'd had sex that afternoon. He'd left a light on in the small kitchen, and it was enough to illuminate a path for her to find other light switches.

The apartment was nothing special. A leather couch and big-screen TV filled the living room. A small bookcase held paperbacks, mostly books on mixing drinks, but he had quite a few trivia books. She imagined trivia was a tool of the trade for a bartender.

A stack of magazines filled a corner. She was pretty sure she didn't want to know where his reading interests lay, so she didn't thumb through the pile.

In the kitchen, she opened a few cabinets to check out the contents and find a glass for some water. The cabinets were empty, but the refrigerator had food. She didn't know why this shocked her, but it did. She'd expected a twelve-pack of beer and maybe a bag of chips on the counter. He had fruits and vegetables in the refrigerator along with a few bottles of beer.

She took her glass of water down a dark hall and found Colin's bedroom. He'd squeezed a king-sized bed into the room, leaving little space. A tall dresser was wedged in the corner. She scooted around the bed and placed her glass on the lone nightstand. She pulled open the drawer and saw a box of condoms. That made her feel better.

On top of the dresser were a bunch of picture frames. His family. They all looked inordinately happy in the candid shots. Her family photos tended to be portraits and no one looked relaxed or happy. She liked the O'Leary version better. She opened the middle drawer of the dresser to find a shirt to sleep in.

She chose an old softball jersey. It was bright blue and the team name BLUE BALLS blazed across the front in white letters. The cotton was soft and smelled like Colin. She took the shirt with her to the bathroom to take a shower. She was sure Colin wouldn't mind, since he'd wanted her here.

The bathroom was as Spartan as the rest of the apartment. She started the water, and while it warmed, she removed her clothes and folded them. Stepping into the shower, she allowed the warm spray to relax her muscles. Between the tension of finding out about the bowling alley and the effort to clean the place, her muscles ached. She used his soap, liking the smell of it. After the shower, she hastily braided her hair and slipped into Colin's shirt.

She was suddenly exhausted. Sleep sounded better than anything, so she crawled into his bed and under his covers.

* * *

Colin sped through the remainder of his evening with a grin on his face. He'd never expected Elizabeth to agree to go to his apartment. He tried to remember how much of a mess he'd left the place and then decided it didn't matter.

They'd had another decent-sized crowd, which somewhat surprised him for a Tuesday night. Elizabeth had done a good job by hiring Mike. He knew what he was doing, which freed up Colin for mingling with the customers after closing up the bowling alley. Plus, Mike was so big, Colin couldn't imagine squeezing behind the bar with him. He looked more like a bouncer than a bartender. As the night wound down, Colin played barback and restocked the shelves so he wouldn't have to do it the following day.

As he looked over the display of hard liquor, he noticed an empty spot. "Hey, Mike, when did you run out of Bushmills?"

"I haven't poured any. I didn't even know we carried it." Mike shrugged and went back to pouring drinks.

Colin knew there had been a bottle; he'd broken the seal himself last night. Suspicion crept into his brain. He'd locked up after Elizabeth left. He struggled to remember whether the bottle was there then, but he couldn't recall. How could someone have lifted an entire bottle without him noticing?

He began to check the bottles against what he remembered putting on the shelf. Elizabeth had tried to reorganize some things in order to make an impression, but he stocked the liquor. He went to Elizabeth's office to see if he could find the original inventory sheet.

The office had Elizabeth stamped all over it. It looked so different than it had just a week ago. Gone were the rickety, rusty file cabinets along with the layer of smoke scum on the walls. Sitting on her desk were three file folders, one clearly marked *Inventory*.

Sure enough, stapled to his handwritten list was a copy of the invoice. They'd only ordered one bottle to see if it would move, but it shouldn't have moved that fast.

He scanned the list and brought it to the basement with him so he could check it against the stock there. They were missing two bottles of Jack Daniel's. He remembered pulling one up toward the end of the night, so they should still have one down here.

Maybe Mike had sold a lot of shots tonight. He certainly hoped so, otherwise someone had to explain where this missing liquor had gone. With inventory sheets in hand, Colin went back to the bar. One bottle of Jack stood in its place and was still half full. "Hey, Mike." When he had the man's attention, he asked, "Have you opened any new bottles of hard liquor tonight?"

"About a half hour after I started, someone ordered a Jack and Coke and there was no Jack here, so I grabbed a bottle from downstairs. That's where Elizabeth told me to get stock. I wrote it down next to the register so I wouldn't forget to tell you."

"What happened to the bottle that was here?"

"There wasn't one."

"I brought it up myself last night."

Mike raised his eyebrows. "I don't know what to tell you."

Anger tumbled through Colin. Someone had to have stolen from them. He eyed Mike and the two waitresses. They had better chances of stealing something than a customer had of getting around the counter. He'd have to check them when they left. If they were good, though, they would've just passed it on to a friend and no one would know.

Fuck. They'd been feeling so successful, they hadn't even thought to worry about theft. How was he going to tell Elizabeth? She was already so stressed about the bowling alley.

Maybe he'd wait until they'd had sex and she was relaxed. The thought of her tense and rigid body made him reassess. Maybe after the second round of orgasms she'd be ready for bad news.

Suddenly, he wanted to go home. Bad news or not, he had a warm and willing woman waiting for him.

Unfortunately, he needed to deal with this problem first. He helped clean up the bar while keeping an eye on all three employees. Instead of sending anyone home early, he kept them all until closing so he could talk to them. Elizabeth would probably accuse him of trying to usurp her authority by having this conversation without her, but he felt that an immediate strike was important.

When the last customer left, he called Mike, Erin, and Marissa to the bar. "First, I want to say that Elizabeth and I are really happy with the way the first couple of days have gone. We've had good crowds and we've kept them moving. I haven't gotten one complaint."

He paused and looked into each of their faces. He was a good judge of character. He'd hired Marissa and Erin, and although Elizabeth had hired Mike before Colin came on board, Colin had a good feeling. "I have found one problem that needs to be addressed. We have two bottles of liquor that have gone missing. A bottle of Jack and a bottle of Bushmills. If it had been only one, I might be able to chalk it up to miscalculation on my part. But both going missing on the second night open points to theft. I don't want to make any accusations, but you need to be aware that theft is cause for immediate termination."

As he spoke, he watched all three sets of eyes widen. Either they were good actors or they were surprised.

"If the bottles suddenly reappear on the shelf, I'm more than happy to forget about this."

"I've never even stepped behind the bar," Marissa said.

Erin added, "I left before you did last night, and I haven't been behind the bar tonight. Mike's a little territorial."

"I think *territorial* is a harsh word," Mike said to her. Then he turned his attention to Colin. "I told you, I didn't even know we had Bushmills. And why the hell would I want to risk my job to steal a bottle of Jack? I don't even like Jack."

"I'm just throwing it out there. We're only on day two of being open. This is not the way I run a business." The words felt awkward and heavy in his mouth. He'd never run a business, but he imagined what Ryan or his dad would say in this situation. Another doubt pricked him. They wouldn't have left brand-new employees in a position to be able to steal.

"When you're done cleaning up, you can head on out. I'll be in the office." He had absolutely nothing to do in Elizabeth's domain, but he thought if he was out of sight, the culprit might return the bottles.

Ten minutes later, he returned to the front and saw no change. Deep down, he knew the bottles wouldn't magically appear. He flicked off the last light and peered around. The bar was clean and ready for a new day.

Now he had to face Elizabeth and let her know they had a thief.

* * *

Colin grabbed his extra set of keys from Ryan's office at O'Leary's and went upstairs. The kitchen light he'd left on still glowed. He glanced around. There was no sign Elizabeth had even stepped foot in his apartment, except for his key ring lying on the counter. He went to the bathroom first, wanting to take a shower before he woke Elizabeth. In the bathroom, he noticed the subtle indications that someone else was in his home. An extra towel hung on the bar. Her clothes were folded and piled neatly on the toilet tank.

He stripped and stepped into the shower. He tried to figure out how to tell her about the missing liquor. Somehow he felt like this was his fault. He'd allowed the bottles to be stolen, and he'd further fucked up everything by the way he'd handled the employees. He toweled off and went to the bedroom.

Thoughts of easing Elizabeth awake and hearing her moan made him hard. He left the bathroom light on and approached the open door. Instead of finding Elizabeth snuggled in his bed sleeping soundly, she was curled into a tight ball.

"Hey," he called quietly, not sure if she was asleep.

"Hi," she answered, her voice strained. She didn't move.

"Are you okay?"

Now she swung her legs off the side of the bed and tried to sit, but doubled over. "My stomach's still bugging me."

Her arms wrapped around her middle and a pained expression blanketed her entire face.

"Can I get you something?" He thought of all the antacids he'd watched her chew on. "Do you want to go to the doctor?"

"For an upset stomach? What's next, want to call my mommy?"

"If it'll make you feel better, sure."

"I think I just need to eat something. Then I'll be fine." She pushed herself up to stand, but it took effort. "Do you have any bananas?"

"Yeah. Sit down, I'll get you one." He walked back into the kitchen and grabbed a banana. It wasn't normal for someone to be in this much pain so often. Maybe she needed a prescription for heartburn. Tomorrow, he'd get her to go see a doctor. Back in the bedroom, he handed her the banana.

The sight of her standing there, wearing his shirt, gave him an odd, comfortable feeling. She'd chosen to wear his old Blue Balls team shirt. Blue balls indeed. He tugged on a pair of underwear, knowing that getting laid was not in his immediate future.

With a mouth full of banana, Elizabeth said, "Why are you getting dressed? We had plans."

"Our plans can wait until you're feeling better." He pulled her close, kissed her head, then climbed into bed.

"I'll be fine in a minute. Once the food hits my stomach, I'll be good."

"Yeah? For how long? You've been a mess all day. Let's get a good night's sleep. I'm not going anywhere." He settled under the covers and waited for her to join him.

She finished the banana and drank from a glass of water. After leaving to get rid of her trash, she lay down beside him. Her hand rubbed his thigh, and he fought the urge to climb on top of her.

Remembering the pained look on her face when he'd walked in, he stopped her hand. "Get some sleep."

"I don't want to sleep. I want to fuck."

"Talking dirty will get you nowhere." God, he sounded like such a chick.

"Afraid you can't deliver on your promises?"

He rolled to his side, grabbing her hip and pulling her body to his. "I can definitely deliver."

He lowered his mouth to hers and kissed her. His tongue swept into her mouth, and he forced his hand to stay at her hip. If he touched her more, he wouldn't be able to stop, and she needed rest.

When he'd adequately proven his point, he pulled away. "I'll deliver tomorrow, when you're better."

"We're seriously not going to have sex right now? Why the hell am I here?"

"I planned on having sex multiple times tonight until I saw you in pain. Lie down and get some rest. You've been working crazy hours and you're under a lot of stress. Is a good night's sleep really a bad thing?"

"Whatever." She pulled the blanket over her and turned away from him.

He pulled her to his body again and reveled in the feel of her curled into him. His dick was still hard, and he tried not to let her feel it, or she wouldn't give up.

"How was work?" she whispered.

The first thing that hit him was how intimate it felt to lie in bed with this gorgeous woman and discuss his night at work. The second thing that hit him was that he was going to have to lie to Elizabeth.

"It was fine. We'll talk in the morning."

* * *

Elizabeth woke to a sunny day, a bright glare shining through the window. She felt well rested and her stomach no longer hurt. Maybe Colin had been right and a night of quality sleep had set her straight.

She looked to her right and saw Colin asleep beside her, his breath even and quiet. She couldn't believe he'd turned her down for sex last night. Wasn't that the point of this . . . relationship outside of work? Getting together to just sleep was not part of the bargain. It was far too couple-ish.

She slid out from under the covers and tried not to wake him. Standing next to the bed, she watched him sleep. It wasn't fair. No one should look that good all the time. Stubble shadowed his jaw, and his hair was mussed in a way that made her want to run her hands through it. And if she didn't know better, he wore a slight grin, a mere flicker of the one he had while awake. The sheet barely covered his hip and the unmistakable bulge told her he was always ready.

Remembering the huge to-do list on her schedule, she made her way to the bathroom to get ready for the day. She opened the medicine cabinet in hopes of finding a spare toothbrush. Colin struck her as a considerate enough lover that he would have extras for whoever might spend the night.

"Didn't your mom teach you that it's not nice to snoop?"

The sound of his sexy, gravelly, just-woke-up voice startled her, and she knocked his deodorant into the sink. She set it back on the counter and answered, "I wasn't snooping. I was looking for a toothbrush."

"Bottom drawer."

"Thanks." It was then that she took in the sight of him in nothing but boxers. He was no longer erect.

"Why are you up so early? I thought we were sleeping in." He scratched at his chest and moved toward the toilet.

"I have a lot of calls to make about the bowling equipment, and I need to deal with last night's receipts. You did bring those home, right?"

He nodded.

As she put toothpaste on the brush, she wondered if she was supposed to leave to give him privacy to pee. From the corner of her eye, she saw that her presence didn't seem to affect him, so she started brushing. After he flushed, he stood behind her and wrapped his arms around her to reach the sink to wash his hands.

She stiffened and tried to concentrate on brushing. The heat from his body relaxed her muscles, and he stepped even closer. He flicked off the faucet and nuzzled her neck. His wet hands dripped on her thighs and he wiped his hands on her shirt. His shirt.

In the mirror she looked at him and he simply smiled. She bent over, thrusting her ass into his groin, and spit the toothpaste out of her mouth.

"Doing things like that will make you late for whatever job you think you're going to do."

"Threats don't scare me." She straightened and wiped her hands on the towel hanging above the toilet, but didn't turn around.

"I don't need to threaten. You look like you're feeling better, so you owe me."

"Sorry, you said you didn't want to be rushed, but I'm on the clock."

He pulled her to his body and his hands crept under the shirt, feeling that she wore nothing underneath. "You can be late. I know the boss."

One hand moved to her breast and the other began stroking between her legs. In the mirror, she saw Colin's blue eyes darken as her body began to melt. He rolled a nipple between his thumb and forefinger and pushed one finger inside her. His palm rubbed her clit, and her head lolled back onto his shoulder.

"You are so damn sexy. I think I just want to watch you come."

She was already panting, her hips wiggling against his hand, but she said, "You're not the kind of guy who can just watch. You like to be in the middle of the action."

A second finger joined the first and his hand moved to the other breast. Elizabeth reached up and held onto Colin's neck. Her legs were trembling. If she didn't move soon, she would be nothing more than a puddle on the floor. She forced her right leg forward to disengage herself from him.

"Uh-uh. Where do you think you're going?" His hand left her breast and held her waist tight against him.

"Back to the bedroom." It was barely more than a whisper, and she sounded defeated because she knew he wasn't going to let her move. His fingers picked up the pace, and her eyes fluttered shut. He was going to make her come standing right here in the bathroom.

His hard-on pressed firmly into her back as she rocked to his rhythm. He bit the side of her neck and then licked the spot to soothe it. The good kind of tension coiled in her stomach.

In that moment she felt nothing but mindless pleasure. Every nerve stretched taut and she balanced on the brink of sanity.

"I've got you. Let go," he whispered against her ear.

And she did.

Every muscle in her body spasmed with her release. When she reopened her eyes, her gaze caught Colin's in the mirror. He wasn't kidding; he wanted to watch her come.

She wasn't sure if her skin was pink from pleasure or embarrassment from having him watch her. She shrugged it off and turned around. "Your turn."

Her fingers circled his thick shaft. He pulled her shirt over her head and started walking.

"I'm not ready for my turn. I'm not done with you yet."

His words sent a shiver down her spine, but she tried to hold her ground. Between her weak knees and his strength, it was a futile attempt. He simply kept walking until they were back in the bedroom. While she walked, she stroked his chest and shoulders, marveling at the toned muscles.

"Being a bully doesn't work for you," she said.

"I make you come, and you call me a bully? Those are fighting words." He gave her a shove and knocked her onto the bed.

A squeal popped from her lips.

"Don't move," he said. "I don't want a black eye."

"Now who's being mean?" She was going to say something else, but the words evaporated because he started kissing his way up her body. Starting at her hip and across her stomach. When his mouth found her nipple, she moaned.

His stubble rubbed against already sensitive skin and it hurt but felt good all at once. He moved up to her neck, kissing, licking, and nibbling. His dick was so close to where she wanted it—needed it. She wrapped her legs around his hips and drew him to her body.

He nestled between her legs, rubbing against her, but not entering. He was clearly intent on torturing her. She whimpered, trying to move into a position to take him, but he pressed her into the mattress.

"What's your hurry?" he asked teasingly.

"Please, Colin."

A low growl rumbled against her skin. She'd found his weakness. Sweet talk.

She softened her voice. "I want you inside me. It'll feel so good. You know you want it too."

"Not. Yet." His words were short but required effort. He was wound up every bit as much as she was. His hands continued to explore.

"Do you want me to beg?" she whispered.

He chuckled. "You wouldn't know how."

She'd show him. She moaned and then added as sweetly as humanly possible, "Please, Colin. I want you inside me right now."

He pulled away, his movements stilted as he reached into his nightstand for a condom. When she heard the wrapper tear, she thought she'd won. Her blood rushed warm and fast. Her nerves pricked with excitement.

He returned to her body and began rubbing his hands over her breasts, down her stomach. Her breath caught in her throat when his fingers traced along her pubic bone. *Almost there.*

He moved his body to cover hers and then stopped.

"Colin, please. I've asked so nicely. What do I have to do to get you to fuck me?"

"How bad do you want it?" His words rasped across her ear.

"I want you inside me so bad, that if you do it right now, I'll owe you. Whatever you want."

"That's a deal I can't refuse." He pushed into her waiting body and stretched and filled her.

Finally. In that moment everything about her body had felt more right than it had in a really long time.

CHAPTER 11

Hours later, Elizabeth awoke tangled in Colin's sheets. His arms wrapped around her waist and a leg lay across her thigh. She stretched and glanced at the clock. She needed to get up and get to work.

"Okay, off." She pushed his arm and leg off her. "I have work to do."

"Yeah, yeah." He rolled over and settled back into his pillow.

She tore her eyes away from his body and headed back to the bathroom. She took a shower and realized that she'd now spend the day smelling like Colin after using his soap. She probably shouldn't have agreed to spend the night. Things between them were getting comfortable too quickly. She should just dress and go back to the hotel to make her calls.

While drying off, she saw her reflection and was immediately reminded of watching herself come earlier. She'd never considered herself a prude, but it was the first time she could remember watching herself. It was erotic and intimate.

She opened the bathroom door and the smell of fresh coffee wafted to her. She checked the bedroom, and sure enough, Colin was no longer in bed. He was pretty good at playing possum. She'd thought for sure he'd still be asleep.

She walked down the hall, the smell of breakfast calling her.

In the kitchen, Colin stood at the stove cooking, still only in boxers.

"Good morning. I thought you'd be snoring away."

He turned from the pan in front of him. "You're the one who snores."

She felt the blush rise. "I guess I should've warned you about that before I spent the night."

"Nah, it wasn't that bad." He turned back to the pan. "Ready for breakfast?"

"Sure, but I'd really love some coffee." Against her better judgment, she knew she'd drink coffee. As long as she limited it to the one cup, she convinced herself her stomach would be fine.

He grabbed the cup from off the counter beside him and handed it to her.

She took a long drink before she realized he'd given her his cup. Again with the comfortableness of the situation.

As if reading her mind, he said, "Don't worry. I don't have cooties."

She smiled. "I'm sure sharing a coffee would be the least of my worries after this morning. I think I've already been exposed to all your cooties."

He slid an omelet onto a plate and passed it to her. Her mouth watered, and she remembered she'd hardly eaten at all yesterday. Her stomach grumbled, but the familiar burn wasn't present.

"Thank you. I didn't peg you for a cook."

He turned back to the stove. "I'm not much of one. My mother was determined that we all learn at least the basics so we wouldn't go hungry on our own. I used to pay Liam to do my share of the cooking."

"Liam?"

"My younger brother."

She sat at the breakfast counter. "How many siblings do you have?"

"Five."

A piece of egg caught in her throat and she choked. She took a swig of coffee. "Five?"

"Irish Catholics. We like big families. How many do you have?"

"Just my brother, Keith." She couldn't imagine coming from a family with six kids. All of the families she knew growing up had only had one or two children.

He joined her at the counter with a plate of eggs and a fresh cup of coffee. "What plans do you have today?"

"Total the receipts for last night, and then I'm going to call and get prices on updating the bowling alley equipment and see about getting someone out there to do routine maintenance to see if it works at all."

"Anything I can do?"

"If you could find a manager for the alley, that would be great. Also, we need shoes. I think all the balls are okay. I don't know what else we need." She finished her eggs and waited for a response.

"I have some ideas about managers. Well, at least where to look for one. I'll focus on that. What's our budget for hiring someone?"

"Hell, I don't know. What's the going rate for a manager of a bowling alley?"

"I'm just the personality, remember?"

"Just make it happen. I need to get this done as quickly as possible. I can't stay in Chicago indefinitely." There would be no way to continue to hide this from her father. Maybe she should just come clean and tell him now. She'd already done half the job. He wouldn't take this from her now. Would he?

"What's the rush? We just got the bar turned around."

"I know, but . . ." How could she explain that she'd taken this job without her family's knowledge or permission?

"Plus, the longer it takes to get the alley up and running, the more mornings we can have like today."

"As tempting as that is, my dad has already mentioned a job that will probably come through soon. I'd like to be able to take a break between jobs."

Taking that break with Colin might be fun.

Where the hell did that thought come from? The hormones must've dampened her brain cells. They'd have their fun while she was in town. No promises of a return or an attempt at a long-distance relationship.

"Okay, then. I'll get dressed and get on it." He pushed away from the counter.

God. Did she really just screw up a potentially good thing?

He turned back with a flirty grin. "I cooked, you clean."

Of course he hadn't been offended; he was a guy. "That's a deal I'll take."

While Colin took a shower, she washed the dishes and left them in the drainer to dry. Then she gathered her receipts and bag to head out. "Hey, Colin, I'm leaving."

He came out of the bathroom with a towel slung loosely around his hips. “Where are you going?”

Damn he was hot. He’d shaven, so he looked less dangerous than he had earlier this morning, but sexy nonetheless.

She forced her mouth to work. “I’m going back to the hotel to make my calls and stuff.”

“You can work from here if you want. You have to be sick of being in a hotel.”

“I’m used to it. Thanks for the offer, but I have a mini-office set up at the hotel with everything I need.”

“Okay. See you later.”

“What time will you be in?”

“When I’m done with visiting bowling alleys. It’ll take me a few hours.” As he talked he moved closer to her.

“Sounds good.” She reached out and grabbed hold of the towel and pulled him to her. She leaned up and kissed him. “Thanks for this morning. It was worth the wait.”

“If you don’t move your hand, you won’t be leaving.”

She released the towel as if it had burned her, and turned to leave.

“Don’t forget. You owe me, and I’ll definitely collect.”

His words sent a shiver down her spine. Lust and anticipation swirled through her. If she couldn’t get her hormones in check, today would be a really long day.

* * *

Colin watched Elizabeth leave and something strange tugged in his chest. They’d had a great morning, not just having sex, although that had been hot, but he liked hanging out with her, discussing their business plans. He’d never had someone he considered a partner before. Certainly no woman he’d ever slept with.

Her reminder that she was in a hurry to get out of Chicago irked him. Of course, he didn’t need her to know that it had bothered him. It would only complicate their relationship. Things were good and he’d keep them that way.

He’d gotten a text late last night from Michael telling him which bowling alleys to check out. Then he remembered that he hadn’t told Elizabeth about the missing bottles of liquor. Should he call her now? Or would it be better in person?

He thought of how happy and relaxed she'd looked before she left. Knowing her, that relaxation wouldn't last, but why should he ruin it now? He'd tell her when he got to the bar later. She wouldn't be able to do anything about it anyway.

After getting dressed, he filled a to-go mug with coffee and headed out. Time to charm a manager into joining his staff.

His staff.

He could get used to the sound of that.

Maybe once the bowling alley was profitable, he might be able to talk to Ryan about a loan. If he had the sweat equity and proof that he could hack it, Ryan might consider it. The thought of asking his little brother for a loan ate at him, but he couldn't hold it against Ryan. Ryan had always been the responsible one.

As much as he didn't want to ask for Ryan's help, he was becoming attached to Brannigan's. In a few short weeks, it had started to feel like his.

Colin visited two bowling alleys. At the second, he hit pay dirt. At least he thought so. The current manager, Bianca, grew up in the bowling alley the way he had at O'Leary's. The business was under new ownership, and she was willing to leave for more money.

He left the alley feeling like he was floating. He had another alley to go to, and he'd go because he should, but he knew in his gut that he could get Bianca to work for them.

Something felt so right about his life right now that he was afraid to jinx it. He was actually looking forward to family dinner next Sunday so he could share his success. Maybe he'd invite Elizabeth.

Whoa. He needed to put the brakes on that thinking. When it came to the O'Learys, you only brought someone to dinner if it was serious. Someone who could stand up to the grilling.

Maybe if he just introduced her as his business partner, things would be okay. Then he thought of Moira and knew better. That girl was a gossip hound and she'd sniff out the truth, whatever it was. But part of him felt sorry for Elizabeth. He remembered how hard it was for the three years he had been gone. To have no one to go home to, to eat most of your meals at a restaurant, to spend nights alone, with only the TV to keep you company. At least he'd been able to settle in a few places for months at a time. She talked like she traveled more than anything, so she couldn't have much.

He'd wait and see how the rest of the week played out and then he'd decide. He pulled into the next bowling alley that straddled the northern edge of the city. As he climbed from his car, his cell rang.

Elizabeth.

"Miss me already?" he asked.

"You need to get to the bar. Now." Her voice was tight and strained.

"What's wrong?"

"This place is disgusting. Did you even bother to clean before you left last night?"

"Everything was spotless when I locked up."

"I have a hard time believing that. Do you suppose the crap fairy stopped by?"

"What are you talking about?" He paused. "Forget it. I'm on my way."

He sped toward Brannigan's as quickly as possible. So much for thinking they were partners. Elizabeth was probably freaking out over some water spots on a glass. It was ridiculous. He shouldn't have to defend himself. He knew he'd done an excellent job. He took pride in his work.

He parked beside the building and went in. Everything in the front looked just like he had left it. "Elizabeth?"

She came out from the back and glared at him.

He spread his arms wide and turned in a circle. "Nothing's out of place. What the hell's your problem?"

A muscle beneath her eye twitched. "Follow me."

She spun on a heel and walked back the way she'd come. She stopped in front of the women's washroom, where she had the door propped open. "There is urine all over the floor."

She took three steps to the left and pointed at the men's room. "Someone defecated in the urinals."

"What?" He couldn't believe his ears. Someone shit in the urinals?

"Check it out for yourself." She pointed in front of her. She clearly was not about to go in with him.

As he came closer, instead of smelling her inviting cinnamon scent, he was assaulted with the stench of a Porta-Potty. Elizabeth had the back door to the alley propped open to bring fresh air in, but it wasn't enough.

"This wasn't here when I left. Everything was clean." He pulled his shirt up over his mouth and peered into the rooms.

He then stepped past her. "I suppose you expect me to clean this up."

"No. I already called a professional because I need to know it's done right and finished in time for us to open."

Her jab poked at him. He'd done everything right last night.

Oh, shit. He hadn't gone back to check the bathrooms after he told the staff about the missing alcohol. He stayed in the office and then left through the back door.

He couldn't imagine any of them striking back because of his accusation. Really, what would be the sense? Especially if they wanted him to believe they were innocent.

"What?" Elizabeth asked.

He turned his gaze to her.

"You just had an oh-my-God look on your face."

"Before I tell you, don't get mad."

"That is never the best way to start a conversation. It means you screwed up." She crossed her arms, and he realized she was back to wearing the boring business suit.

"I didn't screw up. And I was going to tell you last night, but you weren't feeling good, and then this morning, we were . . . busy."

She moved one hand in a quick circle to tell him to move it along. What was with this woman always rushing him?

"While I was stocking last night, I came up two bottles of liquor short. A bottle of Jack Daniel's and the Bushmills I opened our first night. I talked to the staff about it. They all denied taking them."

"You think one of them is a thief. I knew it was a mistake to leave new employees unattended."

She dropped her arms, and he watched as her hands folded into fists before she tucked them into the pockets of her blazer. Muscles that he'd thought were tight when she was yelling at him became granite. She looked like she might shatter.

"What does that have to do with this? Were you so distracted by a couple of missing bottles that you didn't remember to clean the bathrooms?"

"The bathrooms were clean. I told Mike, Erin, and Marissa that if the bottles reappeared while I was busy in back, the incident would be over."

"So you were going to reward a thief by letting him or her keep the job?" Her head shook stiffly like she thought he was an idiot.

"I knew that part would bug you, but everyone screws up sometimes. I think people deserve a second chance. Anyway, the bottles weren't returned, and while I was in your office giving the culprit a chance, they were left alone. One of them could've done it."

She pushed past him and walked out to the alley. She inhaled deeply while staring at a tree in the neighbor's yard. He didn't know if he should follow or just give her time to cool off. He'd known that their management styles would clash at some point, but he didn't think it would happen so soon.

He opted to follow. He wouldn't let her shut him out. She turned at the sound of his shoes scraping the concrete.

"I can't imagine a woman would do something like that," he said. "I know there are crazy women out there, but Marissa and Erin don't strike me as insane."

"But Mike does?"

"No, but he's a guy. We're calibrated differently. Stupid stuff like that is something you'd see at a frat party."

"So I hired an immature idiot of a thief."

"No, he seems pretty normal." He stepped closer and put his arm around her. "You know, as a bar owner, cleaning up messes like that is part of the job. I've cleaned up worse."

Her face turned a shade of green.

He shrugged. "You can't afford to hire someone every time some drunk pukes or pisses all over the place."

They moved to return to the bar and then saw graffiti on the back wall.

In bright orange letters, *Fuck You* stared at them.

"You've got to be kidding me." Elizabeth flinched under his arm.

He sighed. "Maybe the potty patrol you hired will have something to clean this up."

* * *

Elizabeth slid out from under Colin's arm. In her office she crunched on more antacids. She really did need to call her doctor and get a prescription; she just wasn't up for a lecture about her health.

She closed her office door and let Colin handle the mess and the employees. If she jumped in now, she would continue to be the hard-ass, while he tried to be their friend. She began to question if this partnership could work. Colin was great with the customers, but he kept overstepping his authority. As if this was his bar. She didn't know what she wanted. Did she want him to be a partner? To be as much of a boss as she was? Or did she want him to be an employee?

The questions and confusion swamped her. She was supposed to be turning this place around by herself to prove to her father that she could. She settled behind her desk and went back to making phone calls. She needed to get the bowling alley operational.

A knock on her door interrupted her third phone call. Colin stuck his head in.

"Clean-up crew is here. They're handling the graffiti."

She nodded and he left. After the call, she sought him out. She needed to wrest back control, otherwise she'd never get what she wanted.

He stood behind the bar, reading a newspaper.

"We need to talk."

He pushed away from the bar. "Shoot."

"I'm calling Mike in and I'm going to fire him. I want to make sure you can handle running the bar until I find a replacement."

"I could, but don't you think you should talk to him before you fire him? See what he has to say before jumping to conclusions?"

"What could he possibly say?"

"What if I'm wrong and it wasn't Mike?"

Tension tightened every muscle. She was just so tired. Maybe her father was right; maybe she wasn't cut out to be in charge of everything. Every battle tore up her stomach and left her more stressed than the last.

But if she didn't get the company, what would she have? That was her biggest fear—the unknown.

"Are you okay?"

Colin was suddenly standing beside her, his hand making small circles on her lower back. It felt good, but she forced herself to step away. "We had a deal."

He shoved his hands into his pockets. "Sorry. But in my defense, no one's here to see."

"And that's our problem. You always look for a way around the rules. I can't play games here."

His blue eyes iced. "I'm not playing games. I'm taking this business every bit as seriously as you are, but I'm not letting each setback eat me up. You need to be able to relax and take things in stride."

"Please don't tell me what to do."

"Did you find someone to come out to look at the equipment in the bowling alley?"

The sudden change of subject caught her off guard. "Yeah. They're coming out tomorrow."

"Good. I found someone to help with managing. I haven't hired her yet, but it looks promising."

She envied his ease with people. If she could bottle that, she'd be well on her way to having whatever she wanted. She shook her head at the thought. "Let me know when Mike gets in so I can talk to him. Were they able to get the graffiti off the wall?"

"You can see there was paint there, but the words aren't legible. Mike couldn't have done that. I left out the back door last night and there was nothing on the wall. None of this makes sense." He went back to the other side of the bar, closed the newspaper, and set it to the side.

"You're right. It doesn't make sense, but I can't very well pretend nothing happened."

"The old manager had keys. Did you get them back? Did you change the locks after you took over?"

"I'm not incompetent. Of course I changed the locks." She didn't need to admit that it had taken a couple of days. "I'll be in my office."

The stench in the hallway was gone. At least they could open on time and not lose business. In her office she put her head down on her desk. She'd gotten enough sleep, but if she had to be here from open to close every night to keep an eye on the employees, including Colin, she would. Unfortunately, she wouldn't be able to sleep like that. Instead she leaned back in the rickety chair and propped her feet on the desk. If she didn't wobble too much, she could at least relax.

The knock startled her, and her feet knocked the penholder off the corner of the desk. Before she could right herself, Colin swung the door open.

"You're supposed to wait until you're invited in."

"Don't get flustered because I caught you slacking." He closed the door behind him.

She was irritated for that exact reason. The constant burn in her stomach settled in for the long haul. She stood and straightened her skirt, debating whether she should change. Did she look like the owner in jeans? "What do you want?"

He edged closer, and her heartbeat kicked up a notch. His hand cupped her chin and, before she could protest, his mouth covered hers in a slow, sensual kiss. Her sleepy brain accepted the kiss and her hormones weren't going to argue. He pulled slowly away with a smirk on his face.

"I came to let you know Mike is here. I figured we should talk to him together. Show him a united front so he can't try to play us against each other."

Damn, not only had he snuck in a kiss that wasn't supposed to happen, at least not at work, now he was making sense on the business end. "Okay. I'll be out in a minute."

He stepped away but kept watching her. "You know, I like you when you're sleepy and unguarded."

"Don't get used to it."

"Wouldn't dream of it." He turned and left her office.

Something about the way he approached her ate away at her defenses. He always seemed to know just what she needed, whether it was a gentle kiss or space to be alone. Every move Colin made worried her just a bit.

After a few deep breaths, she strode to the front. Mike stood ready for an assault. Whatever Colin had said last night had definitely left a mark. Elizabeth moved to stand in front of Mike, leaving Colin to stay behind the bar. "Mike."

"Look, Elizabeth, I like working here, but I'm sure you know what happened last night."

"What did happen?"

Mike crossed his arms, causing his biceps to bulge. He glared at Colin, who began wiping down the already clean bar. Seeing the two men alongside each other marked their differences. Mike, with his muscles and short light-brown hair, had a tough-guy persona, and Colin remained the laid-back, charismatic guy.

"Colin accused me of stealing. I didn't even know we carried Bushmills. It wasn't on the shelf when I started last night."

"Did Colin mention the other problem we had?"

He shook his head.

"The bathrooms were a mess, and someone spray painted the wall in the alley."

Mike raised his hands. "The bathrooms were clean when I left out the *front* door. The only time I used the back door was when I took out the trash."

"What about the girls?"

"We all left together after Colin accused us. In fact, we stood by our cars talking about whether or not we wanted to continue working for someone who had no trust in us."

Elizabeth paused and fought the urge to look at Colin. She believed Mike. This was a test and surely she'd fail if she made the wrong move. She sighed. "I'm not trying to accuse anyone, Mike. I know every business suffers some loss, but as the main employee behind the bar, I need you to make sure that inventory is accounted for. Just keep your eyes open."

The tension etched across Mike's face dissipated and relief filled his eyes. "I wish I knew what happened, but I have no idea. The only time I left from behind the bar was for a bathroom break while Colin was here and to go refresh stock later in the evening. The bar was never unattended."

"I'll be here from open to close from now on. I know things have been hectic. The other half of the building is a bowling alley that we need to get reopened. It's been pulling some of my time and energy away from the bar."

From the corner of her eye, she saw Colin's jaw flex. A couple of days of slacking had caused nothing but problems.

"I'll be in the office if you need me."

She strode away, and Colin followed her. He didn't say anything and his steps were nearly silent, but she felt him closing in. She left the office door open to give herself a moment to be able to face him.

His opinion shouldn't matter, but it did. More than him just being her partner. The door clicked and she moved behind her desk. More armor.

"I thought you were going to fire Mike."

"I was. But then I listened to him and I believe him. I can't ignore the problem, but getting rid of a good employee on a maybe didn't seem to make sense." She straightened papers without making a difference to the appearance of the desk.

"I agree. Now, about this opening and closing every day . . ."

Her gaze shot up to meet his to let him know this was non-negotiable.

"You can't be here all the time. It's not humanly possible. Especially when you take into consideration the work that takes place before hours."

"I think a strong management presence is important. While the cat's away and all that. They need to know I'm in charge."

He moved closer still, and she backed into her chair.

"No one is doubting that you're the boss. But you can't be everywhere at once, and I don't think the staff is to blame. You have to spend some time next door to get the alley open. Not that I'm complaining about having more time with you." The corner of his mouth quirked up.

"What do you think this is? It's not date central. We're here to work, to run a business."

"Hmmm—mmm." He stared at her lips. "There's no rule against enjoying your work."

She held her arm out straight to prevent his progress. "We just talked about this. If you plan on ever seeing me naked again . . ." His eyes lit. "Then you need to keep your hands off while at work."

He inched against her palm and the warm firmness of his abdomen pressed against her. "How long?"

Her mouth dried up. "Huh?"

"How long until I get to see you naked again?"

Her laugh came out as a snort and she covered her mouth again. "Stop it. I hate that you do that to me."

"What? Make you laugh?"

"Make me forget who and where I am." The words startled him almost as much as they did her. If he didn't have that ability, her words would always have been kept in check.

He took a big step backward.

Now she'd done it. She'd ruined a great casual sexual relationship because she'd said the wrong thing.

Then his smile broadened. "Until tonight then. My place or yours?"

She answered his smile with one of her own. "Mine has room service."

"Okay." He turned and headed for the door. With his hand on the knob, he said, "There's a boxing match this Saturday on pay-per-view. I think we should consider getting it. We can advertise and bring more people in."

"Sure."

He swung the door open and walked through it without a backward glance.

Elizabeth opened her laptop and began Googling sports events. It was great that Colin seemed on top of it, but if this was going to be a sports bar, she had to be on top too.

CHAPTER 12

For the next few days, Colin and Elizabeth worked side by side and slept together each night. He found the biggest problem he had with working with her was not that she was bossy and controlling, but that no matter what she wore, he imagined her naked, which gave him an instant hard-on. They worked so well together, he had moments when he worried about whether he could hack it after she left. Whether he bought this place or another, could he go it alone?

He tried not to think about how cold his bed would be after she left. After less than a week of sleeping together he shouldn't have those kinds of thoughts.

They'd done a lot of advertising to bring people in for the boxing match, and he'd convinced a beer sponsor to send beer promo girls with prizes. Elizabeth chose a company to work on the bowling alley and work would start on Sunday. Bianca had stopped by and impressed Elizabeth enough to get hired.

All in all, his life was finally looking up. Now he just had to decide if he wanted to expose Elizabeth to an O'Leary family dinner. Even if he invited her, she might not agree to come. And he still worried about sending the wrong message to his family.

Maybe he'd wait until after tonight. If the boxing event was a huge success, she might be distracted enough to agree. Plus, having baby Patrick at his first family dinner might dissuade everyone from interrogating Elizabeth.

He decided not to examine the idea that he wanted her to come. That fell under the same umbrella of missing her in his bed after she left.

All things better left for another day.

Elizabeth had already left his apartment to go into work. He'd tried to convince her to wait for him, but she wouldn't hear of it. She still insisted they drive separately so no one would know they were sleeping together.

He really just wanted her to wait so that she might take a nap. She hadn't been kidding when she'd told Mike she would open and close the place. She'd been there around the clock all week, and while she'd been doggedly productive, the hours had been taking a toll on her. Even with spending a few hours at O'Leary's and his time at Brannigan's, he was nowhere near as exhausted as she was.

She thought he didn't know she was still consuming antacids, but he did. He'd tried to get her to go to the doctor, but she just bought some over-the-counter pills that didn't seem to make much difference.

He turned on the ignition in the Jeep and his phone rang. With a glance at the screen, he answered, "Yes, Elizabeth, I'm on my way now."

"Good. Someone broke in last night."

"What?" His tires screeched a little on the way out of the alley.

"The entire bar is trashed. TVs are broken, every glass smashed. I don't know if we'll be able to open." Her voice was tight, but controlled.

"Get out of there and call the cops."

"They're here now."

He exhaled with relief, knowing she wasn't alone. "I'll be there soon."

Speeding through the Chicago streets, he tried to figure out why it felt like their bar had been targeted. First the missing alcohol and graffiti, now this. He pulled up in front of the bar and ran in.

Elizabeth stood in the middle of the room talking with a uniformed cop. Colin glanced at the cop, but didn't recognize him. Elizabeth's back looked like it had a steel pole running through it. Another cop stepped in front of him to stop his progress.

Elizabeth called out, "It's okay, officer. He's my partner."

Partner. He liked the sound of that, especially when it came from her mouth. She walked away from the cop she'd been speaking to and met Colin.

"Are you okay?" He reached out and then dropped his arm, knowing she'd yell at him for touching her.

"No, I'm not fucking all right. Look at this place." She'd lost what control she'd had in talking with the police and the comment came out as a harsh whisper.

He did as she said and looked around. Three of his TVs were smashed, and glass from the barware littered the floor. Puddles of alcohol pooled on the bar and dripped down the side.

He checked the time. One o'clock. If he called in Mike and they busted their asses, they might be able to open.

"How much longer will the cops need?"

"I don't know." She turned and walked away, effectively shutting him out.

He found the cop who had tried to stop him from coming in. "Excuse me, officer. How much more time will you need here? I'd like to start cleaning up and restocking so we don't have to lose a night of business."

"The detectives are talking in the corner. Those are the guys you want to ask."

"Do you know how they broke in?"

"Through your storeroom."

Storeroom? How the hell would someone get in through the storeroom? Colin found the detectives and heard them snickering. One commented on the alarm not functioning.

The alarm worked. He'd set it himself last night when they left. "Excuse me, detectives? I'm one of the owners and I have a few questions."

After another lengthy conversation, Colin found that although the alarm appeared to be working, it wasn't actually connected to anything. The siren itself had been disconnected. Furthermore, the locks on the doors hadn't been broken. Someone had gotten in on the bowling-alley side of the building and come up through the basement.

As the police wrapped up, he called Mike, Erin, and Marissa and asked them all to come in immediately. Then he went to find Elizabeth. In her office, she was doubled over in her chair. He hurried to her side. "Hey, what's wrong?"

She struggled to straighten.

"You need to go to a doctor."

"Shut up." Her words held no vehemence. "Who do we call to cancel the promotion tonight?"

"We can't cancel. This event will be good for us. I have everyone coming in now. If I need to call in friends and family, I will, but we're going to be open tonight."

She shook her head like she wanted to disagree with him. She just looked beat. "How are we going to replace everything in a few short hours?"

"I don't know, but I'll figure it out."

Elizabeth moved slowly toward the door and he walked with her, afraid she'd lose her balance. She gripped the door frame with one hand and her stomach with the other.

"Hey." He touched her cheek, not caring who saw or if she got mad.

With a sudden burst of energy, she pushed away from his touch and bolted across the hall into the bathroom.

A glance over his shoulder told him the cops were gone and they were alone. He stood outside the bathroom door, worried about her. He pushed the door open about an inch and heard her retching. He didn't ask permission to enter. He needed to make sure she was okay.

Seeing her kneeling in front of the toilet was bad enough, but then he saw that she had vomited blood. When she leaned against the metal wall of the stall, he squatted in front of her. Panic pounded in his chest. Blood was never good. "You're going to the hospital right now."

"No, I'm not. I'll be fine." Her face was pale and her voice weak.

"You're not fine!" He stood and tried to calm himself. "Throwing up blood is not fine. Eating more antacids than you do actual food is not fine. Pretending that nothing is wrong is not fine. Now, you either stand up and walk to the car to go to the hospital, or I'm going to carry you out of here." He offered his hand, knowing that she'd take it instead of risking him following through on his threat.

She looked frail and walked with a wobble, but she stayed on her feet. "What about the bar? We need to close up and let people know we won't be open tonight."

"Mike will be here any minute."

Right after the words left his mouth, the front door opened and Mike walked in.

"See? Everything will be fine, including you." He propped her up near the door and talked to Mike to let him know what was going on. "I'll be back as soon as I can. Get everything cleaned up, and I'll work on getting deliveries of new inventory. Can you handle that?"

"Sure. Is she okay?"

Colin shook his head. "She thinks she is, but I'm taking her to the hospital."

He put his arm around Elizabeth's waist. She must've really been feeling like crap to not push him away.

Once in the car, she turned to him, and said, "This is a total waste of time. I know what's wrong with me. I already talked to my doctor, but he wouldn't prescribe anything without seeing me. I thought I could wait until I got home."

Colin glanced at her out of the corner of his eye as he pulled out into traffic. "So now you're an MD too?"

"I know my body. I have stomach ulcers. They've been under control."

"I guess all that stress and lack of sleep is catching up to you."

"Stress doesn't cause ulcers. It just aggravates them." Her arm wrapped around her middle again.

He reached out and patted her thigh. "We'll be there soon."

Unfortunately, they had to wait at the hospital. Stomach ulcers apparently weren't a huge emergency. If only he could convince his heart and nerves of that. He paced in the waiting room, avoiding contact with the sick people sprawling in the chairs.

"I'm fine. Go back to the bar."

"I'm not leaving you in the hospital alone." How could she even think he'd leave? "Do you want me to call someone? Your parents?"

Her eyes widened. "God, no."

The woman was impossible. His entire family would kill him if he was at the hospital and didn't call. The antiseptic smell infiltrated his senses. He needed escape. "Sit here. I'm going to make some calls."

She waved a hand to dismiss him. He walked through the automatic sliding doors and breathed in the fresh air. Being at the hospital for Patrick's birth had managed to erase some of the horrid memories he associated with hospitals, but he still hated the place. He pulled out his phone and called the one person he never wanted to ask for help.

"Hi, Ryan. I really need a favor."

"What now?" He sounded tense, but at least he didn't hang up.

"My bar was broken into last night. Liquor, TVs, and barware were all destroyed. I need to get deliveries within the next couple of hours so that we can open on time. We're airing the boxing match, and we have sponsors coming."

Ryan sighed.

"I know I'm asking for a lot, and I swore I wouldn't need your help, but to top it off, I'm at the hospital right now with Elizabeth."

"What happened?"

"She thinks she's fine, but she was throwing up blood less than a half hour ago. I can't leave her here alone. I've got a manager and waitresses at the bar cleaning, and I'll get back there as soon as I know what's going on here." He ran a hand through his hair. "I could really use your help."

"I have some favors I can call in. Anything specific I need to know?"

"I'll take whatever you can get me."

"Have you called the family?"

Colin stopped his pacing. "No, just you. Why would I call anyone else?"

"A woman you care about is in the hospital, your business is attacked, and you don't think you should let the family know? Maybe you have been gone too long."

How did Ryan know he cared about Elizabeth? He'd never mentioned anything more than them being partners. "Yeah, well, Elizabeth doesn't know them and wouldn't want them here. I could probably use a couple of extra hands at the bar, though."

"You go take care of Elizabeth. I'll make the calls to everyone else." There was another pause. "I still can't believe that you're running The Irish."

Colin chuckled. "It's called Brannigan's Sports Bar now. Wait till you see it."

"Give me a call if you need anything else."

"Hey, Ry?"

"Huh?"

"Thanks. It means a lot."

"That's what family's for."

The conversation had been short, but it was the least stressful interaction they'd had in a long time.

* * *

While Colin was outside, a nurse called Elizabeth into an exam room, if that's what it could be called. She was sick of this stupid crap. She hadn't had an attack like this in a year. She explained her symptoms, filled out all of the required paperwork, and gave them the number to her doctor. It was Saturday, so they'd get the emergency line, but Dr. Walsh would call back.

The burn in her stomach rose up, and she grabbed the yellow plastic pan the nurse had left. She threw up again, hating the taste of bile and blood. She rinsed her mouth with a sip of water, afraid to swallow.

She wished they would listen and just prescribe the antibiotics that would fix this. She sat on the uncomfortable bed and willed her stomach not to heave anymore. The curtain that gave her little privacy moved aside and the nurse returned.

"Your fiancé is here."

"Fiancé?"

The nurse's eyebrows knit, suspicious that she'd been taken.

"Of course. Send him in," Elizabeth tried to cover.

Colin pushed the curtain aside and smiled at the nurse, who blushed. The man could melt chocolate with a glance.

When the nurse left, Elizabeth narrowed her eyes at him. "Fiancé? Couldn't you have said you were my brother?"

A corner of his mouth lifted enough to make a dent in his cheek. "Do you really think they'd believe I was your brother once I got back here?"

He winked and moved closer to the side of the bed. Sitting down, he took her hand and leaned over her.

She turned her head. "God, don't kiss me. I puked again."

He sighed. "Point taken."

He kissed her head and sat back. His thumb caressed her knuckles, and she wanted him to hold her. Not the thoughts of someone in the middle of a temporary fling.

She closed her eyes. "You can go back to work. They're going to need all the help they can get. I'm okay."

His gaze bore into her, calling her a liar without words.

"It hurts. A lot. But I've been through this before. They're going to talk to me, run a test, and then prescribe antibiotics. A couple of weeks on medication and I'm as good as new."

The warmth of his hand soothed her as he continued to stroke her knuckles rhythmically. "I hope you're right."

He didn't say any more, but Elizabeth began to feel smothered by his presence. She was used to being alone. It was how she spent most of her life. Traveling to different cities, working, she didn't have room for a lot of permanent things.

Colin was starting to feel permanent.

She needed space. He had to go.

"You're tensing up again. Relax."

"I'm worried about the bar," she lied. Sure, the bar was a pressing matter, but it wasn't encroaching on her ability to breathe. That was all Colin.

"It's being taken care of."

The curtain swooshed open and the doctor walked in. He nodded at her and looked at the chart. "Ms. Brannigan."

"Do you want me to leave?" Colin asked.

Yes. She squeezed his hand. "No."

The doctor, Dr. Weiss, flipped the chart closed and looked at her. "I've spoken to your primary physician and we both think we should do an endoscopy to make sure the bleeding is under control."

"Can't you just give me the antibiotics? They worked last time."

"I will, but you told the nurse you've been vomiting blood for a few days. We need to make sure the problem isn't bigger than a simple ulcer."

Elizabeth felt Colin's glare when he heard Dr. Weiss. She'd been able to keep the severity of her condition from Colin. In truth, being with him helped. She was always more relaxed around him, and it wasn't just the great orgasms. They shared meals together and his attitude was calming.

And now she was trying to get rid of him.

She sighed. "Okay. What's the next step?"

"As long as you're here, we'll admit you and do the test first thing in the morning. Barring any problems, you should be home by lunch."

"Let's get this over with then."

Dr. Weiss left, and she turned to Colin. "Can you bring me the numbers for the bowling guys so I can cancel them for tomorrow?"

"I'll take care of everything. You rest and focus on getting better."

"I can't do that if I'm worrying about my business." She pushed up in the bed.

He gently pushed her back down. "*Our* business. I told you I'll handle it."

"You can't handle it from here."

"I'm going back to the bar as soon as you're settled in."

"I don't need you here to settle me in. Go to work. Who knows what else might fall apart."

He stood and paced, like he needed to decide. Then he huffed out a breath. "Do you want me to bring you a bag or anything? I could go to your hotel room."

His strange bouts of generosity freaked her out. Her chest tightened and she clenched her jaw so it wouldn't tremble. Thinking about the thin hospital gowns made up her mind. "I'd love to have my own clothes."

"I'll get everything going at the bar and then come back. Where's your room key?"

She tossed her purse at him. "It's in here. I need to go to the bathroom."

He grabbed her arm to help her up. "Do you want me to help?"

"I can manage to pee on my own. Thanks."

She kicked off her heels and walked in her stocking feet to the bathroom. While on the toilet, she stripped off the pantyhose and tossed them in the trash. When she was done, she splashed cold water on her face and rinsed her mouth again. The pain in her abdomen was a dull rumble now. She could function like this.

Hell, she had been functioning like this.

She went back to bed to find Colin putting her purse back on the nightstand.

"You sure you don't want me to call someone?"

"I'm fine. They'll get me in a room, and I'll probably go right to sleep." She sat back on the bed.

"Call me if you need anything."

She nodded.

His fingers tilted her chin until her eyes met his. "Seriously. Anything, and I'll be here."

She managed to croak out a whispered "Thanks."

He left the room as the nurse returned with a wheelchair.

"I can walk."

"Rules are rules, Ms. Brannigan. Let's get you to a room."

* * *

Colin left the hospital, grateful to get away, but swamped by the catalog of things he needed to take care of. First, he'd call Elizabeth's friend. No matter what Elizabeth said, she shouldn't be alone in the hospital. While she'd been in the bathroom, he'd copied Janie's number from her cell phone. Before getting into his car, he dialed.

"Hello?"

"Hi, may I speak to Janie?"

"Speaking." Her voice was cautious.

"Hi, you probably don't remember me, Colin O'Leary, but I'm Elizabeth Brannigan's partner."

"Oh, I remember you, all right." The tension in her voice eased a fraction. "How'd you get my number?"

"I got it from Elizabeth. I'm calling because she's in the hospital."

"What? Why?"

"She says it's stomach ulcers, and they're going to run tests, but she's staying overnight. She pushed me out to go back to the bar because we have some problems there, but she's alone. She didn't want me to call her family." He glared out across the parking lot, wondering why.

"No!" Janie's voice screamed out. "I'm sorry. It's just that Elizabeth's family won't exactly put her at ease. Give me the information, and I'll stop by to see her."

Relief eased into his shoulders as he gave her the details. He said good-bye and started the car. Next up, get back to the bar and see how fast they could put everything back together. Moments later, his phone rang.

"Hey, Mike. I'm on my way now. Any more problems?"

"Uh, no, not exactly. Some guy came in and said he's your brother. I mean, he looks like you, but then he started carrying in boxes of stuff, including new TVs."

Colin smiled. Ryan had come through. "I'll be there in a little bit. Just do whatever he needs."

The knowledge that in a pinch his brother had come through for him made him feel good. For the first time in a long while, they felt like a team again. Colin pulled up at the bar.

Inside, a hive of activity exploded. He scanned the area. Broken glass and puddles had been cleaned, Mike was restocking the shelves with liquor, and Ryan stood on a ladder attaching a new TV to the wall. Although part of him swelled with pride, a small prick of doubt told him he was still unnecessary.

" 'Bout time you got your ass in gear. Get over here and help with this," Ryan called.

Colin shook his head, but headed over and helped Ryan balance the TV.

Once it was up, Ryan eyed him. "How's Elizabeth?"

Colin shrugged. "She says she's fine. It's stomach ulcers she's had before."

"But?"

"She was throwing up blood. It rattled me enough that I forced her to go to the hospital, only to find out that the blood had been going on for days. I knew she'd been chewing antacids for weeks, but I hadn't expected that." Until speaking with Ryan, he didn't realize how scared he'd been. Something deep down tightened, and he attempted to uncoil it without inspection. He stretched his shoulders and rolled his head.

"But she'll be okay." Although it was a statement, Ryan's voice went up at the end in uncertainty.

"Yeah."

Ryan pointed to another TV that needed to be installed. He ripped open the box. "Do you need to go back?"

"I called one of her friends to stay with her. I'll go back later tonight. I don't think they'll let me spend the night or anything." But he'd thought about it. He wanted to. As much as the thought of being in the hospital freaked him out, he wanted to be with Elizabeth.

He worked side by side with his little brother in a way they hadn't done in a long time. The work and companionship settled him. He looked at Ryan. They'd wasted so much time over the past few years.

"Thanks, man. It means a lot to me that you did this."

"We're family. I know I've been critical of you, especially when it came to you getting involved with this bar, but you were right. It looks better than ever, and that's because of you. Dad would be proud."

The words hung between them, a weight neither wanted to acknowledge. Colin hadn't gained his father's approval before his dad's death, and he didn't need Ryan's, but getting it made an impression.

Then Ryan punched him in the shoulder. "So what's this thing with you and Elizabeth?"

"We're partners."

Ryan snorted. "You need to sell that a little better if you want it to work around the family. Moira'll get one whiff and you're toast."

Colin rolled his eyes. "I like her. We're involved, but it's nothing serious. Once we get everything working, she's going back to Florida. We're having fun while she's here."

The words sounded hollow, even to his own ears.

* * *

The entire staff worked together to get the bar open on time and they succeeded. Ryan left right before they opened, and part of Colin wanted him to stay, not to continue helping, but just to hang out. The evening started out slow, but as it got closer to the beginning of the boxing match, the bar filled.

Since it was a pay-per-view event, many of the neighbors walked in, knowing it would be cheaper to buy a few beers here to enjoy the match than to order it themselves. Marissa and Erin buzzed around nonstop while he and Mike worked the bar. The beer girls wove in between tables giggling with every man in the place. The waitresses followed in their wake to up-sell shots. He'd known the sponsorship would pan out.

Even as he chatted up customers, Colin's mind was elsewhere. He couldn't stop thinking of Elizabeth. He'd hoped Janie had stayed with her. He watched the clock and the customers. As much as he wanted this night to be a success, he wanted them all to go home so he'd be free to go back to the hospital.

Colin hadn't known it was possible to be that exhausted. Even with the main event ending in a knockout in the first round, they'd been jammed all night. He'd decided to close a little early. He engaged the slide bolt lock on the basement door that he'd installed as an extra security measure and double-checked each door. Neither he nor Elizabeth could handle another hit to the business. Every inch of him ached and his eyelids had become sandpaper.

In Elizabeth's hotel room, he stared longingly at the bed. The scent of her cinnamon body wash filled the bathroom. He quickly grabbed her stuff and shoved it into the duffel he'd brought. He opened and closed every drawer in search of pajamas. Silky underwear slipped through his fingers. No way was he going to let her wear that in a hospital.

He closed his eyes and pictured her. She slept naked beside him every night. The only time he'd seen her wear anything was when she pulled on one of his T-shirts. He shrugged and grabbed the shirt she seemed to favor and a pair of shorts. He checked the closet and only found her damn business suits. She'd want something comfortable to wear home tomorrow. But the woman didn't own anything comfortable.

It was after one in the morning. Maybe he could find an all-night Walmart. Wouldn't Elizabeth of the I-only-wear-designer-clothes love that? But he couldn't stomach the thought of shopping with the crazy people. Not tonight. He shook his head and decided she could make do with his clothes. He'd stop at his apartment for a pair of sweats.

He made it to the hospital by two. He knew visiting hours were over and chances were good that he wouldn't be able to see Elizabeth, but he at least wanted her to get the bag and know he'd followed through. Lucky for him, the cute young nurse on the floor was a sucker for a love story. Once he pled his case about wanting to say good night to his fiancée, she sighed and told him he could have a few minutes.

The soft glow of the light above the bed illuminated Elizabeth's pale face. Her expression was still pinched, so he knew she was in pain.

"Hey. Thought you'd be asleep," he whispered.

"How'd you get in here? Visiting hours are over." She gave him a reprimanding look, but smiled.

"The nurse said I could come in. I brought you clothes."

"Thank God." She extended her arms for the bag.

"I don't know what you're so excited about. You don't own anything comfortable."

She lifted her gaze to meet his with her hands still on the zipper of the bag. Her shoulders slumped.

"Never fear. I brought my clothes for you to wear." He grabbed the bag and pulled out the shorts and T-shirt.

She reached behind her and tugged at the gown. She peeled it away from her body with no thought of getting naked in front of him and what it might do. He turned away to grab a chair and drag it close to the bed. By the time he sat, she was dressed and he was hard.

"So tell me about tonight. How bad was the bar?"

"We opened on time. The event was a success. Everyone went home happy. No worries."

"How did you get everything replaced so quickly? The glasses, the liquor, the TVs . . ."

"My brother's been in the business long enough to have connections. He came through for me." He stretched his arm out and held her hand. "How are you feeling?"

"Like crap. I can't eat because of the tests tomorrow, so there's no buffer against the pain. There's nothing good on TV, and I can't sleep. At least earlier, I had Janie to keep me company." She paused. "I told you not to call anyone."

"I'm not good at doing what I'm told."

She offered a half smile. "I'm glad. Janie was just what I needed."

Her smile faded into a grimace. He stroked her hand again.

"What can I do?"

She sighed. "Not much. Can you just talk to me until I fall asleep?"

"I'm good at talking." He scooted his chair closer and kept his voice low. "I remember when Ryan had to have his tonsils taken out. . . ."

He told her stories of his childhood until she faded off to sleep with a slight smile on her lips.

Morning light brightened against his eyelids and he blinked. The feeling of sandpaper still grated against his eyeballs. Elizabeth snored loudly in bed. The woman sounded like a truck. She was a contradiction. Usually full of poise and manners and grace, but then she had a raucous laugh and she snored. And then there was the clumsiness. Although he hadn't seen any of that in a while. No crashing into him, no spilling drinks, no tripping.

When had her awkwardness stopped?

He straightened out of the chair and brushed a kiss on Elizabeth's forehead. She stirred but didn't wake. He needed to go home and shower before heading back to the bowling alley. Luckily, Bianca would be in, so he wouldn't have to stay the whole time. He'd be able to come back to pick up Elizabeth. Dinner with his family was out, but he'd make sure she stayed where he could keep an eye on her.

CHAPTER 13

Elizabeth stretched out on the uncomfortable bed, dying of thirst, but her throat was too scratchy to risk a drink. The nurse had promised she'd be released within the hour, but she felt totally abandoned. No one had come in to check on her, no one had come with paperwork, and worst of all, no one had arrived with the dreaded wheelchair so she could escape. The doctor had already given her a prescription and guidelines.

Rest for the remainder of the day should be easy enough; she was exhausted. Mushy foods for the next couple of days didn't appeal to her, but if it meant no more vomiting blood, she'd suffer through. Colin had called and promised he'd be here to take her home, but given how often he was late, she began to consider calling Janie.

The door opened, and she pushed herself into a sitting position. The nurse came in with paperwork.

"Good, you're up. Your fiancé is here to take you home. Talk about perfect timing. Here are your release papers. I'll be back in a minute with your wheelchair."

Colin stood behind her looking as beat as she felt. He hadn't shaved, and even in her weakened condition, she thought of the delicious whisker burn he liked to leave on her inner thigh. "Hey," she managed, hating the scratchy sound to her voice. "I was beginning to think you forgot about me."

"Not possible. How are you doing?"

"I'm fine. It's ulcers, just like I said. I have a prescription. I'll be back on my feet tomorrow."

He opened his mouth and she knew he planned to argue, but he was cut off by the return of the nurse.

"Here you go. Hop on."

They said nothing on the way out of the hospital. Colin left her at the door and went to pull the car around. She was pleasantly surprised when he drove up in her rented Mercedes instead of his Jeep.

He walked around and opened the door for her, placing the duffel bag in the back.

She sank into the soft leather and enjoyed the air-conditioning blowing on her. She closed her eyes and hoped Colin wouldn't want to start a discussion, or worse, an argument. The silence allowed her to doze, and she didn't open her eyes until she heard him put the car in park.

They were at O'Leary's.

"Why are we here?" Her voice had become even rustier.

His eyes narrowed. "Did you really think I was going to dump you off at your hotel all alone? I want you where I can keep an eye on you."

He wanted her to stay at his apartment? "I'm fine. I'm just going to sleep."

"You'll sleep here." He opened his door and walked around the car, leaving her stunned.

Nothing about his reaction over the past two days felt like the happy-go-lucky Colin she knew. Every night they'd spent together smacked of coupledom, but this felt worse. He wanted to take care of her.

While she processed the thoughts, Colin opened the door for her and extended a hand to help her out. The idea of sleeping at the hotel didn't appeal to her. It was just a way of life. But feeling this crappy made her want to crawl into her own bed, which she couldn't do. Colin's bed would more than suffice.

She accepted his hand and slid from the car. Her stomach rumbled and she wanted to eat. "Can I ask you a huge favor?"

"Anything."

His response came a little too readily. No caution for what she might ask.

"I'm starving, but I can't eat real food yet. Can you get me a vanilla milk shake?"

"That's it?"

She nodded weakly and wondered if she'd be able to stay awake long enough to get the shake. Colin kept his arm around her as they went up to his apartment.

He unlocked the door and said, "Go get settled. I'll be back with the shake."

She mustered a smile. "Thanks."

Inside the apartment, she wanted to go to the bedroom, but knew she wouldn't stay awake, so she sat on the couch. A soft blanket lay across the back. She'd been in this living room and he'd never had a blanket on the couch. Reaching for the remote, she saw a vase of flowers on the end table. The card sticking up read, *Get well soon.*

She didn't know what to do with this sweet version of Colin. He was trying to get too close and that spelled disaster. Why couldn't he keep things as they were? Casual and fun worked for their relationship.

Cuddling the blanket, which was a huge improvement over what the hospital offered, she dozed.

What seemed like minutes later, Colin sat beside her, brushing a strand of hair out of her face. She had definitely fallen asleep and snoring made her throat even more dry and scratchy. She attempted to clear her throat, but even that hurt.

"Here." He put the straw against her lips.

She sucked gently and the creamy coolness slid down to ease the irritation.

"Thanks. That's perfect. You really should've taken me to the hotel. I don't belong here."

"What if you start bleeding again?"

"I'm fine. The doctor fixed everything."

"Yeah, well, as much as I'd like to believe that, it's not like you'd tell me anything different. You were throwing up blood for days and said nothing." Anger crossed his face.

"I knew what the problem was and I had talked to my regular doctor. What was the point in telling you?"

"What would be the point?" He shoved off the couch and stepped away. "The point is, when you care about someone, you share the important shit."

She knew it. Things were getting sticky between them. "You're not supposed to care."

"Bullshit. Beyond having sex, we're partners and friends. You should've told me. Everything that happens to you affects me and our business."

He had a point there. If he hadn't taken her to the hospital, she probably would've gone herself. She would've missed work, and he wouldn't have known. "I'm sorry. I thought I was handling it."

He crossed his arms. "You're not supposed to handle it alone."

"Got it. I'm not used to having other people to answer to. I work alone."

"No one works alone all the time."

She raised her eyebrows and took another sip of her shake. "I do. I only have subordinates that I work with, and I certainly don't answer to them."

"What about your dad or your brother?"

"They do the front-end work, and I go in when they're finished making changes. I make sure the new staff follows the plan and the business remains successful."

She busied herself with another sip, hoping he wouldn't figure out this was the first time she was in charge of an entire project.

"Lonely life. Don't you ever get sick of it?" He sat back beside her and caressed her leg.

"Yeah. I'm more than sick of it. That's why it's so important for this business to work."

"Why?"

She'd never really talked to anyone about her plans. Of all the people in the world to confide in, Colin felt right. And really, who would he blab to?

Taking a deep breath, she let it pour out. "My father is planning to retire. I want his job. I've been working toward it since college."

The memories of that summer working in competition with Keith flooded back. "Since Keith is the oldest, and male, I've always had to work to prove myself. Every job is a test, but this one is the ultimate trial."

"Why?" He picked up her legs and laid them across his lap.

"Because I'm here without my father knowing. He bought this bar more than a decade ago and has done nothing but let it languish. I have no idea why. When I found it in his holdings, I came here to check it out and decided this would be the project that would prove my ability."

She waited, but he said nothing in response. Exhaustion tugged at her now that her belly was full of milk shake. "I need to prove that I'm as good as Keith."

Colin looked deep in thought, and she hoped she hadn't given him pause to reconsider their partnership. It wasn't as if she'd hid her inexperience, but the idea that he might think less of her set her nerves on edge.

"I'm really tired, so I'm going to lie down."

As if startled by her announcement, he jumped up and offered her a hand.

"I don't need you to help me walk. I'm fine." She walked alone into his bedroom and curled under his covers. The sheets were fresh and didn't even hold a hint of his scent, which she found disappointing.

* * *

Colin watched Elizabeth leave the room, and his foggy brain tried to piece together the conversation. Something had shifted between them. She'd told him something she hadn't wanted him to know. He wondered why she'd decided to tell him now.

He understood being in competition with a sibling, and he definitely knew what it was like to have to prove himself. He just couldn't reconcile the accomplished woman he knew with the woman he now saw as afraid of failing. No wonder she had stomach ulcers.

She really was all alone.

No matter how much he butted heads with Ryan, they would always be there for each other. Their dad had instilled that in them. He had never wanted his sons in competition. He certainly wouldn't have set them up to compete. Patrick O'Leary had wanted a team. Colin's own ignorance had ruined it.

The information filtered in, and he realized that she had said that she'd come here without her family's knowledge. How had she been funding this project? How would her secret affect their success?

He filed the questions away to ask her when she was feeling better. He went to the kitchen to find something to eat before checking back in with Mike and Bianca. A knock at his door stopped him. He peered through the peephole. Moira.

He swung the door open, but stayed in her path. "What are you doing here?"

She held out a wrapped plate. "You couldn't make it to dinner, so I brought dinner to you."

He wanted to snatch it and close the door, but knew that wouldn't work with Moira. She was here on an expedition and wouldn't leave without bugging him.

He took the plate and went into the kitchen. "Keep your voice down. Elizabeth is trying to sleep."

Moira bounced on her toes. "Oooo, she's here?"

Colin shook his head and peeled back the foil on the plate. Roast beef and potatoes, a staple of his childhood.

Moira sobered for a minute. "How is she? When Ryan told us she was in the hospital, I got worried."

"She's okay. Stomach ulcers."

The mischievous gleam reentered her eyes. "So why is she here?"

He forked potatoes into his mouth before answering. "Because I thought she'd be more comfortable here than in a hotel by herself."

"And you're still trying to sell this relationship as purely business? Keep dreaming."

He put his fork down. "We're business partners and friends."

"With benefits?"

"None of your business."

"So that's a yes."

"That's a stay out of it. You delivered the food and irritated me enough. Isn't it time for you to head home?"

"I can hang out here. You have to go back to work, right? I can keep Elizabeth company."

Colin chewed his meat and considered Moira's proposition. He didn't like the idea of leaving Elizabeth alone to go back to work, but she'd ream him a new one if he left everything unattended to care for her. Moira was a good bet since they'd already met and liked each other. As long as Moira didn't decide to write an exposé on Elizabeth.

"Fine. You can stay to keep Elizabeth company, not to grill her for information. I think she could really use more friends. If you need to leave, tell her to call her friend Janie. And watch her do it, otherwise she'll say she will, but won't." He finished off his food without tasting much.

Moira studied him. "You're really worried about her. You said she was fine."

"She is."

Moira continued to stare, and he felt himself breaking just like he did when his mother gave him that look.

He sighed. "She was throwing up blood yesterday. They kept her in the hospital to run tests. So although they released her, she has to make sure the bleeding doesn't start again. Keep her relaxed, because stress makes things worse."

"Well, then, I guess you should be thrilled that my nosy ways led me here tonight. I'll keep an eye on her. We'll hang out and watch TV."

"Thanks." Having the burden of worrying about Elizabeth lifted, he relaxed. His family had stepped up. Again.

Colin snuck into his room and grabbed fresh clothes. Elizabeth snored away and he smiled. The little things about her always surprised him most because they seemed like they didn't fit. He ducked out to take a quick shower and head back to work. Moira had already taken possession of his remote and made herself at home.

The shower refreshed him some, but he was dog-ass tired. Mike was behind the bar and Erin served a couple at a table. It was Sunday and business was slow. Maybe he should talk to Elizabeth about whether it was worth staying open on Sundays. It made sense during football season, but he didn't know if afternoon baseball would be a big-enough draw. And after how busy they were last night, they could all use some time off.

He checked the register and the stock at the bar and nodded at Mike. Then he went over to the bowling alley, where he found Bianca strolling down a lane and sliding a ball for a perfect strike.

His loud applause made her jump.

With her hand over her heart, she said, "Thanks, but next time, don't sneak up."

"I didn't realize I was sneaking. I thought the repairmen would still be here working."

"Nope. They just left, so I figured I'd give it a test run."

"That was some fast work." He looked up at the monitors and saw that Bianca had logged her name in and it showed a strike.

"We still need to get the floors waxed, but most of the equipment here was in good shape. It just needed to be updated." Her ball had returned, and she turned away from him to roll it again.

This time she left a seven–ten split.

"No way I can pick that up." She went behind the counter and reset the machine before turning it off. "When do you think we'll open?"

"We're waiting on the order of shoes. The floor guys are coming tomorrow. So maybe later in the week? I'll talk with Elizabeth and see what her plan is. She always has a plan."

"How is she? You said you had to pick her up from the hospital. Did something happen?"

He shook his head. Elizabeth would freak if everyone knew her business. "No. She was sick, but she'll be back in a couple of days."

He followed Bianca out and locked up. She had agreed to come back and supervise the floors getting done during the day, so all Colin had to do was show up and let them in. Since the locks had been changed, he didn't want too many people having access.

The thought brought him back to the damage yesterday. Had it really only been a day? His body felt like many more than twenty-four hours had passed. Sitting at Elizabeth's desk, he put his feet up as he had seen her do many times. The position was surprisingly comfortable.

He leaned back and closed his eyes. Just as his mind began to turn off, his phone rang. He jolted up. No, not his phone, the business line.

"Hello, Brannigan's Sports Bar."

"May I speak with Elizabeth Brannigan, please?"

"She's unavailable right now. I'm her partner, Colin. Is there something I can help you with?"

A throat cleared on the other end. "Partner? This is her brother, Keith. Do you know when she might be available? She's not answering her cell phone."

Shit. He had to think fast. After what Elizabeth had told him this afternoon about her family, he knew he'd just stuck his foot in his mouth. "Uh . . . I'm not expecting her to be in until tomorrow. Can I take a message?"

He didn't want to have to deliver a message. He didn't want to admit to Elizabeth that he'd told her brother they were partners.

"No. I'll call her tomorrow."

Keith hung up, leaving Colin feeling slightly relieved.

* * *

Elizabeth caved and spent an extra day in bed, catching up on sleep and eating mushy food. Colin managed to both keep an eye on her and run their business. For the first time in weeks, she'd been able to relax.

Now, though, she needed to get back to work. She had to check on the progress of the bowling alley and figure out a plan for the grand reopening. She also had to nag the insurance company about getting her a check for the damages after the break-in. Colin wouldn't let her pay him back out of her own pocket, but she knew he couldn't afford to foot the bill for everything he'd replaced while she'd been sick.

Dressed in her new business attire of jeans and a T-shirt, she felt comfortable. Colin had already left; he'd been keeping longer hours than she did. She packed her meager possessions and locked up his apartment. Continuing to stay when they hadn't been sleeping together sent the wrong message, no matter how easy it felt. She didn't want to assume she belonged living in his space. She was better and should get back to her own life.

Colin had left her car parked in the same spot when they came from the hospital. After not driving for three days, the car felt awkward, but it only lasted a moment. She relaxed her body and drove to the bar. She parked on the bowling alley side and went to check on the progress there. The door was propped open, allowing a breeze to blow through. Her eyes adjusted to the dim interior and she looked around. The place looked clean if not inviting.

"Hello?" she called out, hoping Bianca and Colin hadn't left the place unattended.

Bianca shot up from behind the counter. "Elizabeth. Hi. Colin said you were going to be out for a few more days."

Elizabeth figured that was what Colin had hoped. "No, I'm back. Where are we with getting this place going?"

Bianca held up a shoe. "Shoes just arrived, so I'm organizing back here. Computer systems are up and running beautifully. Floor guys are coming out to wax later today, so we won't be able to do anything for another day or so until they're done."

Elizabeth stared and barely prevented her jaw from dropping. She'd expected everything to come to a halt while she'd been out.

"Is there a problem?"

"N-no," Elizabeth stammered. "Good job. It looks like Colin definitely hired the right person."

Bianca beamed. "Thanks."

Loud pounding and thunking against the wall stopped both of them.

"What is that?" Elizabeth asked.

Bianca shrugged. "I'm not sure, but it's Colin."

A moment later, a sledgehammer broke through the wall behind what used to be a bar of some kind.

"What the hell?" Elizabeth edged closer.

Two more smacks and Colin's face poked through the hole. His wide, silly grin filled the space, and her heart gave a little jump.

"Ha! I knew it," he said.

"Knew what exactly?" she asked, trying to muster the anger she knew she should feel.

His face twitched. "Elizabeth? What are you doing here? You're supposed to . . . Hold on. I'm coming around."

She crossed her arms and readied for a fight. At the moment she wasn't quite sure which fight would happen first: the one where she argued the necessity of her presence or the one about him busting a hole in the wall.

As Colin strode through the door, she turned to Bianca. "Why don't you take your lunch break? I think Colin and I have some things to discuss."

Bianca's eyes widened, but she nodded and hurried out the door.

The happy grin on Colin's face had been replaced with grim irritation. Maybe even anger. Like he had a reason to be mad? He was the one who'd just put a hole through her wall.

"What are you doing here?" they both asked simultaneously.

Elizabeth's jaw clenched. "I'm here to work. I'm trying to build and run a business, not tear it apart."

"No, I mean why are you here now? You're supposed to be recuperating."

"I'm fine. The doctor said I could've returned to work yesterday, but I didn't want to deal with your nagging. Now, please explain why you're busting a hole in the wall."

Concern shadowed his face. "We knew the two businesses shared the basement, but I figured that there had to be more than one way to connect them. I couldn't imagine them running as two completely separate businesses. After poking around in the storeroom, I noticed that one wall seemed newer than the rest."

He stared at her like that explained the hole.

He smiled and grabbed her elbow to lead her to the wall. "When they closed up the bowling alley, they threw up a sheet of drywall on each side. These spaces are supposed to be connected. That's why our storeroom is so small. It's not a storeroom; it's a small kitchen. There's a gas line for a stove and a hookup for an exhaust fan."

"Why is this important? We have enough work to do."

"Don't you get it? We can really increase our profits if we can offer food. Both the bar and the alley would share the same kitchen. It encourages people to stay longer if they can have a meal. Nothing fancy. I'm thinking burgers, wings, and nachos. Maybe hot dogs for kids."

His excitement was infectious as usual, but she grasped at rational thought. "First, we agreed a long time ago that all decisions were supposed to go through me. Second, adding a restaurant, even small scale, is a huge headache. We have to get permits and inspections and then hire more people in the hope that it will increase business."

"How many bars have you gone to that don't offer food?" He didn't wait for an answer. "I know I'm supposed to talk to you first, but I got excited and broke through. Even if you don't want to offer a food menu, connecting the two businesses is the right move."

She waved a hand at him, knowing his argument made sense. "Whatever. How long until you get the wall fixed?"

"That's a day's worth of work. Then we can walk from one side to the other."

"Fine. Before you do anything else, we need to check into permits and inspections. I can't afford to be shut down over something stupid." She walked behind the counter and picked up where Bianca had left off organizing the shoes.

He followed her, and she could smell sweat and man combined with dust from the wall. What should've had her wrinkling her nose made her want to step closer.

"Go back to my place and get some rest. We have this handled." His palm landed on her hip.

When she brushed it aside, his print left a mark on her jeans like she'd been branded. She didn't tell him she'd taken her things from his apartment. She certainly didn't need a babysitter. "I need to keep working. This is too much for you to do alone, and every day I'm gone slows things down."

Slows down her return to Florida.

The words were unspoken but hung between them.

She hefted shoes from the box and placed them in cubbies according to size. "I'll call Keith and ask him about the food issue. He'd have the background on it, even if it has been years."

Something flashed across Colin's face, and his gaze darted back to the hole in the wall.

She ignored the nagging feeling his look gave her and stacked more shoes. "Have you heard from the police at all?"

"Yeah. They don't have any leads, but whoever broke in didn't really break in. He came in through the bowling alley and came up through the basement. They need to know who might've had access to keys for the bowling alley."

This was all her fault. She hadn't thought to change the locks on the bowling alley. She'd been so overwhelmed and distracted. Well, no more. "I'll check with Keith and see if he has any clue, but it's probably hopeless, given that the place had been pretty much abandoned for years."

Tension curled in her stomach. So much for trying to stay calm and let the medicine do its work.

As if sensing her discomfort, Colin moved close again. "Go home and rest. We can handle this."

"I'm not leaving."

She sounded like a bitch and she knew it. He didn't deserve it, especially after he'd gone out of his way to take care of her and the business. She looked up into his eyes. "I'm sorry. I'm just not myself yet."

"Bossy is who you are. Since when do you apologize for it?" He cupped the back of her neck and pulled her into a kiss.

She melted against him, tension unfurling and disappearing. This man was too good. She didn't even want to push him away, which told her she was getting in too deep.

He pulled away and she forced herself to focus.

"Better?"

Damn him. He knew she was, but she didn't want to give him the satisfaction.

He smirked when she didn't answer.

"So what's with *Highlander*?"

The change in subject threw her. "Huh?"

"For the last two nights *Highlander* was cued up to watch on my TV." He was studying her face, making her uncomfortable.

"I like it. I used to watch it with Keith. It kind of became our credo." Again, she faltered under his scrutiny and talked more than she preferred, but she knew Colin would expect more explanation. "From the time I was in high school, Keith and I have been in competition. At first Dad thought it would just push us to better ourselves, but it became more."

She couldn't talk about how ugly it had gotten, especially with her ex-boyfriend Matt in the mix, or why they no longer went head to head.

"So you chase each other around with swords trying to chop off each other's head?"

"Not quite. We just did whatever we had to in order to be the best."

She finished unpacking the shoes under Colin's vigilant eyes. How was she supposed to work with him watching her every move? "Don't you have a wall to fix?"

"It'll keep for a while. How about a game?"

"What?"

"Wanna bowl?"

"The lanes aren't ready. And even if they were, we're supposed to be working."

"A little fun won't kill you. The floors will withstand a couple of frames. Come on. Let's bowl. What's the point of having a place like this if you can't enjoy it?"

She stared at him. He'd been so responsible and together that she'd almost forgotten this side of him and she'd missed it. She surprised them both by saying, "Okay."

She tossed him a pair of shoes and grabbed her own. He pulled her to the rows of balls. She picked a green marbled one and he chose hot pink, drawing another smile from her. While she laced up the shoes, he turned on the lane and entered their names. ELIZABETH stared at her from the monitor, stiff and formal. She wished she were here with Janie because then, for at least a little while, she could be Libby.

Screw it. Why couldn't she be Libby with Colin?

While he put on his shoes, she changed her name. Nervousness skittered through her as soon as she hit Enter.

"Libby?"

The way he spoke the name was even better than when he said the full version. It was so personal, it should've bothered her, but it didn't.

"Yeah. I figured if we're going to act like a couple of irresponsible kids, I might as well go back to being Libby."

He moved in on her again, wrapping his arms around her and nuzzling her neck. "I like it. Who calls you Libby?"

"No one. Except Janie and Lori. They refuse to use my full name." Her answer came out a little breathless because he began nibbling on her ear and worked his way down to her collarbone.

"Can I call you Libby?"

So unfair to ask her now and he knew it. She was always at his mercy when his mouth was on her. "No."

"Please."

The whisper coasted along her skin. She smiled and pushed his shoulder to escape his touch. "You can call me Libby whenever we bowl."

He tugged her back and whispered in her ear. "And when we're naked. I want to see Libby come."

He released her waist but pulled the rubber band from her hair.

"What are you doing?"

"Libby strikes me as the kind of woman who likes to let her hair down." He picked up his ball and threw it down the lane. About halfway down, it slid into the gutter. "Practice frame," he said when he turned around.

"You're only saying that because you suck. I'll let you have your practice frame, but that's it. No more do-overs."

"I suck? I haven't bowled in years. I don't think a practice frame is too much to ask." His ball came up through the return. He picked it up and looked at her with a gleam in his eye. "How about we place a little wager on this game?"

"Like what?"

"If I win, you have to go back to my place and rest."

She bit the inside of her cheek and considered the possibility.

"Naked," he amended.

The single word made parts of her pay attention. "And what do I get if I win?"

"What do you want?"

It was like he was daring her to say she wanted him naked. Which she did, but she wasn't going to give him the satisfaction of admitting it. "I win and you can't mother me anymore. You have to trust me to take care of myself."

"Like you've done such a good job so far."

She ignored his jibe and thrust her hand out to shake. "Deal?"

"Sure." He held the ball in his left hand and shook her right hand, gripping a little tighter than necessary.

Although he always appeared to not care about anything, she was suddenly seeing a competitive side to Colin, and she wasn't sure she liked it.

CHAPTER 14

Bowling was a lot harder than he remembered. They were in the tenth frame and although he was ahead by eight pins, Libby could catch him. It was only fair to employ the same strategies she had. He whispered in her ear, "Nervous?"

"Nope. I got this in the bag."

That's what he was afraid of. He pushed her hair off her shoulder and placed a wet kiss on her neck. "Wouldn't want you to get distracted."

She shivered and stepped away to pick up her ball. She hoisted it and focused.

"Naked sounds pretty good."

She stepped up and faltered. The ball slid into the gutter. "Stop cheating."

"I don't cheat."

"You're trying to distract me."

"Me? You groped me before I took my turn."

Her face reddened and she turned away. Her ball came back, and he sent up a little prayer. Before the ball reached the end of the lane, she turned away. "Shit."

Her curse was quiet, and he peered around her to see that the ball ran crooked. It knocked over four pins. Not enough to win.

He tried not to smirk. "Good game."

"Whatever."

Talk about a sore loser.

She put her ball back on the rack and sat down to change her shoes. He sat beside her and she edged away.

He changed his shoes and watched her pull her hair back into place. Just like that, Libby was gone.

* * *

An hour later, Colin wiped the sweat from his forehead. He couldn't believe that he'd not only beat Elizabeth at bowling but that she'd honored their bet and left. She looked better, but not herself, regardless of what she thought.

After sending her on her way, Colin checked in at the bar and closed himself in the small storeroom that would become the kitchen. Ever since they'd cleared out the basement, most of their inventory went there. With the door closed, Colin hoped the customers at the bar wouldn't hear his noise.

His sledgehammer slammed through the last bit of drywall and he smiled. Libby. He never would've guessed that she'd been a Libby. The simple switch to a nickname changed who she was. Libby was the girl dancing at the club. Libby was the woman who tried to pick him up for a one-night stand.

The light went on in his head. Libby was the snorer. The obnoxious laugh and the clumsy behavior belonged to her.

There was a lot to like about Libby.

Knowing that she would probably try to find a loophole in their deal, he said he wouldn't nag her if she went back to his apartment. She could make some phone calls, but then she had to nap.

He worked until he had the wall opened up. Tomorrow he'd finish it so it would be a walkthrough. He taped plastic over the opening and let both Bianca and Mike know that he'd be back in few hours.

Before putting in a whole night of work, he needed a shower and a nap, hopefully next to a warm, naked woman. The thought made his dick jump. He'd been afraid to do anything more than give Elizabeth a kiss on the cheek for days now. He didn't want to risk any activity that would land her in the hospital.

But she was almost back to normal. She fought with him and she bowled like she wanted to win.

If he took it slow and easy, she would be fine.

He swung open his apartment door. "Honey, I'm home."

It was meant as a joke, but it felt right. Elizabeth peeked around the corner from the breakfast counter. "Hey."

When she stood, he realized that she was wearing a pair of his shorts, hanging precariously on her hips. She'd taken his shirt and rubber-banded it tight around her waist, showing a hint of skin where it should've met the shorts. He tugged at the shorts and saw that she was bare beneath. Maybe the shower could wait. "The deal was you'd be naked."

She grabbed his hand at the waistband. "I decided a compromise was fair. I know how much you like me in your clothes."

Instead of scooting away she pushed into his body, their hands clasped at her waist. She ran her tongue across his lips, pulling a groan from his chest.

"Take a shower with me."

Now she did pull away. "I haven't done enough today to warrant a shower."

"Then let's get you sweaty enough to need one." He pulled her toward the couch, shoving the shorts down along the way.

She stepped out of the shorts and pulled the shirt over her head. Looked like he was going to get the warm, naked woman he was looking for. He kissed her neck and smelled the cinnamon scent on her skin.

She pushed him onto the couch and straddled him. He held her away from his dusty jeans. He wanted to go slow and make sure she was okay, but Elizabeth, as usual, didn't seem to agree with him. She tugged at the button of his jeans like she hadn't gotten laid in a year.

"Slow down." He picked her up and set her down on the couch before taking off his jeans.

Her hair lay in a pool spread out over her shoulders, blending in with the smooth leather of the couch. Her hands began to rub across her stomach and head south, and he whipped off his shirt. No way was she going on without him.

He grabbed her hands and held them at her hips. He kissed his way down her torso, following the path her hands had taken. She moaned when he stopped at her belly button. Her hips thrust up letting him know without words what she wanted.

So he gave it to her—lips and tongue, fast and smooth until she was writhing and panting his name.

He released her hands and moved to sit beside her on the couch.

He pulled a condom from his jeans. Elizabeth looked a little boneless lying next to him, and he was about to slide over her body when she pushed up to straddle him.

"Where do you think you're going?" she asked.

"Absolutely nowhere." He buried himself in her and let her set the pace until they were both sated and relaxed.

She had her nose pressed against his neck, and he wrapped his arms around her.

"I've missed that."

"Me too," she mumbled against his skin.

"Are you okay?"

She pushed on his chest to look into his eyes. "I told you I'm fine."

He wanted to believe her, but she'd really scared the shit out of him.

He stood, putting her carefully on her feet, and kissed her forehead. "Why don't you order us some dinner while I take a shower?"

She grimaced, and he realized that she hadn't eaten any regular food in days.

"The doctor said you can eat, right?"

He thought it wasn't possible for her to look more miserable, but she did.

"Yeah, but part of me is afraid to. I want pizza so bad, but I think I need to wait until I'm done with medication." She stood and gathered the clothes they'd tossed over the living room, while he headed toward the bathroom.

Colin decided that he'd take her out for the biggest and best pizza he could find as soon as she thought her stomach could handle it. Then he had an idea. "How about shepherd's pie?"

"Huh?"

"We serve it downstairs. Mashed potatoes over ground beef and vegetables. Pretty simple, but filling." He was already at the phone calling Mary. "Hey, Mary, it's Colin. Can you put in an order for shepherd's pie and a burger and fries?"

"And why can't you come down and put it in yourself?"

"Because I'm about to step into the shower. My friend Elizabeth will be down in a few to pick it up. Thanks. You know I love you." He hung up and smiled at Elizabeth. "She loves me like a brother."

"Uh-huh."

Elizabeth stared at him like she was still hungry for more than dinner. If she traveled all the time, how many men did she do this with? Did she have a guy in every city? Jealousy pinched him, and he pushed it back. They were having a good time. It wasn't as if he hadn't had plenty of other women.

The problem he had now was that he wasn't sure any of them could ever measure up to Libby.

* * *

Elizabeth stretched out in Colin's bed. The rest of their week had gone off without a hitch and life was looking good. Especially the sight of the naked man sprawled beside her. For an entire week, Colin had taken care of her. He made sure she'd eaten regular meals, kept her from working too many hours in one day, given her multiple orgasms. All in all, a pretty damn good week.

Of all the things she'd miss in Chicago, this would top the list. Lazing around in bed on a Sunday morning. No rush to get the paper, no hurry to get something done, to be productive.

Colin had accomplished the one thing no one else ever could.

He'd taught her to slow down and relax.

The proof was in her lack of accidents. She hadn't broken anything in weeks. She hadn't stumbled or fallen.

Except for him.

The thought came out of nowhere like a slap in the face. A shiver tumbled through her body. She slid from the bed and went to the bathroom, hoping that a warm shower would erase the shiver and the thought.

She wasn't supposed to fall for him. They had great sex and an even better partnership. It wasn't supposed to be anything more. Stepping under the hot spray, she tried to come to terms with her new knowledge.

How had she not seen it coming?

Worse, did Colin see it? Did he care?

Of course he cared. Colin cared about everyone around him. She knew she should've gotten some distance from him, but he drew her in and she was caught.

The water removed the shiver, but the idea of falling for Colin stuck. She wouldn't go so far as to say she loved him—she couldn't be that stupid, could she?

The bathroom door swung open, interrupting her questions. Berating herself would have to wait.

Colin pulled the shower curtain aside. "Are you planning on saving any hot water for me?"

"If you didn't sleep so late, you could've been here first. Early bird gets the hot water."

"Oh, yeah?"

He reached for her and she let him pull her into his embrace. He claimed her mouth with his, and she forgot about being cocky. He licked water from her neck, and she felt his erection against her stomach.

Suddenly, he pulled back, leaving her feeling cold again. "As much as I want to continue this, we need to get going. We're on dessert duty, and if we don't hit the bakery early enough, all the good stuff will be gone."

She heard the words and they made sense in theory, but she had no idea what he was talking about. "Huh?"

"Dinner with my family. My turn to bring dessert."

She vaguely remembered him telling her he had some family dinner thing to go to, but she had no intention of being part of that. She twisted past him in the tub. "I'll let you finish up then."

He grabbed her wrist. "Don't try running out of here. You have to go with me to dinner. My family is expecting you."

Running out was exactly what she'd planned. "I'm not crashing your family dinner."

"It's not a formal thing. We eat together as a family at least once a month. Since I couldn't make it last week because you were sick, we're doing it again. If you don't show, then I'll have to listen to Moira complain. And she'll probably track you down and drag you there." He gave a careless shrug. "For some reason, she likes you."

Elizabeth stepped from the shower and dried off. She liked Moira as well. Moira was the first friend she'd made in a long time.

"Call her," Colin said from behind the curtain.

"Why?"

"She'll tell you to come. It's as close to an invitation as you're gonna get."

The water cut off, and he yanked the curtain open. The man looked even more delicious when wet. She handed him a towel so she could think straight.

He wrapped it at his hips and stepped out. The look he gave her in the mirror told her he had the same thought she did every time she looked at the damn reflection.

She shook her head. "Look, I appreciate the invite, but I'm not going to a family gathering."

"It's not a gathering, it's dinner."

She hung her towel up and left the room. Hopefully, he'd get the hint that the conversation was over. She couldn't do a family thing with him. Their relationship would become even more complicated. She dressed quickly.

He followed her into the bedroom, water still sliding down his chest. How she wanted to follow that trail with her tongue. "If you want to talk, get dressed."

He chuckled low. "I think I do better at negotiating when I'm not."

"That's the problem."

"What's the big deal about dinner?"

"I don't want to offend anyone by not eating the food. I'm still a little cautious about eating. You know that."

"Trust me, my mother's food is good, but there's no way it'll upset your stomach. The only seasoning she owns is salt and pepper. The food is about as bland as you'll find."

She threw a pair of underwear at him. "That's not a nice way to talk about your mom's cooking. Plus, you said it was her recipe they use for the shepherd's pie, and I really like that."

His smile spread across his face. "I never said you had good taste. Although it started as her recipe, Liam doctored it."

She gave him a shove, knowing it wouldn't actually move him, but it gave her an excuse to put her hands on his chest. "We also have the bowling alley opening tonight. One of us should be there."

He pulled her to his chest, and water began to soak into her T-shirt.

"We'll both be at the alley tonight. Dinner isn't an all-day thing. We eat, we talk, we leave. Plus they all know the alley is reopening tonight. They plan to come."

She groaned and twisted away. "As much as I appreciate you filling our establishment with your family, I'd much rather have paying customers."

Colin pulled clothes from his dresser. "They'll pay. And they'll bring friends who'll pay."

She sighed. This conversation was getting them nowhere. She

went to the living room and gathered the notes she had on licensing the bowling alley to serve food. It was all so complicated because no one could verify what licenses the bowling alley had or used to have. She'd avoided calling Keith. She really didn't want to get him involved.

"Ryan will be at dinner. I'm sure you can talk to him about the food issue. He probably knows people who can help." He grabbed his keys from the counter. "Let's go."

They stood staring at each other for a minute. He wasn't leaving without her. He'd made that clear. She finally caved.

"I still don't understand why you need me to come." She left her papers on the table and walked toward him.

He slung an arm over her shoulder and kissed her head. "I like hanging out with you, and if I leave you here, you'll just stress about licenses and forget to eat."

* * *

An hour later, Elizabeth was sandwiched between two of Colin's brothers on the couch in their childhood home. She'd met Ryan, of course, when she'd first offered him the chance to partner with her. The other one, Liam, looked nothing like the other two. Moira was helping her mother in the kitchen.

According to Colin, they were short a couple of siblings, not that she'd notice, but they'd gained in-laws to fill the gaps. Gaps? He'd talked about having a big family often enough that she should've known what to expect, but there was no way to prepare for being crowded into a bungalow with this many people. It wasn't normal.

Just as she'd started to talk about the bowling alley license, the baby in Ryan's arms began to squawk. Ryan shifted to rise, but Colin came from the other side of the room.

"I'll take him."

Ryan's face wrinkled. "He needs to be changed."

"I can handle it." Colin stretched out his arms and took the baby.

"I'm not going to argue. Have at it."

Elizabeth sat stunned for a minute, knowing that she should gather her thoughts to get Ryan's input, but the sight of Colin cradling a baby surprised her. He appeared to be totally at ease with holding a newborn.

"So you were saying . . ." Ryan prompted.

"Your brother busted a hole in the wall between the bowling alley and the bar. They used to be connected and the storeroom was a small kitchen. He'd like to start serving food, but I'm not sure. I can't figure out how difficult it would be to get the correct licensing. He suggested I talk to you." She eased back on the couch, and although she listened to Ryan's answer, part of her brain was cued in to watching for Colin's return.

Ryan indeed had friends who might be able to help with her dilemma, and he promised to call them first thing Monday morning.

When he finished, she said, "I haven't had the chance to thank you for your help with the break-in. I'm sure Colin told you that I'd gotten sick. I'm really grateful you stepped in to help him."

He shrugged, like he hadn't been expecting her to acknowledge his help. "It's what family does." He braced his elbows on his knees and leaned toward her. "You're good for him. I haven't seen him this focused in . . . ever."

"That's not me, it's the business. He really wants to build something of his own."

"Don't we all," came a voice from behind her.

She'd forgotten Liam was there.

"He could've started or taken over any number of businesses. There's a reason this one stuck with him. I owe you some thanks too. Colin hasn't been around much, and this project of yours has kept him close to home. It means a lot to my mom."

But not to you? She wanted to ask, but didn't. She'd never understand the dynamic between these siblings.

Colin returned with the baby, but didn't move to hand him over to Ryan. The infant was curled under Colin's chin, comfortable and quiet. Elizabeth couldn't argue with that. She knew how nice that exact spot was.

"Dinner," Moira called from the kitchen door. She walked over to the dining room table and placed a plate of ham in the center. Her mother followed with what looked like mashed potatoes.

Colin held out his free hand to help her up. "It'll be fine," he whispered as she walked past him.

Elizabeth inhaled deeply. Was that homemade bread she smelled?

In the dining room, Moira pointed to a chair. "Sit next to me. I haven't seen you all week and I want to catch up."

"Can I help with something?" Elizabeth asked.

"Nope. Sit." Then Moira disappeared back to the kitchen. When she returned, she was carrying two round loaves of bread.

Colin nudged her and took the seat at the head of the table, baby still in his arms. Another woman, Ryan's wife, if Elizabeth remembered correctly, came in.

"I'll go put him down."

"If you move him, he'll wake up. Eat."

Quinn eyed him with a raised brow. "Are you sure?"

Ryan had taken his seat. "Don't question it. He already changed a diaper. I think he's trying to impress our guest."

"Fuck you," Colin said with no anger.

Quinn moved away to sit, but pointed a finger at Colin. "I do not want those to be my son's first words, so watch your mouth."

Unbelievably, the reprimand worked, and Colin mumbled an apology.

Elizabeth looked at Quinn. "Can you teach me how to do that?"

"Years of being a teacher." She smiled broadly at Elizabeth. "So tell us about yourself."

"Not much to tell. I'm here fixing a mess of a business my father bought a long time ago and left neglected. With any luck, the bowling alley will open successfully tonight. If I can get the right license in place, we'll start offering a small menu, and I'll be done."

Quinn's eyes narrowed. "Colin already told us that. I meant tell me about yourself, not your work."

Colin's mother, Eileen, entered the room, wiping her hands on a towel before taking her seat opposite Colin. Conversation stopped.

"Colin, say grace."

Everyone around the table held hands. Since he was still holding the baby on his chest with his right arm, only Colin's left hand was free, which he extended to her. She placed her hand in his.

He stroked her fingers before he spoke. "Lord, thank you for family, good friends, and a good meal. And thank you for healthy baby Patrick. Amen."

He squeezed her hand once more and, for a minute, she thought he wouldn't let go.

She slid her hand from his grasp and took a sip of water.

"You still haven't answered my question, Elizabeth."

Water slid down her throat and she began to choke. She'd hoped that questions would stop once people started to eat. Apparently, Quinn was a multitasker.

When her throat cleared, Elizabeth tried to answer. “There’s still not much to tell. I live in a suburb of Miami, but I’m not there often. I travel for work probably about eighty to eighty-five percent of the time.”

“What about your family?” Eileen asked.

“My father has the business headquarters in Miami.”

“So you don’t see them?” The thought appeared to really bother Eileen.

Elizabeth shrugged. “I see my father and brother on various job sites. I live in the coach house that my brother owns, so when I’m home I see my sister-in-law and nieces.”

Eileen tsked.

“I didn’t bring Libby here for an inquisition.”

As soon as she heard him use her nickname, Elizabeth felt the wave of attention shift back to her. Her cheeks flamed.

Eileen didn’t falter. “We’re just getting to know your lady friend.”

Moira gave her a nudge under the table. “Libby?”

Elizabeth turned to Moira and knocked her fork off the table. Then when she bent to pick it up, she whacked her head on the underside of the table.

She clenched her teeth to prevent the curse word from slipping out. She was embarrassed enough without Quinn scolding her too. When she resurfaced, everyone had begun to eat and conversation had continued as if she hadn’t just made a total fool of herself.

Except Colin. He smiled, and her muscles eased a little.

Unfortunately, Moira also kept her attention on Elizabeth. She leaned close and whispered, “So what exactly is going on with you and my brother?”

“What do you mean?” Elizabeth didn’t want to lie, but she certainly didn’t want to fuel any gossip or place any unrealistic expectations on her relationship with Colin.

“You’re sleeping with him.”

Elizabeth felt everything from her chest to the tips of her ears burn red. “Even if I wanted to talk about this, it would never be at a dinner table with your entire family.”

“Moira, stop whispering at the table. It’s rude,” Eileen reprimanded.

“Sorry, Mom.”

The apology might as well have come from a snotty teen because, at a glance, Elizabeth saw the corner of Moira's mouth lift as she tried to hide her smile.

With excellent timing, the baby began to squirm and cry. Quinn stood. "He's probably hungry. I'll take him."

Colin handed over the bundle and focused his attention on loading his plate. In between bites he filled his family in on the progress of the bar and the bowling alley. Colin had been right, the food was pretty bland, not that it mattered. Elizabeth didn't taste much after Moira's declaration.

Except for the bread. That was truly delicious. "What kind of bread is this?" she asked Moira.

"Irish soda bread."

"I thought that had raisins and stuff in it."

"Shh . . . don't let my mom hear that. *Real* Irish soda bread is bread and not dessert."

"Whatever it is, it's fabulous."

"It's an old family recipe, passed down from generation to generation." Moira wagged her eyebrows. "Maybe we'll get a copy for you."

Elizabeth sighed. This was why she didn't want to come to a family dinner. There were always expectations when a date is brought to the family home.

She poked at the remaining food on her plate and glanced at her watch. They had no idea how many people to expect at the bowling alley. They'd sent out flyers around the neighborhood and done some basic advertising, but it was a bowling alley. It wasn't like they were introducing a new nightclub.

She envisioned a senior center sending a bus full of old people who would haggle over prices. Maybe the local high school might start using it as a hangout. She couldn't imagine which would be worse.

Colin leaned over and touched her arm, sending a warm pulse up. "I'm done. How about you?"

She nodded and stood so quickly her chair almost toppled. After rescuing the chair, she turned to grab her plate, but Colin already had it in his hands.

With a smirk he said, "My mother's fond of these plates. I'll take them to the kitchen."

His mild teasing didn't help. She was grateful that she'd left her hair down so that her red ears couldn't be seen. "Eileen, thank you so much for dinner. We need to be going."

Eileen stood and took her hand. "Thank you for joining us."

Elizabeth managed to carry her and Colin's glasses to the kitchen without incident. At the sink he smiled and took them from her.

"See, you survived. No big deal."

Before she could respond, Moira and Liam entered carrying their plates. Colin pointed to the bakery box. "Enjoy. Don't forget you guys promised to come to the bowling alley tonight."

"Colin, you shouldn't strong-arm your family into coming."

Moira nudged her. "We're used to it. Besides, I think we have things to discuss. Things much more interesting than *Highlander*."

"Keep the traffic moving," Ryan yelled from behind his siblings.

Elizabeth shifted to allow them access to the sink and turned to leave.

"Elizabeth," Ryan said, "I'll call you tomorrow when I have some information."

"Thanks." On her way out, she said good-bye to Eileen and Quinn.

The house was so full of people and . . . love. It was weird and overwhelming. And as much as she wanted to escape, she also wanted to burrow in.

She didn't need these complications.

CHAPTER 15

Colin was disappointed that the bowling alley hadn't seen as much success as the bar did its first night. His family had shown up, just as they'd said they would, but the number of strangers didn't make him smile. If they wanted this to work, they'd have to find another avenue of advertising.

Days had passed and they'd had very few customers. If they didn't find more, they wouldn't be able to continue paying Bianca.

What made it worse was watching the stress take its toll on Elizabeth. She kept saying she was fine, but he knew better. She still wasn't eating much, and she looked like she was losing weight. She assured him she wasn't, but he knew the feel of her body. The more he watched her, though, the more irritated she became.

At night, after the alley was closed, sometimes he could talk her into a game. It was the only time he got to see a genuine smile.

Of course it helped that they usually played for sexual favors, which was definitely a win-win for both of them.

Something had changed today. Elizabeth had left his apartment after taking a phone call that he couldn't overhear. When he caught up with her at the bar, she didn't want to talk. Although she was dressed casually, she moved with the brisk, businesslike air that she had when they first met. She barely spoke to anyone.

An hour before they opened, he'd had enough. She was fussing with everything in sight from the bottles to napkins and straws. She wiped down clean tables and tripped—over nothing but her own feet. He finally grabbed her hand and dragged her into her office.

"Let go of me," she ordered and tugged.

He wouldn't let go. He couldn't possibly work with her like this. He closed the door behind them, pressed her against it, and kissed her like his life depended on it. At first her lips were tight and immobile with anger, but as he pushed his body into hers, she let out a moan and that was all the encouragement he needed.

His tongue swept in and he slowed his pace, stroking her mouth patiently while his hands caressed her neck. He didn't pull back until he felt her stiff muscles give way to softness.

"Now," he whispered, "do you want to tell me what the hell is wrong?"

She sighed and leaned her forehead on his chest. Why couldn't she just talk to him?

"We're not going anywhere until you talk." He said it as gently as he could, but she needed to understand that he meant it. When she raised her head again, he added, "And at some point, people are going to think we're in here fucking."

She smiled, but it wasn't real. "My dad is coming."

He waited, but that was all she said.

"And?"

"That's it. I'm sure Keith told him what I'm doing."

"Wait. You still haven't told him?"

"Well, he knows now. And he'll be here to check it out."

Colin smoothed a hand over her hair, which she'd been leaving down. "That's a good thing, right? You've built a great business."

"It's not good enough yet. The bowling alley is dying. If he sees that, I'm still a failure."

He growled and pulled her away from the door. He yanked it open and shoved her into the hallway. "Look out there. What do you see? It sure as hell is not failure."

"You don't understand. You couldn't possibly understand. Keith would never show this to Dad. I have to be better than Keith."

Colin flexed his hands and shoved them into his pockets. He wanted to shake her, but knew it wouldn't do any good. "Why? If you're both so good, why not run the company together? It's what my dad always wanted for me and Ryan, but we fought and fucked it up. Now my dad is gone and can't see us."

"Because."

"That's not an answer. Why not?"

She stomped her foot. "Because there can be only one."

He stared at her for a long moment and then burst out laughing. "Did you seriously just quote *Highlander* to me as the basis for why you and your brother can't work together?"

She huffed, spun on her heel, and slammed the office door in his face. He swallowed his grin and opened the door. "I'm sorry I laughed. But you have to admit, it's a little childish. And that says a lot coming from me."

Elizabeth stood in the middle of the room, wooden and composed. "Yes, it is childish. I told you you wouldn't understand. Keith and I made that agreement when I was still in college. You can't possibly get it. You have a problem and an army of people are waiting in the wings to offer help and support. You don't know what it's like to have no one to count on except yourself."

The hell he didn't. He'd spent three years running from his family, afraid he wouldn't be able to measure up. But now that he was back, he'd been taking full advantage of that support and loving every minute of it. Mostly.

Her shoulders slumped. "That's not my life."

"It could be." He said the words and his heart lurched.

"What?"

He wasn't sure what he was saying, but he continued, "If your life is so miserable and your family doesn't stand behind you, why go back? Stay here. We make a great team, and I have family to spare."

The more he talked, the more he wanted her to say yes. He didn't want his life to change. He didn't want her to go back to Florida.

She gave him a look of total disbelief. "I can't stay here. My life is in Florida. I've worked my ass off for years to build a career in my father's company. I can't just walk away."

A spear of disappointment shot through him. Although his mind understood, his heart wanted a yes. He'd known all along that she was driven by her goals and wouldn't be waylaid by the likes of him. Throwing an offer out without thought was what had always gotten him into trouble.

He covered his unease and asked, "When's your dad coming?"

"Next week."

He sighed. "What can I do to help?"

"I wish I knew. He usually only shows when it's time to sell."

Sell? But they weren't ready. He wasn't ready. Not to sell. Not to say good-bye to her.

Colin left her in the office and returned to the bar. She might not know how he could help, but he'd figure it out. He wouldn't let her think she'd failed, not when she'd taught him and given him so much. He'd do whatever was necessary, even if it meant calling the one person she didn't want involved.

* * *

After a long night of Elizabeth bristling against everyone, Colin had finally gotten her to leave. He claimed he was worried about her health, but the truth was that no one could stand her when she got like that. They closed the alley early, and he offered Bianca the chance to waitress at the bar so she wouldn't lose out on hours. She declined, saying she was going to look into other avenues to bring in customers.

Mike had the bar under control, so Colin went back to Elizabeth's office. She'd offered to bring a desk for him into the cramped space, but he knew she didn't really want him there. Over the past weeks, she had taught him how to organize all the paperwork and do the spreadsheets on the computer. But they'd done it all from his kitchen counter.

He sat behind her desk and scrolled through his phone to the number he'd saved from more than a week ago. It would've been so much easier if Elizabeth had a sister instead of a brother. He knew how to charm women.

It was late, but he didn't care. He dialed the number and waited.

"Hello?"

He didn't sound asleep.

"Hi, may I speak to Keith?" Colin's mother would be so proud that he remembered his phone manners.

"Speaking. Who's calling and why so late?"

"This is Colin O'Leary. We spoke briefly when you called here to talk to your sister."

Shuffling occurred on the other end, and Colin began to wonder if the man was going to hang up on him.

"I remember. What's this about?"

Unfortunately, Colin hadn't really thought about how to phrase the rest of what needed to be said. "Have you talked to Elizabeth?"

"About what?"

Colin sighed. This wasn't going to be easy. Reticence ran in the Brannigan family. Maybe he should've had Moira call. "Look, I'm calling because I'm worried about her."

"Why? What's wrong?"

"She's fine now, more or less. She was diagnosed with ulcers, and although she was doing better, whatever crap you have going on with her is stressing her out."

"Who the hell are you to call and blame me for Elizabeth getting sick?"

Colin hung his head. "I'm not blaming you. She's been working her ass off trying to turn this place around, and she feels like you're working against her. I'm just asking you to lighten up a little."

"I don't know you, and I don't know what your relationship with my sister is, but you know nothing about us. I keep trying to help her and she won't let me."

The man went from sounding irritated to worried. Good to know he wasn't the only one with a screwed-up family.

"If you want to help, get your dad to cancel his trip here. She doesn't feel ready, and she doesn't want to fail."

"So what else is new? The bar isn't the reason for my father's visit, so I won't be able to stop him. I'll come to Chicago in a couple of days, as soon as I clear my schedule. I'll see what I can do. Don't tell her I'm coming."

"Don't tell her I called you."

The man laughed, and the tension Colin held lightened. Maybe Keith wasn't as bad as Elizabeth made him out to be.

"You're Colin O'Leary."

"Yeah. We've talked before. I think I just mentioned that." Colin began to wonder about the man's sanity.

"It just came to me now. We talked a few months back about you wanting to buy The Irish Pub, didn't we?"

"That was you?"

"Yeah. Now you know why I couldn't sell. The place was always supposed to be for Elizabeth."

The information interested Colin. It explained why she took

everything so personally. It was much more than a competition with her brother.

"So why is your dad coming?"

"It's her birthday."

That tidbit changed Colin's attitude altogether. Elizabeth hadn't mentioned anything about her birthday. Maybe she didn't celebrate it. But her dad was coming. Colin no longer had to worry about making sure her father knew she was successful; he just needed to make sure she enjoyed her birthday.

* * *

Four days later, Elizabeth struggled with everything. Her dad had made dinner reservations at a swank downtown restaurant, but she really didn't want to go. How would she be able to eat when the fate of her career was here, ready for Dad's discerning eyes? Things were not going her way. Although the bar continued to turn a profit, the bowling alley sat empty every day. The place had been abandoned for so long that people had forgotten it existed. She needed a way to wake up the neighborhood and get them to invest time and money in her business.

Bianca was out pounding the pavement, trying to get local businesses to join a summer league. If the league brought people in, they would continue it in the fall. Elizabeth had planned on being long gone before the fall.

Now, she wasn't so sure.

She'd told Colin that she wasn't ready for her dad's arrival because she wasn't successful enough, but the truth was she was afraid Dad would want to sell immediately. If he gave the green light, she'd be back in Florida within a week.

She wasn't ready to go. Colin's offer for her to stay kept her up at night. She knew getting involved with her business partner would be a mistake. They'd grown close in so many ways, but they were business partners first. What would happen if she stayed and then they grew tired of each other? At some point, surely, he wouldn't find her snoring cute. He wanted someone who would give him a family.

Running the bar might not be enough for her either. She knew she wanted more balance in her life, so she could actually have a life, but she didn't want to remove all challenges. Once she figured out how to make the alley profitable, would running a single business be enough?

She'd thought the only thing she wanted was to be CEO. Again, she was no longer sure.

No matter what thoughts entered her mind, she needed to do something. She grabbed the box of glasses Colin had left in her office. Once in the hallway, she noticed that the back door was open and she heard voices. Colin's laugh echoed in the alley, bouncing off garbage cans and probably carrying into the neighbors' yards.

She took a step forward and opened her mouth to call him, but then she heard another voice. Keith's. A bubble of panic welled in her chest. She propelled her body toward the door, wanting to stop them from talking, because she had no way to predict how Colin would react to Keith. Colin extended his hand and she froze. She was too late, so she just eavesdropped.

"Sounds good," Colin said.

"Make sure she doesn't find out."

"You don't have to worry. I don't want to face that wrath."

"She'd hold it against me, not you. You're sure everything is handled?" Keith asked.

"Got it."

Colin started to back up, and panic zinged through her whole body. She spun and lost control of the box she carried. It sailed across the hall and bounced off the wall. Glass clanked and jingled and then shattered. Luckily, the box was closed.

She knew Colin heard. How could he not?

"Are you okay? What happened?"

Her head spun with thoughts; emotions swirled in her chest. She cleared her throat. "Oh, uh, nothing. I accidentally dropped the box of glasses. You really shouldn't have left them in my office."

Colin grabbed her shoulders and turned her to face him. "Are you okay? Did you get cut?"

Concern filled his face, and she couldn't reconcile that image with the idea that he was just conspiring with her brother. "I'm fine. I hadn't opened the box yet."

One more thing to add to the trash. She couldn't imagine what she wasn't supposed to find out about. It couldn't possibly be anything good, though. Keith enjoyed back-alley deals. Suddenly, her breath shortened. "Can you handle this? I need some air."

His fingers tightened on her shoulders. "What's wrong? You don't look so good."

"Don't worry. Elizabeth always gets upset when she's clumsy," Keith called from the door behind Colin.

She peered around Colin's shoulder and feigned surprise. "Keith? What are you doing here?"

"I came to check out the progress."

His smug smile rocketed her confused emotions straight into the pissed-off range. She knew that look. The one that said he'd won. How dare he do this to her again?

She inhaled sharply and refused to let him know he'd gotten to her. "Well, I'm sure Colin can handle showing you around. I have some things to do. I'll be back later."

Elizabeth walked slowly past both men and grabbed her purse from the office. Then she went out the back door where she'd overheard them cementing their deal. Her movements were stiff and awkward.

The stagnant heat inside her car pressed against her and breathing became difficult. She started the engine and pulled away from the bar. She drove without a destination in mind. She just knew she needed to get away from Colin and Keith.

Seeing them shake hands was like reliving everything with Matt. Sadness burned her throat and choked her, so she pulled over in the lot of a convenience store. Tears poured down her face. She cried until she shuddered and hiccupped, then dried her face.

This was not the same. Even if Keith had decided to employ the same tactics he had when she was in college, she was no longer that naïve, trusting person.

But you are, a little voice in her head called. True, she had mostly trusted Colin, but she'd learned her lesson with Matt. She and Colin were business partners first and foremost. She had a contract that would protect her assets.

Her heart was a different matter, however. But she'd overcome those issues. She had before.

She scrubbed her hands over her face and headed back to her hotel. After freshening up to remove the evidence of her crying jag, she put on a business suit. Then she tried to catalog what she'd left at Colin's apartment because there would definitely be no more sleepovers.

Her stomach did a little flip. She would miss the sleepovers.

Being with Colin had taught her what relaxation really felt like. Just because she would no longer be getting regular orgasms from him didn't mean that she couldn't still relax. She could learn to let go of the stress and anxiety from work. At least that's what she wanted to believe.

She shook her head. She needed to focus on the problem at hand—beating Keith at his own game. If only she could figure out how he planned to sabotage her, she could get out in front of it.

A chilling thought speared through her. What if the sabotage had already started? Everything that had gone wrong so far—the missing liquor, the disgusting bathroom episode, the break-in—had all occurred on Colin's watch. Keith could've put him up to it.

And then he let her feel guilty for the break-in because she hadn't changed the locks on the bowling alley. All the while comforting her and making love to her.

Her heart beat so fast it felt like it might burst. Colin had never struck her as phony. He never put up a façade to be different. Looking back on what had happened with Matt, she saw the signs, the little things she should've been suspicious of, but convinced herself not to be.

She sat and thought about every moment with Colin and came up empty. But the doubt took hold so tight it strangled her. What if Colin was just better at deception than Matt?

Maybe he played the game too well. Colin had taken care of her when she'd gotten sick, brought her to his family, allowed her to make friends with his sister. What about Moira? Was she in on this too?

No, Moira wasn't that sneaky. Elizabeth briefly wondered how Moira would react if she knew what her brother had been up to. She'd love to see some of that Irish temper unleashed on Colin. She'd record it and it would be an instant YouTube sensation.

Knowing that there was nothing to be done this minute, she readied to go back to the bar to face the enemy. Keith, she could fool. Unfortunately, Colin had gotten very good at reading her, and she wasn't sure how she'd pull that off. If they suspected she was onto them, they might rush things before she could get the upper hand.

She still had time. Dad wasn't coming for days. She'd play their game and figure out her next move.

When Elizabeth returned to the bar, she still didn't have a plan.

She knew Mike was scheduled to work, which would make her night easier. She still wasn't sure how to hide her newfound knowledge from Colin.

Entering the building, she kept her head high and her path focused. *Make it to the office.* En route, she made the mistake of glancing at the bar. Colin stared like he was dissecting her. She gave him a single nod and continued on her way.

Once she was safely behind her desk, she relaxed a fraction. She needed to get rid of Colin. Her office door swung open without notice and Colin strode in.

"What's with the suit?"

"What do you mean?"

"You haven't dressed like that in weeks."

Just one more mistake she'd made. Taking off her suit made her forget who she was.

"Did you need something?" she asked as a way of brushing aside his question.

"Mike's here, so I'm going to check in at O'Leary's. I'll be back later tonight."

"Don't bother," she snapped before she caught herself. "I mean, take the night off. I'll close with Mike."

"You sure?"

She nodded and hoped he wouldn't come closer.

"See you later then. I'll be well rested." He closed the door behind him.

He'd get plenty of rest since he had no shot of seeing her tonight or any other night.

* * *

Elizabeth had no idea how Keith managed to live like this. For two days, she'd avoided Colin as much as humanly possible and it had been sheer torture. Every morning she dressed in a power suit, resolved to look at him like any other employee, to keep her distance.

But he chipped away at that resolve with a grin and a wink. She clung to the image of him making a pact with Keith so his charm wouldn't melt her. She'd never been faced with such a challenge.

She sat in her car, staring at the ugly-ass building, shoring up her defenses. Keith left town again with a promise that he'd be back for her birthday. Neither he nor Colin mentioned anything about their time together. Surely, if everything was on the up-and-up, they would've said something, offered a report, or even a comment in passing.

But they were both tight-lipped, which was truly uncharacteristic for Colin.

Her heart was ripping in two. She wanted to believe in Colin. There was ample evidence to support his feelings as genuine.

But reality, her reality, had taught her that appearances could rarely be trusted.

Feeling sure of herself, or at least as sure as possible at the moment, she opened her car door to go to work. Her phone rang and she hesitated. Dad. If she spoke to him now, she might lose the strength she'd just built up, but it was usually better to get it over with. "Hi, Dad."

"Hi, sweetie, how are things?"

Weird. Dad never led a conversation with pleasantries. "I'm good. How are you?"

"Good, good."

Oh, no. He was repeating himself. He almost never did that, but when he did, it wasn't good. She leaned against the car, the afternoon sun beating down on her, blazing a path across her cheek. "What's up, Dad?"

"Well, I've been talking with your mother, and she really wants me to retire this year."

No, no, no. He couldn't make this decision now. Not after putting it off for a couple of years. Not now that she'd put in all this work.

She swallowed hard. "I know. She mentions it every time we talk. She's under the misconception that I hold some sway over your decision."

"She's issued an ultimatum this time. She's planning a cruise around the world, with or without me." He let out a chuckle as if he couldn't believe Mom would go without him.

Elizabeth had no problem believing it.

"What does this mean for us? I'm assuming you're going with her, right?" Elizabeth turned the other cheek to the sun. If she was going to burn, she might as well make it even.

"We bought tickets for January. I've already let Keith know."

Of course Keith was informed first.

"I'll start transitioning power at the end of the summer."

So she still had a chance.

"We'll talk more when I get to Chicago. I just wanted you to know."

Really he just needed to tell himself he wasn't playing favorites. "Okay. Thanks. See you soon."

She disconnected. At least her strength hadn't been sapped by the conversation. She had even more of an incentive to show her dad how well things were going, and neither Colin nor Keith was going to take this from her.

* * *

Colin was a mess. He'd spent a day planning with Keith under the guise of showing him the business. He didn't see the competitiveness in him that Elizabeth claimed was there. The man seemed to care about his little sister. He wanted what was best for her, but even Colin could recognize that there was something else neither of them talked about.

Call it his bartender's intuition. Keith and Elizabeth carried some deep secret, and it weighed on their relationship.

And she was dodging Colin. For the two days since Keith's departure, she worked around his schedule, as if she didn't want to see him. Now, she'd been holed up in her office for hours. He couldn't take it anymore. He wasn't as good as she was at this game. He went into her office and closed the door behind him.

At the sound of the click, she looked up from the papers in front of her. "Yes?"

"Where have you been? You didn't come to my place for the last couple of nights, and you didn't answer your phone."

She cleared her throat. "I'm too busy for distractions right now."

Distractions? He was a distraction? The words sucker punched his chest and constricted everything.

"My father will be here soon, and I need to have everything in place so I can go back to Florida."

He still couldn't find words. She was leaving.

She stood and, for the first time, he realized that Elizabeth Brannigan was back—full suit, high heels, hair pulled back tightly. The stick up her ass completed the image.

"If you'll excuse me, I have to check on the delivery of the kitchen equipment."

When she came close, he reached out to stroke her cheek. He wanted a reaction and he got one. She pulled away.

She'd stopped pulling away from him a long time ago, even while at work. This was a clear message. He just didn't understand the reason for it.

"What's going on? Talk to me."

She opened her mouth to answer, but someone knocked on the door at his back. Instead of responding to him, she reached for the doorknob.

He stepped back and Mike said, "Hey, Elizabeth, the delivery truck is here."

"I'm coming." She left without so much as a backward glance, but she did stumble on her heels.

She could tuck Libby away as tightly as she wanted, but he knew where to find her.

Colin had no idea what had happened, but there was no way he'd let his last days with Elizabeth be like this. He was having a hard enough time coming to terms with the fact that she was leaving. Maybe that was it. She wanted space to make leaving easier. He couldn't tell which of them it was supposed to be easier for.

He went back to the bar to work his shift. At least if she wasn't talking to him, keeping her birthday party a surprise would be simple. Bianca had done most of the planning since her days were slow. Elizabeth didn't notice because getting the kitchen together garnered most of her attention. That, and worrying about her dad's visit.

Colin wanted to ease that worry for her, but Keith was against it. Elizabeth wouldn't want to be rescued. Still, Colin was concerned about how the added stress would affect her stomach.

The night dragged, and although he thought Elizabeth would leave so he wouldn't confront her again, she stayed. Sure, she locked herself in her office all night and didn't interact with anyone, but she stayed. Colin sent everyone else home and finished cleaning up alone.

When Elizabeth finally stuck her head out of the office, he smiled. "What have you been up to all night?" he asked.

"Getting orders together for the kitchen." She walked through the bar and checked to make sure everything was clean.

"You can head out. I'll finish up."

"I was just going to suggest that to you." She grabbed a rag and began wiping down the nearest table.

One he'd already finished.

"I almost always close."

"I managed without you last night. You should go." She continued to wipe, looking completely efficient and out of place in her heels and skirt.

"What the hell is going on?" He rounded the corner of the bar to get closer to her. Even from a few feet away, he could smell the cinnamon on her skin that made him crave her.

"Nothing is going on. I'm closing."

"Talk to me." Another step.

She glanced at him. Her eyes changed from cold to cautious.

"I want to be here to make sure there are no more problems." She turned away and walked to the next table.

"Problems like what?"

"The missing liquor, the break-in . . . I want to be sure everything is the way it's supposed to be." Swipe, swipe, swipe.

He grabbed her elbow and spun her around. Her eyes widened and she clamped her mouth shut. The pulse at her neck throbbed.

"Are you implying that I'm not doing a good enough job? That it's my fault that someone broke in?"

She dropped the rag and took a step out of his reach. "Screw it." Her stance straightened even more and she locked her eyes on his. "I heard you talking to Keith. I don't know why I thought I could play this game. He's the master. You win. Congratulations."

Nothing she said made sense, but his gut told him to be pissed off. "What are you talking about?"

"Look, it's over. I overheard you and Keith. I know how he operates. Can you please just give me some credit? I might be slow on the uptake, but I'm not stupid." She crossed her arms over her middle. Although she was obviously accusing him of something, she wasn't angry. She was hurt.

If she'd overheard the party plans, why would she be upset? And who could ever mistake her for someone stupid?

He needed to change his tactic. He leaned a hip on the table. "What exactly did you overhear?"

She rolled her eyes. "To put it nicely, I know you're in cahoots with him."

He snorted a laugh. "Cahoots?"

She narrowed her eyes. "I heard you tell each other to make sure I didn't find out or I'd hold Keith responsible. He's right. I just can't believe you'd do this to me. I expect it from him." Her voice lowered to a near whisper. "Not from you."

She was serious. She didn't know it was plans for the party that she'd overheard.

"I need more here, Libby."

"Don't call me that." Her voice was sharp. She'd found her anger.

"What do you think we were conspiring about?"

She closed her eyes and dropped her head. "He'd do anything to make me lose. I thought that, after last time, he wouldn't go there again. I was wrong. I hope whatever he's giving you is worth it. I'm not going to let him—or you—do anything else to sabotage this. I've worked too hard and come too far for it to be ruined because I trusted you."

She raised her head and stared at him.

He couldn't believe his ears. She believed he was behind all of the sabotage. "I'm not doing anything to ruin our business. I wouldn't do that."

"My business."

"*Ours.* I'm a partner."

"Funny way of showing it. Now please leave so I can lock up."

"Sabotaging this business takes money from my pocket too."

"I'm sure Keith's paycheck would balance it out."

"You're not making sense. You think I'd come in here and break the TVs and glasses? For what purpose?" His own anger began to show itself.

"To make me look incompetent. You pretty much accomplished that, didn't you? Making sure the break-in came through the bowling alley where I hadn't thought to change the locks. Then you were able to swoop in and fix everything because I couldn't. Hell, we didn't even miss a night." She sidestepped around him, safely keeping her distance.

Heat radiated from her skin, amplifying the cinnamon smell. He grabbed her arm, but she shook free.

"I'm not going to let you lay this on me. I didn't do anything. I've worked my ass off to make this place a success every bit as much as you have. It might not mean anything to you, but this place is everything to me." Fear swallowed him. Everything slipped from his grasp. "I couldn't do that to you."

"Why would I believe that?"

"Because I love you." He blurted the words out, and his brain scrambled to keep up.

She froze and a flicker of pain crossed her face. "That's rich. Nothing else works, so you prey on my emotions? Go home, Colin. I'll make sure I fulfill our contractual agreement, but I don't want you here anymore."

She was throwing him out? Fuck that. "No."

"I wasn't asking. I'm still the owner and boss. Go back to O'Leary's. You're not needed here." She walked away, quietly adding, "I don't need you."

Her words did more damage than he'd thought possible. His anger boiled, but he clung to enough control to keep his mouth shut. Anything he said would only make things worse. "Fine. Have it your way."

He stormed out, determined not to look at her. So she didn't need him. Just like everyone else. He got into his Jeep and sped toward the highway. He put in a call to Keith and left a message. Whatever crap Keith had going on with Elizabeth was ruining everything Colin had. He wanted answers, and Elizabeth wouldn't talk. Without real reason, what he wanted more than anything was to punch Keith's face. He didn't need the whole story to know that Keith had been the cause of Elizabeth's pain.

The wind whipped around him as he increased speed on the Kennedy, driving toward downtown. Air slapped at him, but he struggled to breathe. He hadn't told any woman he loved her since his lust-crazed adolescence. He learned quickly the power of those words. And now, the one time he'd used them, he'd been tossed aside. Part of him wanted to keep driving until he crossed state lines, to escape. He'd done that plenty.

He turned his car around and headed back to O'Leary's. Elizabeth might not need him, but he knew his family at least wanted him.

He was done running.

CHAPTER 16

Elizabeth released a shuddering breath. Telling Colin to leave was harder than she'd anticipated. The man was an excellent actor. She'd give him that much. When she'd confronted Matt all those years ago, he'd immediately looked ashamed. Matt thought it was a harmless game. He hadn't been the brightest bulb in the chandelier.

She shook off thoughts of the past. She debated whether she should call Keith and let him know she was onto him. No, Colin had probably already made that call. Their dad wasn't due in until late to-morrow. She could sleep in and then plan how to approach him.

After finishing the closing routine, she looked over the bar again. She'd done good work here. Maybe it wasn't perfect, but it was a complete turnaround. Keith had to grant her that much. In some ways, she'd accomplished at least as much as Keith did with most of his projects. Maybe on a smaller scale, but she'd done enough to be proud.

She double-checked the lock on the front door and flipped off the last lights, allowing the glow from the hallway to guide her. The light glinted off the nearest TV and a niggle of doubt pricked at her. If he wasn't guilty, why hadn't Colin told her about his conversation with Keith? She stared at the black screen and tried to imagine Colin swinging a bat to smash it. The picture couldn't form in her head. The damage done here struck her as the work of someone who was angry.

Even after her accusations, Colin didn't seem angry enough to strike out like that.

No, maybe it wasn't anger. If he'd wanted it to look that way, he could've faked it. She wondered how much of their relationship had been for profit. Her heart sank. Everything had felt so real with Colin. What had Keith offered him to make him prostitute himself?

She couldn't think about that. If she held on to the anger, she'd be fine. The minute she let herself feel anything other than the anger, she might fall apart. And she no longer had anyone to turn to.

No, that wasn't true. She had Janie and Lori. When she got back to the hotel, she'd send them an e-mail to make plans to get together this weekend. After her father's visit, she would definitely need comfort. A last trip out with the girls before going home. A night of dancing and drinking would fit the bill. Well, maybe not the drinking, but dancing with strangers, people who wanted nothing more than the temporary use of her body . . . She could get behind that.

Her mind wandered back to the first time she'd wanted Colin to use her body. She wished she had followed through that night. If they'd slept together then, she never would've allowed it to go further. She would've laughed him out of the conference room when he proposed becoming her partner.

Hindsight and all that. Time to move on.

She locked her office door, just in case, and set the newly installed alarm at the back door before leaving. She walked to her car with her keys in hand. Exhaustion swamped her, and her bed called. But it wasn't really comfortable. Noises would be heard in the hall. A Friday night meant people would be coming back from a night out. Doors would slam, people would talk, yell, moan. She longed for the quiet of her little house.

Or Colin's apartment. His place was always quiet. Or maybe it was the comfort of sleeping next to him that gave her the feeling of peace.

Two blocks from the hotel, her cell phone chirped. Who the hell would call so late? She checked the screen. No one she knew. She hit Ignore. A few seconds later, it rang again. "Hello?"

"Elizabeth Brannigan?"

"Yes."

"This is Metro Security. The alarm at your building was triggered. Are you on the premises?"

"No. Send the police."

She turned her car around. Nerves gripped her stomach. Colin was upset when he left. Would he come back now to do something else? But he wouldn't have tripped the alarm. Unless that was part of his plan to throw suspicion off him.

Maybe she shouldn't have called the police. If she went there alone, she would have all the proof she needed. His actions would be cause to terminate their contract, and she could prove to her father that she could handle everything.

But what if it's not Colin? the voice whispered quietly in her brain.

By the time she returned to the bar, two squad cars were in the parking lot beside the bowling alley, blue and red lights flashing. She pulled in and approached the nearest cop. He looked vaguely familiar, and then she realized that he was one who showed up for the bar fight when she first took over.

He smiled, putting her at ease.

She shrugged. "At least it's not a bar fight this time. What triggered the alarm?"

Part of her hoped it was a malfunction, that no one had tried to break in.

He pointed toward the door. Sitting on the ground, hands cuffed behind his back, was Mitch, her old manager.

"He was trying to get in the door when we showed up. He had a key in hand, saying he didn't know why the door wouldn't open. He's pretty drunk. He got loud and pushy, so we cuffed him, but we wanted to check with you before hauling him in."

"Did he by chance admit to breaking in before?"

The cop snickered. "He thinks he has every right to be here. He said he's the manager and just forgot something inside." The cop leaned forward and added, "I get the impression that you're new to the business, but allowing employees to drink on the job doesn't usually turn out well."

She bristled at his accusation. "He's no longer an employee for that very reason. I'd already fired him when you were here for the bar fight. But thanks for the advice."

"So you're pressing charges?"

"Hell, yes."

He signaled to another uniformed officer who grabbed Mitch's elbow and hauled him to his feet. Mitch swayed and started to yell, but then he caught sight of her.

"You," he shouted, hitching his chin in her direction. "You never shoulda fired me."

His eyes were filled with hatred and anger.

In that moment, she knew she'd been completely wrong about Colin. Colin hadn't destroyed their bar. Mitch had. He was pissed off over getting fired.

She couldn't force enough air into her lungs. She sucked hard, but they wouldn't fill. How could she have been so wrong? And if she was wrong, Colin's declaration of love had been real.

She'd completely screwed up everything. She turned to leave, hoping movement would bring air rushing back. Instead, she plowed right into a hard body. Colin stood with his hands tucked in his pockets, but when she stumbled back, he quickly caught her arms to steady her. The warmth of his hands calmed her, and air filled her lungs.

She'd expected a smile and a quick remark about how clumsy she was, but his blue eyes were ice, his face blank.

"What's going on? The alarm company called. They said they couldn't reach you."

"They got me on the second call, so I came back. Mitch, the old manager, was trying to break in." She looked into his eyes. She couldn't read anything. "With a set of keys."

He nodded his understanding. "You have everything handled?"

Now she smelled the faint whiff of alcohol on his breath. He'd been drinking. In all the weeks they'd been together, he rarely drank.

Her head reeled, juggling notions of love. Before she answered, he turned to leave. He got as far as his Jeep before she could make her voice work. "Wait," she called.

He paused with one leg in the car, ready to hoist the rest of himself in and drive away.

She hurried over to him. "I'm sorry." The words choked out, and she knew they were inadequate.

He eased his leg out of the car and leaned against the side. He crossed his arms, but didn't say a word.

"I'm sorry I accused you. I know I was wrong. It was Mitch who did everything, I'm sure of that now. He had a key to the bowling alley and used it to do everything I accused you of."

His icy stare chilled her. "I'm glad you have the proof you need. It would've been nice to have that before you started believing the worst."

"I know. But you don't understand. I heard you talking with Keith. You don't know."

Colin shoved forward so quickly, she stepped back. Anger sparked in his eyes. "You're right. I don't know anything because you won't talk to me. About anything. But I never pretended to be anything other than who I am."

He leaned close enough that she could feel his breath on her face.

"I've done some fucked-up things in my life, and I've let a lot of people down, but I've never betrayed anyone. Especially you." He backed away and climbed into his car. "Good-bye, Elizabeth."

He started the engine and flicked the radio on, much louder than necessary. Probably to make sure he couldn't hear her if she tried to talk.

But she had nothing to say. Colin was right. He never had a chance.

* * *

The single shot he'd had in his apartment hadn't numbed him nearly enough for facing Elizabeth. He drove away from her for the second time that night, and even with her apology fresh in his mind, he didn't feel any better. She'd said from the beginning that they wouldn't have anything more than sex. Business and pleasure didn't mix.

Now he understood why. She couldn't trust anyone enough to build a relationship. It had nothing to do with her living in Florida or the amount of travel she did for work. It was all about her fucked-up family and her inability to trust.

The woman should've come with a warning label.

He tossed his keys on the counter and grabbed the bottle of whiskey, not even bothering with a glass this time. Taking a swig, he plopped onto the couch. The leather couch Ryan had left behind. The couch where he'd made love to Elizabeth. Another swig, this one to make him forget.

Shit. Maybe he'd just get a new couch. He stood and walked to the bedroom. She'd been gone for only two days, and evidence of her lingered. He'd washed the clothes she'd left and they sat on his dresser.

He looked at the stack. Half the clothes he considered hers were actually his.

He picked up the Blue Balls T-shirt and thought about putting it back in his drawer. Then he realized that he'd never be able to wear the shirt again without thinking of her.

A softball team. They should sponsor one. They were a sports bar after all. That would give them an extra group of regular drinkers.

He put the bottle on the dresser. He had to stop thinking about how to improve business. Elizabeth had made it clear that he was hands-off from now on.

But she'd apologized. Was that enough for him to want to continue to work with her?

No, she'd made it clear that he worked *for* her, regardless of how he felt. It was time to move on. He'd made money on this venture, added it to the savings he had. He'd talk to Ryan about adding another business. His brother was a partner he could count on.

He'd proven it time and again.

And this time, Colin knew he could pull his own weight and wouldn't have to lean on Ryan more than as a partner.

He guessed he'd gotten more than just some money out of his dealings with Elizabeth. He grabbed the bottle again, but put it back. Alcohol wasn't going to cure anything. He stripped and crawled into bed.

* * *

The phone rang, and Colin sat up in bed. Sun glared through the window, and he scrubbed a hand over his face. The numbers on the clock were blurry, but he was certain it was early enough that he couldn't seriously consider staying awake.

The phone stopped, and he flopped back. Then it started again. What the fuck? He crawled to the edge of the bed and fumbled for his jeans. As he yanked the phone from the pocket it stopped.

He checked the call log. Keith. Didn't that just figure? Why bother being courteous to people who had to work late? Not that Colin had been courteous in calling Keith at two a.m. No messages, so Colin dialed.

"Hello?" Keith's voice was the smooth sound of someone who'd been awake for hours.

"It's Colin. What did you want?" His own voice was rough and cracked. He stood and got a glass of water from the bathroom.

"What the hell happened last night?"

"What *didn't* happen?"

"Elizabeth won't take my calls. You left some cryptic, threatening message. Then I get a call from my former bar manager saying he'd been arrested."

Where to begin? "Mitch was arrested for trying to break into the bar, well, technically, the bowling alley. We think he was behind other problems we've had since reopening. I have no idea why he called you."

"I know why he called me. He wants me to bail him out. He said Elizabeth was an unreasonable bitch, which, of course, she can be, but he tried to say it was all a misunderstanding."

Anger rose in Colin's chest, and he wanted to defend Elizabeth. She was no more a bitch than she needed to be. And even if she was, shouldn't her own brother stand up for her? "No misunderstanding. He was trying to use an old key to get in. Based on the damage he did last time, I don't want to know what he would've done last night."

Colin felt weird having this conversation with Elizabeth's brother while naked, so he pulled on jeans.

"Fine. Now tell me why Elizabeth won't take my calls and you threatened me."

He sat back on the edge of the bed. "It wasn't a threat. It was a request for information. Before we closed last night, Elizabeth accused me of sabotage. She said she overheard us talking. I assumed she meant she'd heard about the party. But she said she knew I was conspiring with you, that you were setting her up to lose again."

"Shit."

"That's not an explanation."

"It's a long story."

"Since she accused me of betraying her, I think I'm entitled to that story, don't you?"

"Fuck." A long stretch of silence followed. "Can we meet for coffee?"

"That long of a story?"

"Unfortunately."

Keith agreed to come to O'Leary's in a half hour, which would give Colin enough time to attempt to look human. As long as he was up, he called Bianca and made sure everything was set for Elizabeth's party. He wouldn't attend, but he wanted her birthday to be a good one. He just hoped her brother wouldn't screw that up.

Down in the bar, Colin found the quiet that used to make him enjoy being here. He still loved working at O'Leary's, but he'd become accustomed to working with someone. The quiet didn't soothe him the way it used to.

A knock sounded at the front door, and he unlocked it to see Keith standing in the sunlight wearing a suit. What was with this family? He couldn't come for coffee dressed like a normal person?

"Come on in. Coffee's ready. We don't open for lunch for a few hours, so I can't offer you anything else." Colin locked the door after Keith walked past him. Keith looked at him and Colin pointed to a table near the bar. "I'll be right back. How do you take it?"

"Black's fine. How did you end up meeting Elizabeth?"

"She came in here and we got to know each other."

Colin grabbed two cups and sat across from Keith. They stared at each other. Colin had nothing to say, so he let the silence fill the space.

"I don't know where to start."

"How about you start by telling me whatever you did to make Elizabeth be leery of anyone wanting to help her."

The man sighed and hung his head. "The year before Elizabeth graduated college, my dad thought it would be fun to have us compete for work. We'd both worked with him, but I'd had more experience. My dad bought two properties in Tampa. While they were in similar neighborhoods, he leveled the playing field by giving Elizabeth the place that would require less work.

"At first I didn't care. I knew I'd win."

"Should I bother asking what the prize was?"

Keith shook his head. "I don't even remember. It might've been bragging rights. It was supposed to be fun. A way to spend our summer. After the first two weeks, I knew I was in trouble. Elizabeth is good at what she does."

Colin knew that already. He focused on Keith. He didn't like sharing this story, but Colin was glad that he didn't back out.

"Our dad did his weekly visit of the two properties and was sure that we were neck and neck. He was prepared to call a tie." He took a swig of coffee. "I was pissed. A tie would've been fine, but then Elizabeth opened her mouth. *There can be only one*."

Colin remembered her saying those words to him and how he'd laughed at it.

"The quote is from—"

"I know. Get to the point." Colin knew things were going to head south.

"She pushed the issue, and I became willing to do whatever was necessary to win. I couldn't let my little sister show me up."

Keith stopped again, and Colin wanted to shake him. No story could be that long. "Finish."

"I sent a friend of mine to work for her. She didn't know I had sent him. He was supposed to spy and let me know what her plans were so I could top them. She fell for Matt and they started to date. I used it to my advantage."

"What exactly did you do?" Anger bubbled in his chest. That Keith could do anything to his own *sister* burned him. It was his job to take care of his sister. He should be the one man she could always count on to have her back.

"I paid him to sabotage her work before the end of the competition. She looked like a fool in front of my father."

Colin shoved away from the table and paced, afraid that if he didn't move, he might hit Keith. This was their family crap, and he had no business putting his nose into it, plus it was more than a decade ago.

"I was young and stupid. I didn't think about what it would do to her. I just wanted to win."

So much made sense now. She saw this as her chance to redeem herself. She could prove to her father that she was as good, if not better, than Keith. He only had one question left, and depending on the answer, he might find himself spending the night in jail for beating the crap out of Elizabeth's brother.

"Were you behind the problems we've had? Did you set Mitch up to make her fail?"

"What?" Keith stood, his eyes shooting daggers, as if he had the right to be offended. "Fuck no. I've been trying to make up for it ever since. I love my sister. I want her to be happy."

Even as angry as he was, Colin could see the remorse on the other man's face. It was easy to recognize because he'd seen the same look in the mirror.

"What's all this to you, anyway?" Keith asked. "What's your relationship with Elizabeth?"

I love her. The admission swamped him and he felt light-headed. He pushed it back, knowing that it didn't matter. "We're partners. My contract stipulates that I get a cut of profits and a bonus when we sell. I obviously want the business to succeed."

"The place isn't for sale."

Colin bristled again. "That's Elizabeth's call."

"It's mine. The business is mine, not hers."

Tension filled Colin's muscles. In addition to accusing him of being a criminal and of betraying her, Elizabeth had lied to him? "You said it was supposed to be hers."

"It's not yet."

"Thanks for telling me. The party's ready for tonight. You might want to talk to your sister before she's blindsided by the party. She's preparing for battle, not a birthday."

"You're not coming?"

Colin shook his head. He, too, wanted Elizabeth to be happy. If he showed up at her party, he would probably ruin it. He didn't know what to do with his emotions. He felt sorry for Elizabeth, but he didn't know if he could forgive her lack of faith in him. He'd definitely confront her about lying about owning the bar. What a clusterfuck.

"You're welcome to come. I'll make sure she knows you had nothing to do with any sabotage."

"She already knows that," Colin answered. "We have other issues."

"Okay." Keith turned and left.

Colin began the prep for opening O'Leary's. Here, he knew exactly what to expect and people knew what to expect from him. Family offered that.

The nagging little voice in his head reminded him that Elizabeth didn't know that feeling. He brushed it aside.

He was done trying to prove himself worthy.

* * *

Elizabeth was beyond tired. She'd barely gotten any sleep between dealing with the cops and worrying about her dad. And Colin. She'd screwed that up, but she'd apologized. She didn't know what else to do, how to fix it. He walked away without accepting her apology. She didn't know what to do about his declaration. Her own feelings were murky, so she ignored them to face the problem at hand.

Keith had been calling all day, but she dodged the calls. Surely he knew what had happened by now. During one message he said he'd talked with Colin, which meant that he knew exactly how she'd messed up and could toss it back in her face. So she'd accused the wrong man. It didn't matter much now.

There had been no sign of Colin at either the bar or the bowling alley. Although Mitch had been caught, she wouldn't put it past Keith to have someone else waiting in the wings. She'd feel better if she didn't have to leave Mike in charge. She was fairly sure Mike would be on her side. Neither Keith nor Mike had showed even a flicker of recognition when they'd met. She couldn't afford any more problems.

Maybe she should call Colin and ask him to work while she was out. But her pride wouldn't let her make that call. She'd told him she didn't need him.

Such a liar.

Everything would be fine for a few hours. She'd eat dinner and then get her dad to go back to the bar tonight. She might as well get it over with. It wouldn't look any better in the morning. At least tonight she had her birthday working in her favor.

Her father sent a car to pick her up. God forbid she should drive herself to the restaurant. When the car pulled up, she groaned. A limo. Really? What was he thinking? Unless it was Mom. This was totally something she would do. Dad hadn't mentioned anything, but maybe Mom traveled with him.

She looked down at the navy suit she wore. If Mom was at dinner, the first thing she'd comment on was her attire.

Why don't you put in a little effort? You're so pretty. Let a man see that.

Elizabeth headed toward the back of the limo while trying to contain a giggle. Her mother would keel over if she found out about Colin. She could almost hear the *He's beneath you*. Maybe she should invite him to dinner. Riling her mother was an excellent way to spend her birthday.

Then she remembered that inviting Colin anywhere was no longer an option.

She swallowed past the lump in her throat and steeled herself for the meal ahead.

The car pulled up in front of the restaurant. Sure enough, her mother stood beside her father. Unfortunately, Keith waited with them. She took a deep breath and climbed from the back of the car.

She could almost hear her mother's *tsk*. Her stomach roiled with a pain she hadn't felt in weeks. She wished Colin were here. He'd put her at ease with one of his smiles. Then he'd win her mother over with his charm.

Keith walked to meet her. "We need to talk."

"Not now." She moved to skirt by him, but he caught her elbow.

"Yes, now." He turned and waved to their parents. "Go on in. We'll be there in a minute."

Keith propelled her to the side of the entrance.

She yanked her arm away. "What do you want?"

"First, I had nothing to do with whatever Mitch did to the bar. Neither did Colin."

"Your lies mean little to me." She turned away. She'd expected him to say that.

"I told Colin everything. Even about Matt."

That caught her attention. The entire episode had been swept under the rug for years. They never mentioned it. She looked into her brother's eyes. He wasn't lying. "Why?"

He shrugged. "It seemed like he deserved an explanation, and he wasn't getting it from you. He cares about you."

He loves me. The lump returned to her throat and she couldn't speak, so she nodded.

"He told me that you planned to sell the bar and the bowling alley."

She cleared her throat. "What else would we do with it? It's not like it fits in Dad's portfolio."

"You can't sell it. It's mine and you know it."

"If you're not going to let me sell, why did you let me do all this work? That's not fair. Not even Dad will side with you on this one." She gripped her purse. With all of the extra work they'd done, she'd never be able to pay Colin if they didn't sell. They hadn't put a time clause in the contract, but it was understood that they would sell as soon as they were turning a profit. The way things stood between them now, she didn't want to tell him they couldn't sell.

Keith's voice brought her back from those thoughts. "I know what

I did back then was reprehensible. If someone ever did that to Mel, I'd kill him and his body would never be found. I don't get you."

"What?"

"You never told Dad what I did."

"He wouldn't have believed me." She crossed her arms. She didn't like where this conversation was headed. They didn't talk about emotions and the past and other useless things.

"But you never came back at me. You just let it slide."

No, she hadn't let it slide; she'd been holding a grudge ever since. Obviously, she wasn't very good at it if Keith was unaware. "Water under the bridge, right? Life goes on. What does any of that have to do with selling the bar?"

"I bought it for you. After you let me win, even though I cheated and after everything I'd done. I wanted you to forgive me. I bought The Irish Pub because it was in Chicago and it had a bowling alley. Those were things that I knew made you happy. You had real friends here, and being away from Mom is good for you."

Her mind was stuck on the fact that he'd bought the bowling alley for her. "Why didn't you ever tell me?"

"I was waiting for the right time. It never seemed to come. I didn't want you to think it was a consolation prize. Then after you graduated, you threw yourself into work, and at first I thought you really liked it. Now I know better." He put his arm around her shoulder and turned them toward the restaurant. "I was right the first time. You're happy here."

She thought of what made her happy in Chicago. Colin. She didn't know if she could run everything without him. She didn't want to. "What did Colin say when you told him about Matt?"

"Not much. I thought he was going to hit me, but he didn't. He asked if I'd initiated the sabotage and he mentioned selling the bar. I told him it wasn't for sale."

Shit. In one conversation, Keith had told Colin more than she'd ever had. "If the bar is mine, then I can sell it."

He sighed and shook his head. "Give it a few days. If you still feel that way, go ahead and sell."

She didn't need a few days. The business would go on the market first thing Monday morning. Colin had a right to go his own way.

CHAPTER 17

Dinner had been mostly painless. They ate at a quiet table with their multiple forks and linen napkins. She would've preferred a good pizza to the fancy fare her father had chosen. By the time dessert was finished, all she wanted to do was crawl back into bed.

But she was determined to show her father the business and get it over with. Regardless of his opinion, she knew she'd done a good job. "Are you ready to look at the bar?"

"Bar?" her mother asked.

Her dad looked almost as confused.

"Didn't Keith tell you?" She looked at Keith, who shook his head. Damn, she'd been so sure that Keith had told him everything.

"What are you talking about?" her dad asked.

She let out a breath. "Remember when you asked me to do an audit of your personal holdings? I found a property that I knew nothing about. One that was losing money. I came here to check it out. Then I decided to take it on as a project."

"Without telling me?"

"Yes. I wanted to do it all on my own, from beginning to end."

"She's done a great job. Wait until you see it," Keith chimed in.

"Do we really need to discuss business now?" Mom asked.

Keith jumped in to deal with Mom. "You know, Mom, you'll probably be bored. Why don't you take the car back to your hotel, and Dad and I will take Elizabeth to the business."

"Sweetie, it's her birthday. She should be out celebrating, dancing, and drinking. Not standing around with her brother and father looking at a tavern."

Elizabeth closed her eyes and tried to remember what her mother had been like before Dad had become successful. Over the years, the image had become dimmer and dimmer. She was a woman of means and, to her, that carried with it certain expectations.

"It's a bar, Mom. Not a tavern. A regular neighborhood bar. A sports bar, in fact. And it's attached to a bowling alley. We're putting in a kitchen so we can sell nachos and hot wings. Things that don't require a fork. It's exactly how I want to spend my birthday." The knowledge sank deep into her bones, unsettling every inch of her. She'd enjoyed almost every minute of being at the bar. Being there on her birthday made sense. Being with Colin made sense.

Elizabeth stood and tossed her napkin on the table. "Thank you for coming all this way to have dinner with me on my birthday." She walked around the table and planted a kiss on her mother's cheek. "It means a lot. I do have to get back to work, though, regardless of whether you join me. I'm closing."

Keith rose. "I'm coming. Dad, you need to see this."

"Can't your father visit in the morning?"

Elizabeth rolled her eyes.

Keith saved her from having to answer. "It's a bar, Mom. If he wants to see how it works, he needs to come at night."

"Fine. I'll see you back at the hotel. Don't forget we have an early flight tomorrow."

Her mother air kissed the three of them and walked to the front of the restaurant.

"Are you sure I wasn't adopted?" Elizabeth said the words aloud that she'd often wondered in her head.

"No such luck, Libby." Keith's tone had softened.

He hadn't called her Libby in years, unless he was trying to tease her and get under her skin. Something was in the process of shifting between them, but she didn't know what or how, much less why.

Keith drove and parked in the lot beside the bowling alley. Elizabeth started walking toward the bar, wanting to put her best foot forward, but Keith said, "I think we should see the bowling alley first."

She shot him a dirty look that he ignored. Well, at least when he saw the bar after the alley, her dad would be really impressed.

She pushed through the door of the bowling alley, preparing excuses for why it wasn't busy. Inside the dark space, she became speechless. Balloons and streamers dangled everywhere. A sign hanging above the shoe counter read HAPPY BIRTHDAY, LIBBY.

Her eyes became misty. Her father hugged her and so did Keith.

"Surprised, huh?"

"Yes." She pulled away from them and was immediately surrounded by Janie and Lori.

Their yells and hugs were a welcome distraction from the emotional wave she was riding. Bianca announced her arrival over the loudspeaker, and the few patrons that were there raised their glasses in a toast.

She looked over the faces with their attention on her and searched for the one face she wanted to see more than any of them.

Colin's.

He was behind this. She knew it. She scanned each person through her watery eyes with no luck. She said hi to Bianca and asked where Colin was.

She shrugged. "I haven't seen him all day. He called this morning to make sure everything was on track, but that was it. I thought he would've been here a long time ago." She put a pair of shoes on the counter. "Hurry up and change. Cosmic bowling starts soon."

Elizabeth took the shoes. Keith stood behind her.

"He's not coming."

She didn't pretend not to know who he was talking about.

"I told him that I would make sure you knew he didn't do any sabotage, but he said he wasn't coming. That you had other issues."

Other issues. Like laughing at him for saying he loved her.

Colin not showing up to her birthday party, one that he obviously had a hand in planning, spoke volumes. He wouldn't forgive her.

She wanted to cry. But she had a roomful of people counting on her to have a happy birthday. She blinked and swallowed hard.

Pulling her phone out, she dialed his number, hoping he'd answer. He didn't, so she left a message. "Hey, Colin. Thank you so much for the party. It's really amazing. Uhh . . . I don't know what else to say. I wish you were here."

With shoes in hand, she turned to find a place to sit and change. A blur of orange flew at her, and she found herself engulfed in Moira's embrace. Moira had come to her birthday party, but not Colin.

"Happy birthday! Did you really think we'd let you get away without celebrating? The O'Learys love a good party. Were you surprised?"

Surprised was an understatement. She forced a smile and slipped off her heels. "I never would've guessed. The Brannigans are not party people."

"That's a shame. Come on, let's bowl." Moira spun and headed for the nearest lane.

It looked like she'd already befriended Lori and Janie. The three of them stood at the table typing their names into the scoreboard. Keith and Dad held back, watching from the sidelines, but they stayed while she bowled.

Bianca piped some dance music through the speakers, and it was loud enough to drown out most conversation. Too bad she could still hear her own thoughts.

Ten frames of bowling and laughter with friends relaxed her more than a glass of wine. After the game, she changed back into her shoes, knowing her father wouldn't stay much longer and she really needed to show him the bar. As she changed, Moira plopped down beside her.

"So what's up with you and my brother?"

Elizabeth swallowed again. "What do you mean?"

"I mean, he's not here. He's totally into you, but he's not at your birthday party that he planned?"

"We fought. I screwed up, and now he wants to have nothing to do with me." With her shoes in place, she added, "And I can't blame him."

Moira jumped up and gave her a quick squeeze. "Colin never stays mad for long. Trust me. I've been pissing him off my whole life, and he likes you a whole hell of a lot more than he likes me."

"Thanks. Another game after I talk to my dad?"

"You got it. I think some of my other siblings might be stopping by."

Elizabeth didn't believe that Colin just needed a cooling-off period. He was plenty cool. The way he'd looked at her after she'd apologized . . . No, she couldn't go there now. She needed to focus on the bar and showing her dad all that she'd accomplished.

She found Keith and her dad talking by the shoe counter. Their heads tilted toward each other conspiratorially, but Elizabeth did all she could to push that fear down. The alley was noisy, and they could be discussing anything. By now she should've learned not to jump to conclusions.

She tapped her dad's shoulder. "Ready to look at the bar?"

He narrowed his eyes, and she knew he was thinking that it was unnecessary, but as usual, he would indulge her. They made their way around the counter and through the walkway Colin had put in.

The bar wasn't much quieter than the alley. The TVs blared with a White Sox game. She paused, a little impressed with herself for even recognizing that. After pointing out the improvements that they'd made in the bar, she brought them to her small office to talk money.

"The bar is turning a profit, Dad. It's not huge, but given that it's been neglected for a decade, this is an amazing difference. We have a steady flow of customers, and as the summer goes on, we have plans to increase that customer base." She turned her computer screen so her father could see the spreadsheet.

"You've done a good job here, Elizabeth. I don't particularly like that you went behind my back to do this, but I'm impressed."

Those were the words she'd wanted to hear, but the look in his eyes did not express what he was saying. His words were the equivalent of a pat on the head. "I went behind your back because you've never given me the same opportunities you've given Keith. So I stole this one. It was supposed to be mine anyway, right? I did more than you ever thought I was capable of. Why can't you give me that?"

"What are you talking about? I just acknowledged your hard work on this business."

She just nodded.

They said their good-byes, and Elizabeth walked them out. In truth, he had acknowledged her work in the same way he always had. It had just been a long time since she'd paid attention. The weeks she'd spent here, away from the stuffy Brannigan attitude, had softened her. She actually expected some praise. When had she ever gotten praise from her father?

Had she really expected a prize for doing her job? She thought back to her early days of working with Colin when he'd thought he deserved a thank-you for doing his job, and she smiled. She had screwed up with him from the very beginning.

Everything was much clearer now. She needed to make some changes in her life. She'd take what she'd learned here and move on. Her life would get better. It couldn't get worse.

Tonight she'd pretend to party. Tomorrow, she'd move on. Without Colin, there was nothing left to keep her here in Chicago. It was time to get back to the real world, where silly bowling shoes didn't fit into her life.

* * *

After her plane landed, Elizabeth went home to unpack and figure out what to do with her future. The more she thought about her meeting with her father, the more she was convinced that he was ready to hand over control of Brannigan Enterprises to Keith. She'd have to suck it up and move on.

The problem was that she'd never come up with a contingency plan. Being CEO had been her one and only goal. Did she want to work for Keith?

Not by a long shot. Not even after they'd moved in a positive direction. They'd had a lengthy discussion over bowling. She'd been surprised to see how much her brother liked to talk once he had a few beers in him. He kept apologizing for being a bad brother. He thought it was his fault that she didn't have a family. He wanted her to fall in love and make a new life.

He wanted her to keep the bowling alley.

But she couldn't. She couldn't continue to hold on to something that wasn't meant to be. Holding on to the alley meant holding on to Colin. That wasn't fair to either of them. They'd been clear about that up front. Best-case scenario, they'd have fun while she was in town, but then they'd be over. Her accusations had ruined an amicable parting. He'd never called her back after the party.

She could admit she'd taken the coward's way out. She couldn't face him again. His cold indifference tore at her.

After changing into an old T-shirt and a pair of boxers she'd stolen from Colin, she crawled into bed ready to sleep for a week. Before she even closed her eyes, the tears started and, for a change, she didn't try to control them.

* * *

Colin avoided his entire family for the next two days. He'd worked around the clock to keep his mind off Elizabeth. He'd listened to her message a dozen times. *I wish you were here.* Like some lame postcard. Not "I'm sorry I fucked up." Certainly not "I love you." And then she had just left. She went back to Florida without a good-bye, like a toddler who'd lost her favorite game. As if he didn't have a good reason for being pissed off and hurt. She obviously didn't want to speak to him, so he got to work to forget her.

He'd received a very businesslike e-mail informing him that the bar and bowling alley would be on the market immediately. She kindly asked him to return to Brannigan's and complete the kitchen so it would be ready to sell.

The kitchen was finally finished for the bar, and they had a temporary license. Mike and Bianca took it upon themselves to organize and do a taste test for menu items. He heard them laughing and joking in the back. Every now and then, Mike would stick his head into the hallway and ask if Colin needed help.

He needed too much. He'd fallen in love with a woman who didn't trust him, who lived thousands of miles away, and who planned to sell his business out from under him.

No, there was nothing Mike could do.

The door to the bar opened and his mom came in. For someone who had worked in a bar for years, Eileen O'Leary looked completely out of place.

"Mom. What are you doing here?"

"I came to see what you've been doing with your life." She sat on a stool and looked around the bar, as if she could offer an official appraisal.

His mom nodded. "He would approve."

There was no need to clarify who she was talking about. Colin had always sought Dad's approval.

"He'd be proud."

He felt his face flush. "Thanks."

"Where's Libby?"

He cleared his throat. That was as emotional as his mother would get. "Florida."

"Vacation?"

"For good. That's where she lives, remember?" He busied himself with wiping down the counter.

"Her business is here with you." His mother's back stiffened. It wasn't often that he witnessed his mother going into mama bear mode, but this time was unwarranted.

"She's selling the business. That was always the plan."

"What about you?"

"What about me?"

"You just let her walk out."

How did she manage to spin this back to an attack on him? "What was I supposed to do?"

"Do you remember what you told Ryan after he had brought Quinn to the house for dinner the first time?"

He thought back to almost a year ago and shook his head. "I think I called him a stupid shit for letting the best thing in his life walk away."

Eileen slid from her stool. "You should take your own advice."

What the hell did that mean? He couldn't tell his mother that he and Elizabeth had agreed to sleep together and when the project was over, so were they. Talking about sex with a parent was creepy. But beyond that, he knew she would call him on being a liar. His relationship with Libby had evolved, and his mother obviously knew. He just didn't know what to do about it. Telling Elizabeth he loved her had meant nothing.

He couldn't offer Elizabeth what she wanted. CEO of Brannigan's Sports Bar wouldn't be enough for her.

* * *

Sleeping for a week wasn't in the cards for Elizabeth. She tossed and turned and cried. Being in bed by ten p.m. had become a foreign concept. She sat awake watching *Highlander* until two every night. She'd tried to meet with her father twice, and both times he put her off.

She was supposed to be using the time to figure out her life, but she couldn't focus. Every day she went into the office and pushed papers around but accomplished nothing. She checked and rechecked her bank balance and began searching for a project of her own.

Maybe striking out with her own company was what she needed. She'd proven, at least to herself, that she could do it. Starting over was a frightening prospect.

When her father called her into his office, she prepared for his verdict. Her mother had started planning his retirement party, so Elizabeth knew a decision was imminent. She knocked on the door.

"Come in."

From the door, she saw her father standing in front of his desk, with Keith by his side. Nothing in Keith's expression hinted at what they'd been talking about.

Her father picked up a box from his desk. "This is for you."

He handed it to her. A brown box, nothing special. No paper or ribbon. She slid the side open and pulled out a nameplate.

ELIZABETH BRANNIGAN, CEO

"For a long time, I assumed Keith would take over, being the eldest, but I saw a spark in you in Chicago, Elizabeth. You showed some gumption. That'll take you far in this business."

Her heart stuttered. Tears welled and she smiled at her father. "I don't know what to say."

"Don't get too excited yet," Keith said, flashing a nameplate of his own.

"What?"

"Dad wants a trial run. I think it's a stupid idea."

Their father bristled. "Nonsense. How else am I supposed to know if you can handle the job? I've spent most of my life building this business."

No, not another competition. She couldn't do that. "Thanks for the vote of confidence."

"I quit," Keith said, startling everyone. "We shouldn't have to jump through hoops for you. We've continuously proven we can handle the business. It's not fair to pit us against each other."

Both Elizabeth and their father stared in stunned silence.

Keith grew a pair, who knew? He stood and walked out of the office, leaving his nameplate on the desk.

Her plaque weighed heavily in her hand. What the hell?

"Well, Elizabeth, looks like you're it. Congratulations."

Suddenly, she wasn't so sure she wanted to be it. At least not this way. She'd wanted her father to choose her. She didn't want to be given the position by default. All the work she'd done wasn't so she could win by forfeit. She wanted more than an empty victory. "I quit too."

"What?"

"You heard me. Keith was right. I'm done competing for everything." She thought of the O'Learys. "We're family, but you'd never know it to look at us. I'm done."

She slapped the nameplate on the desk beside Keith's and quickly left the office before she could falter. Working without a plan had never been her forte.

Down the hall, she knocked on Keith's office door. "Hey."

He looked up from his desk. "I guess congratulations are in order."

"Not quite. I quit."

"Why would you do that? He was going to give you everything you wanted."

She stood in front of his desk, fingering the small items sitting there. "I didn't want it as runner-up. Plus, you made an excellent point. He shouldn't pit us against each other. We're more effective when we're on the same side."

The thought sparked an idea, then another. She and Keith did work well together.

"What's that look about?"

"Were you serious about quitting?"

"The competition, yes." He swung his arm out. "But this is my home. I'm fine with my position. Dad can hire someone to be CEO."

"I have a proposition for you." A jolt zinged through her at the thought of a challenge, much as when she'd first decided to take on The Irish Pub.

They made plans to meet for dinner to discuss a new business venture. Colin was right; there was no reason why she couldn't work with a partner.

* * *

Colin had spoken to the real estate agent that Elizabeth signed with. The asking price for the bar was out of his reach, but if he had a new partner, he could swing it. Something his mother had said about letting a good thing go stuck with him.

There was no getting Elizabeth back. She'd made it clear that her goal of CEO was more important than anything. He'd gone into their relationship with his eyes open. It was never supposed to be a permanent thing. They were always supposed to go their separate ways. He might not be able to get the woman, but he could hold on to what they'd built. It wasn't as good as having her, but it would do.

He knocked on Ryan's office door. "Got a minute?"

"What's up?"

"Elizabeth left town and put Brannigan's on the market." He moved into the room and sat in front of his brother. "I want to buy it."

"Why? I thought the place was a mess."

"It's better." Colin paused to gather his thoughts. This had been so much easier in his head. "I helped build that place. I really want it, but I can't afford it on my own."

Ryan started to shake his head.

"Before you jump all over me, look at this." He placed his carefully crafted proposal on Ryan's desk. "This is not some scheme for me. I'm looking for a silent partner. Emphasis on silent. I just need the financial backing."

"I told you before—"

"This isn't like before. Look it over. If it's a no, it's a no. I wanted to give you first stab since we're family. I'm not looking for charity. This is a business arrangement."

Colin stood and left the office. He had no idea what Ryan was thinking. To Ryan, Colin would always be the family fuckup. Colin didn't know how to change that; he'd earned the title. Eventually, he would prove to everyone that he'd changed.

He drove back to Brannigan's and let himself in the back door. The place felt like his, more than O'Leary's as of late. One way or another, he'd own this bar. He'd tried to take over Elizabeth's office, but no matter how he rearranged the few crap pieces of furniture, it still felt too cramped. The biggest problem was that he couldn't rid the space of her.

He worked the bar every night and took his laptop home with him to complete the office end. The business stuff still wasn't his idea of fun, but it also wasn't as difficult as he'd thought it would be. He gave himself a mental pat on the back. Hell, if no one else could recognize that he had succeeded, he would.

The delivery of food for their newly opened kitchen arrived, and Colin started unpacking and organizing when Ryan walked in.

Showing up the same day that Colin had asked for a partnership could only mean one thing: Ryan was going to shoot him down. He probably hadn't even looked at the proposal.

"Hey," Ryan said.

Colin looked at him and waited.

"Your proposal makes sense. You obviously put a lot of thought into it."

He'd actually read it?

Colin waited for the "but." He knew it was coming.

"But I wonder if this place is worth the asking price."

Colin set down the box he held on the stainless-steel table. "We'd obviously negotiate a better deal, but I'm willing to pay for this place. It will be successful. I've worked too hard for it not to be."

"Why now?"

Colin leaned against the table. "What do you mean?"

"Why should I trust you now?"

He shook his head. He knew he couldn't win Ryan over. What a waste of time. "It's pretty sad that a total stranger had more faith in me than my own brother."

"Sometimes a clean slate is easier to work with." Ryan inhaled deeply. "I don't understand why you left, but you expect me to forget you did. Why didn't you stay and prove O'Leary's should've been yours?"

The fear Colin had buried crept up again, and he wanted to lie as he had been but couldn't. He sucked in air before forcing out the words. "I left because I couldn't hack it. Without Dad here, I knew everyone would look to me to be in charge. And I was a fuckup. I knew I'd let everyone down. So I left."

"Leaving let us down."

"I'm sorry. I owe an apology to you more than anyone. I never considered what my leaving would do to you, but I knew, no matter what, you'd handle it. It's who you are."

Colin turned back to the box of food. "I can't make up for not being here, but I can promise not to leave again. Every day for three years, I wanted to come home, but I didn't have the balls to do it. I'm not the same man I was. Hell, I wasn't much of a man then."

He dropped burgers into the chest freezer and waited for some response from Ryan.

"What about Elizabeth?"

That sure as hell wasn't the kind of response he'd expected. Hearing her name caused another arrow of pain in his chest. He unclenched his jaw. "She's gone. What about her?"

"Did you think about going after her?"

Colin turned back to his brother. "Honestly? Yeah. But I can't walk away from home again. Even if I did, what would I do? She has a career. She travels nonstop. She doesn't have room for me."

"Did you ask her to stay?"

"Yes." But he didn't push. He should've made it a real invitation. He should've made her believe he loved her.

"Then I guess you're screwed." Ryan's stance finally relaxed.

Colin saw the look of pity on his face and tried not to cringe.

"But you do have a partner." Ryan stuck out his hand to seal the deal.

Instead, Colin grabbed him in a bear hug. It felt good to have his brother back. "You plan to be a silent partner, right?"

"Shut the fuck up."

Yeah, it was definitely good to have him back.

* * *

Three days and five failing businesses later, Elizabeth questioned her own sanity. Every site she'd visited held some promise, but nothing excited her. She was exhausted and still didn't have a plan.

And Keith was little to no help. He'd offered to partner with her, but he really only wanted to write a check and then reap the profits. Keith planned to continue doing business the same way their father had.

She wanted to do things differently.

She wanted to get her hands dirty, to be a part of something, to build something. Simply putting the Brannigan stamp on a business wouldn't be enough for her. She knew that now.

She needed real involvement. She wanted what she'd found in Chicago with Colin. Could she figure out how to replicate that?

Her phone rang. It was the real estate agent in Chicago. "Hello."

"Elizabeth. Good news. We have an offer. I'll e-mail you the details now. I think it's the best we're going to do."

Elizabeth heard the words, but couldn't quite grasp them. Sure, she'd wanted a quick sale, but she wasn't ready yet. She looked around her room in her brother's carriage house. A bottle of antacids sat on the desk beside her frogs. She picked up a frog made of painted rock. Like her, they didn't have a real home. "Take it off the market."

"What?"

"I've changed my mind. I don't want to sell. So decline the offer and take it off the market."

"But—"

Elizabeth didn't wait for reasons why she couldn't or shouldn't do that. She sat at her computer, whipped off an e-mail, and scheduled a flight.

* * *

Colin got off the phone and depression stabbed at him. He called Ryan. "The deal's off. Our offer was rejected."

"So offer a little more. That's the way negotiations work."

"I tried." Part of him wondered if Elizabeth had found out he'd made the offer and she didn't want him to have it.

"Sorry, man. Let me know if you find something else. I'm still willing to work with you."

"Thanks." Colin hung up. He was so upset that even Ryan's support didn't make him feel better. He faced his routine for opening the bar with a grimness that took hold of his whole body. His movements were sluggish, and he couldn't even muster a smile for Bianca, who came in to offer him a taste of the burger she'd cooked.

The front door opened, letting the afternoon sun streak into his gloominess. Without turning around, he said, "Sorry, we're not open yet."

"That's too bad. I could really use an Irish coffee."

Colin spun so fast at the sound of Elizabeth's voice that he lost his balance and smashed against the bar.

She smiled. "That's usually my schtick."

"What are you doing here?" He realized he sounded like an asshole, but he didn't know how to fix that. Jumping across the bar wouldn't be the best thing to do, but it's what his instincts pushed for. Keeping the desire in check meant he couldn't necessarily control his mouth.

She tugged at her blouse and cleared her throat. "We had an offer."

"I know."

"You do?"

"I was the offer you turned down without negotiation."

"You—" She froze, and confusion ran across her face.

She hadn't known he'd tried to buy the bar. Why did she turn down the offer then? While she took a moment to stare at him, he studied her. Dark circles showed she hadn't been sleeping again. Good. At least he wasn't alone.

"Give me a minute." She ran out of the bar toward the bathroom, gripping her bag to her side.

He followed, afraid that she was going to be sick again. "Are you okay?"

"Fine. I'll be right out." Within a minute, she emerged from the bathroom wearing a Brannigan's Sports Bar T-shirt. One of the skimpy ones that showed great cleavage. She'd let her hair down and wore a smile that exuded happiness.

She extended a hand. "Hi, I'm Elizabeth Brannigan, and I have a proposition for you."

Hearing those words again made him smile. He rocked back on his heels. "As good as the first proposition I made to you?"

She took a step forward, and her cinnamon scent tickled his nose. "Better."

"Really?"

"I'm here to offer you a fifty-fifty partnership."

"That's a good deal, but I wouldn't say that it's better than my offer."

Another step. "I'm proposing a fifty-fifty split in both business and pleasure."

Blood drained from his brain, and he struggled to focus on her words. "What about your dad's company?"

"He made me CEO."

That sobered him, and he edged away from Elizabeth. "Congratulations."

"Thanks, but I quit."

This conversation was giving him whiplash. "Why?"

"It wasn't what I wanted. It turns out my brother knows me better than I know myself. He bought this place for me as a graduation present because he thought I could make a good life here."

Colin absorbed everything she'd said. She'd come back for the business, but how did he fit in? "What about us?"

"I want there to be an us. I'm sorry I didn't trust you. I hope you can forgive me for thinking that you'd do something to hurt me or our business. Being here, building this business with you, made me happy, and I didn't know how to trust that. But I'm learning."

His throat felt raw. "How do I know it won't happen again? Or that you won't take off when things get rough?"

"You'll just have to take my word for it."

"That's a lot of trust you expect. The kind that's reserved for a select few."

She moved closer again, putting her body within an inch of his. "Would it help if I said I love you?"

His heart jumped into his throat. "Maybe. Are you going to say it?"

"I love you, Colin. I shouldn't have left. I thought I screwed this up beyond repair. I should've fought for us, but I was afraid you didn't want this."

He reached out and cupped the back of her neck. "How could you think I wouldn't want you? I've loved you for a long time. I didn't want to hold you back from your dreams."

"My dreams were blurry. I didn't realize how good I had it here until I left. So, do we have a deal?"

Words couldn't express what he felt. He leaned in and kissed her until they were both breathless. When they came up for air, he said, "One condition."

She raised her eyebrows.

"You only wear this shirt for me."

Her laughter echoed in the hallway until she began to snort. "Deal."

Traditional Irish Soda Bread

3½ cups flour
1 teaspoon baking soda
1 teaspoon salt
1¾ cups buttermilk*

Preheat oven to 425 degrees Fahrenheit. Grease and flour a round cake pan (8- or 9-inch).

In a large bowl, sift the dry ingredients together. Pour in 1½ cups of buttermilk and mix quickly. Add in remaining ¼ cup buttermilk and mix. Turn dough out on a lightly floured surface and knead for only a few seconds to make sure it holds together. Shape into a round disk and place in the prepared cake pan. Cut a cross into the top of the bread. Cover with another inverted cake pan.

Bake for 30 minutes. Remove top cake pan and bake an additional 15 minutes. When bread is done, you will hear a hollow sound when you thump the bottom of the loaf.

Slice and enjoy with butter.

**Although the recipe can be made using regular milk, the taste and texture are much better if you use buttermilk.*

Photo: Nicole Morisco

About the Author

Shannyn Schroeder is a former high school and middle school English teacher. She holds a BA in English and MAs in Special Education and Gifted Education. After having her third child, she decided to stay at home. She has since worked as an editor for a couple of e-publishers, and currently works as an editor for an education company that publishes online current events assignments. She juggles writing around the kids' schedules.

In her spare time, Shannyn loves to bake and watches far too much TV, especially cop shows. She started her first book on a dare from her husband and has never looked back. She came to reading romance later than many, but lives for the happy ending and writes contemporary romance because she enjoys the adventure of new love.

Readers can visit Shannyn online at www.shannynschroeder.com and follow her on Twitter @SSchroeder_.

MORE THAN THIS

Is love between friends worth the risk?

SHANNYN SCHROEDER

A Good TIME
The O'Learys
He's got game, but can she play for keeps?
SHANNYN SCHROEDER

CPSIA information can be obtained at www.ICGtesting.com
Printed in the USA
LVOW08s0931060414

380507LV00001B/189/P